Drug Money

Alan Lewis

Prologue

"The Asians," as they were known as, had not started their lives as criminals. They were intellectuals and professionals who were on the run from a country that had gone to hell. Many of them came from Vietnam, Laos or Cambodia at a time when good people were being moved from the cities to the country-side and into "re-education camps" and what the communist governments called, "new economic zones". Executions by the thousands and deaths in the slave labor camps forced young men and women to flee their homes in order to survive. And the struggle for survival turned desperate humans into savage animals.

Sometimes, government officials were bribed so as to secure night passage out of their home countries in whatever sailing craft they could find, make or hijack. With nothing more than the shirts on their backs and whatever gold they could smuggle with them, these families set off to a country as foreign to them as the language spoken.

The adversity and suffering of weeks at sea forged friendships that would last them until death. They were academics, economists, chemists and mechanics and together they developed systems of procuring the essentials of life. By the time those that survived the Thai pirates, the rape gangs and the atrocities of a society without laws arrived in their new country, they had their own new ways of survival.

A consequence of the insane journey across the Pacific, countless families became separated. Some of the family members ending up in Vancouver, Toronto or Montreal. Later, this misfortune became opportunity. The naive people in the new world had no way of seeing what was coming their way.

Utilizing the already established connections of friends and family, the boat people started small, but their climb up the criminal ladder was meteoric. They did their best to stay out of sight from the mainstream society that didn't understand them and was racist against them. Out of necessity, the small groups of friends from the boats became strong gangs. It was easy to do when nobody cared about you or paid attention to you.

Years later when the separated families reconnected with their lost members from across the country, they established a criminal foothold that had the potential to become a global network. By the time the "Boat People" made it onto the radar of the established gangs and the police forces, it was too late. They had delivery systems, shipping and receiving, warehouses and real estate. Legitimate lawyers were getting involved to tie up legal issues. They had foot soldiers and sergeants willing to do dirty work and no shortage of young guys that just wanted a piece of the action.

Donny watched "The Asians" become powerful and he was wise enough to stay out of their way in their hunger to establish themselves, prove themselves and to compete with the big gangs. He liked the guys from Vietnam and he especially loved the food from the people from Laos. The "Boat People," now "The Asians" had always worked well with him and his boys. They paid him market value for the drugs he supplied and they were all making decent money together.

But, with money and power control to be the "Big Man" frequently created struggles within the "Asian Families". Overt violence in neighborhoods and pool halls for ownership of territory forced Donny and the boys to lay a little lower than usual.

One afternoon while Tim, Donny's son was outside watching the Harleys, Donny and the boys tossed around ideas of how the new power struggle was affecting them. Sipping on bottled beer, Don leaned back on his chair, ordered another round of beers and said, "Let them fight it out, boys. As long as they keep the money coming our way all is cool. Hey, lets face it, it's their money that's buying this beer." And the boys cheered and ordered another round before the just ordered one arrived.

Chapter 1

Present day

Kat stood in the fetid, humid hallway, looking down the gun in her trembling hands. Her dirty, stringy hair hung in her face, but despite the dim lighting, she could see the trails of sweat running down his temples as he cowered on the ground in front of her.

His eyes darted to the right for a moment, toward the little backpack lying on the filthy floor, then his pleading eyes came back to her. She almost pulled the trigger right then.

"Come on, Kitty Kat. I'm all you've got."

She thought about that a moment and decided that, no, he wasn't all she had.

Her finger twitched, and the muzzle sparked.

The sound was deafening, seeming to explode throughout the building.

Grundy's chest took the 9 mm bullet, and he flinched, mouth gaping before he toppled over onto his side.

If he wasn't dead, he would be.

There was a bloody mess on the wall, and a hole about the size of her index finger. This registered through the quickly receding rush of drugs. She smelled the gunpowder, and it seemed to clear her head momentarily.

The drugs.

The backpack.

Gotta go.

There was a sense of elation, finally being free of the scumbag, and a push of adrenaline got her moving.

She knelt quickly, snatched the little backpack, and scurried to the stairs. It felt heavier than she expected. This was good because it meant she had enough cocaine to last the next two weeks, three if she was conservative.

As she hurried down the stairs, the feeling came over her that life was perfect. Things would be so much better with Grundy gone. But only if she stayed out of jail.

Hugging the little backpack with both hands the way a small child would wrap its arms around a teddy bear, she scampered out of the stairwell, down the hall and out into the bright sunshine.

It stung her eyes, and she stopped on the sidewalk, blinded, trying to get her bearings. Sirens screamed in the distance.

Damn that was fast.

One of the scummy residents played good citizen, though knowing the low-lifes she encountered, it was probably an anonymous call. Kat decided to walk calmly, so as not to draw attention, and stuffed the handgun into her waistband, pulling her green muscle shirt over it. She stepped between two cars and, like a good girl, looked both ways, heading across to the shade of the big cypress tree at the corner. She needed to figure out something fast. As she leaned against the trunk, allowing her eyes to adjust, two police cars roared past, only to squeal to a halt in front of the apartment building. A uniformed officer bolted out of each car, sprinted up to the apartment entryway, and paused, guns drawn. They frantically exchanged some sort of plan, one opening the door while the other entered, weapon first.

Okay, now what?

It was difficult to put together a coherent thought because she was on the wrong end of a drug binge. She knew she had to get off the street and out of sight . . . but where? She turned right and crossed the quiet road, aiming herself for the building across the street.

Kat kept her head down, focusing on the sidewalk, watching her worn boots take turns walking. The pavement turned to lawn, then the lawn turned into a cobblestone path, then wide, low steps that led up to a pair of big heavy doors. She looked up.

A pair of teenage girls stared at her, looking her up and down. They were holding books to their chests.

Kat's eyes went up to the words over the doors.

Havermyer High School.

More sirens were signaling their impending presence.

The girls sneered at her as if she were disgusting.

She glanced around, and heaved on the metal handles, entering the large cavernous hall. More teens milled about, and Kat made her way straight ahead as if she knew where she was going.

She was young enough to pass for a student, but not exactly looking her best, which was a pretty big deal when she attended Mountain Hawk High. It wasn't a good time then, and it wasn't a good time now. She needed a safe place to take a hit.

For a fleeting moment, a she saw herself sitting on the floor with Grundy in the apartment, staring wide-eyed at each other across the coffee table, bags of coke lined up and ready to sell. That was the problem, she knew. It was meant to sell, but they turned out to be their own best customers. Or worst, since they only lost money on what they snorted.

The bag was getting heavy and she let it hang from one arm. Kids were staring at her, but she pretended to ignore them. Her head started to throb and the repetitive thud of a basketball being dribbled on a hardwood floor off to the right only added to the pounding in her brain. She rubbed her eyes with her empty hand and turned left, up the first flight of stairs to the second floor.

Light blue student lockers lined either side of the wide empty hallway. She looked for a woman's washroom and found one down the hall. She hoped it would be a quiet place to get a well-deserved fix.

She glanced in the mirror, then immediately turned away from her reflection. She was disgusting. No wonder they stared. She smacked open the door of the last stall, quickly locking the latch. She sat down, leaned back and took a deep breath. The little pack sat on her knees, and she stared at the worn zipper. Her fingers fumbled with the tab and she looked up as indistinguishable voices drew close, then faded down the hall.

She closed her eyes and immediately regretted it. The image of Grundy's fist coming out of nowhere took over her brain. Her head snapping. That wasn't the only time, just the most recent. She tenderly felt her still-sore ribs from the kicking he'd given her. If he hadn't kicked her, she thought, it might have worked out. But probably not. He'd always been an asshole and if she hadn't killed him, somebody else was eventually going to do it anyway. Who knows, maybe he would have killed her first.

Kat breathed heavily, calming herself down, finding just enough peace to get down to the job at hand.

Her fingers rummaged through Grundy's drug bag and she felt a sense of anticipation and euphoria almost as sweet as the drug itself. Inside were small plastic baggies ready for sale, larger bags for the personal stash, a few glass pipes, a black lighter and two thick folds of cash. She suspected business had been good lately and the cash reinforced that. He had been lying and hiding money from her.

"There's one small bundle left," he said last night. She didn't believe him, suspecting it was a big bundle. She was relieved she was wrong in a good way.

She had the drugs, a fix, a gun, and a lot of money.

Fuck him. It's mine now.

She used one of the small packets to get what she needed, wiping her nose with the edge of her forearm.

She pulled the stall door open and looked into the mirror.

"Much better," she said to the smiling reflection.

Kat hooked a swath of hair with her finger and tucked it behind her ear. She walked out of the washroom and turned left, moving down the hallway to find a way out of the school. She felt great. There were more people around than before, but she didn't care, she knew she could take any of these pretty punks out, any time.

It seemed like it had been a long time since she had been in a high school, but it seemed better now. Maybe it was being older. Maybe it was having more confidence. Maybe it was the gun or the money. But she decided it was none of the above. Drugs just make everything better.

She made her way straight through the hallway, smiling lightly at the stares, turning left, then right, then left again, straight into the open doorway of a classroom.

Chapter 2

Ainle Lorcan looked at his watch and saw he had a little more than an hour until the first of the students arrived with their inane chatter and tales of heartbreak. Teaching English literature was fun for him, and he always enjoyed reading, but the chaos the students brought to class made him wonder if he really actually taught anything other than how to manage their self-created life problems.

He considered his own issues, for what they were worth. Grace was right -- he needed a haircut. He was looking more like "Labowski" than the neat, professional high school educator he imagined. He forgot his lunch. Again. And while the pulled muscle in his thigh was healing, it still tugged at odd moments. He may have to skip his next martial arts class. Again.

The sound of sirens drew his attention to the open windows. Vancouver was not immune to crime, especially this low-income inner city area, but this sounded like more than usual. And close. Ainle looked out the second story window and saw an ambulance pull up behind two parked police cars. It made him think again of having a class somewhere that wasn't quite so . . . messy. Somewhere in the country, where the air was clean, the people weren't scared and there were fewer sirens.

Of course, the pay would be less, and maybe they wouldn't be able to afford their neat little suburban home. Grace, also a teacher, would understand -- but would she be able to take the trade off? While he doubted his effect on the students, she made a difference here. She might not like the area, or the neighborhood, or even the school, but she liked the students.

There were always compromises. Always.

He look over his classroom. The only organized thing was the rows of students' desks. Books were stacked on shelves a little too haphazardly, the dictionaries were falling apart -- which he guessed was a good thing since if they were pristine he wouldn't be doing his job -- and his own desk was cluttered with ungraded papers. Something that would only get worse after this morning's test.

When he looked out the window again, he saw another police car pull up, and a large woman in a flower-patterned nightdress standing on a lawn across the street, hands covering her mouth.

The sound of teenagers laughing in the hallway brought an odd disparity to the scene unfolding outside. Something really bad had happened, and they were oblivious. By tomorrow, though, they would fill him in on every gory detail, with a lot of conjecture and rumor thrown in for added spice.

Maybe he'd go to class tonight anyway, even if he couldn't physically participate. It was supposed to be an introduction to Filipino stick fighting, and if there wasn't much -- if any -- kicking involved, he could take his turn being a student instead of the teacher. Yes, he would go, even if he just stood there all suited up and absorbing. He grabbed the stack of exams and began placing them on the desks.

When he was done, he checked the time again and saw he had time for coffee. Oh, the little things could mean so much. He turned to leave when the door flew open.

The unbelievably thin woman with wild maniacal eyes smacked him square in the face.

His head jerked back, his brain fuzzed up with a blaring pain, and he could immediately feel wetness come out of his nose.

She hadn't even hit him with her hand, but the top of her head, like a whirling dervish that had gone even more out of control than usual.

While he had stumbled back a few steps, she completely stiffened and jerked backwards onto the floor, her head making a loud and nauseating smacking sound.

Ainle stood in a wobbly stance, trying to take in this bizarre sight, when his blurred vision caught an even more strange thing: A gun spinning on the floor like a dangerous version of Spin The Bottle. His immediate reaction was to get it -- oddly, not out of any sense of danger or self-defense, but out of concern of the kids who would be filtering in shortly.

The scarecrow woman, apparently unaffected by the certain concussion she must have sustained, also saw it, and they both had the same idea. She stayed low and crawled under desks, while he came in from above, over the top.

It dawned on him that they would both reach the general vicinity at the same time, risking another head-splitting impact. He hesitated for the briefest of moments, allowing her to snatch the gun and begin pulling the trigger even before she lifted the weapon off the linoleum.

Ainle dove backwards, holding his arms out as if to ward off the bullets.

One round went through the palm of his right hand, and he screamed, sending him deeper into panic mode. It fired him up.

He managed to lunge, pushing his bloodied hand at the gun as she fired another round that raced across the room and burst his computer monitor.

With his other hand, he punched at her, hammering down at her squirming, wiry body. He pummeled her shoulder and neck, and then tried to kick his good leg at her stomach, but his foot caught in one of the desks, and she managed to half-turn.

He grabbed at the gun, missed, then took a different tact and smashed down at it. He missed, and his fist connected with her pale, sweaty face.

The pistol went off a third time, the bullet going somewhere, but at least not into him.

He saw her eyes lose focus, and Ainle went for the barrel, twisting the gun viciously to the left, trapping her forefinger in the trigger guard. He heard her finger snap, and she screamed, arching her back in pain.

He pushed her down to the ground, managing to kneel on her chest with his right knee as he wrenched the gun free.

The smell of gunpowder was heavy and strangely sweet. Blood dripped out of his nose, and his hand throbbed around the new hole in it. She seemed to be bleeding from her mouth, but between his face, palm and her lip, it was impossible to tell whose blood was whose.

Ainle fumbled with the gun, trying to point it at her defensively, but it was warm and sticky. He managed to point it at her, and he saw she was shaking. Despite feeling nauseous and about ready to puke, the lucid thought came to him that he would need to tell his martial arts instructor that unless one is attacked in an open field or empty parking lot, the training in a dojo or MMA club is nothing like reality. They should put some shopping carts or desks around the room for real-world application.

The sobbing from under him helped bring everything back into focus.

"Hey, don't move," he said trying to sound like a cop, but instead imitating a scared middle-aged man with a bloody nose and a gunshot wound.

The young woman just looked up at him with blue bloodshot eyes, staring at him with a mix of pain and anger. She raised her hand, staring at her dislocated finger. Her other hand went to her face and came away with blood. She suddenly looked distressed. "I'm bleeding," she mumbled.

"You shot me!"

She seemed to deflate, and give up. "I'm sorry," she whispered. "Can I get up?"

He realized his knee was in the middle of her chest, so he managed to get up while still wobbily pointing the gun in her direction. "Go sit over there," he said, waving his bad hand at his messy teacher desk.

She rolled on her side and slowly got to her knees, then her feet. She looked around, dazed, then moved toward the head of the classroom.

The alarm went off, much like a fire alarm, but different. Lock down.

She froze for a moment, head cocked as if to say *What's that?*, but then she pulled off a little backpack she'd been wearing, setting it on the floor, and settled into his chair.

If he had been paying attention and not trying to save his own life, he might have heard the sound of children in the hall screaming and running from the sound of gunfire. But he had been a little preoccupied.

He knew the procedure for a lock down: Bolt the doors to keep the intruders out, and get the kids safely into classrooms until the police could come and secure the area. But they hadn't planned for the intruder to be locked inside the school. Hopefully, someone would have figured it out and everyone was running for the hills while he sat here with a crazy woman. He stared at her. She looked at everything else.

Underneath the blood, sweat and grunge was a pretty girl -- tall, slim, attractive. Her old stained t-shirt was tough to make out, but said, "LET'S PARTY!" He sensed she was lost not just in the physical sense -- she obviously didn't mean to burst into his classroom as she had -- but lost in every other way as well. He nodded at the box of tissue near the corner of his desk, and she grabbed at it, stuffing a wad at her mouth.

"It's not my gun," she said.

He could have replied a few different ways. *Possession is nine-tenths of the law.* Or *Yeah, guns magically appear in this room all the time.* Or *You could have fooled me.*

All he could do was nod.

His hand throbbed. His nose had stopped bleeding, but it was all over him. His brain was only now starting to get a grip.

"Well," he said, "we should probably get you fixed up."

She stared at him for several moments before bursting into tears.

"Hey, hey, hey," he said, a little alarmed. "It's okay. It will be okay."

"No it won't," she said thickly. "I shot your hand!" Then she pointed off toward the corner to her left. "And I killed your computer!"

He nodded and took a deep breath. "Yeah. Yeah, you did." He tried to smile, but probably looked like a ghoulish zombie with all the blood on his face. "Come on, let's head downstairs."

She stood awkwardly and sniffed loudly. "Will it really be okay?"

"Yeah," he lied. "It will be okay."

She turned and headed for the door, and he followed, gun still pointed half-heartedly at her.

They turned to the right, and what he thought was an empty hallway suddenly became filled with a booming voice:

"Stop right there, raise your hands and slowly turn around."

The girl, either working off animal instincts or stupidity, turned and ran.

She only made it to the end of the hall when two men appeared and tackled her like defensive linemen on a football team. She went down hard, and was handcuffed before she managed to work up a complaint.

"You, with the gun. Drop it. Now!"

He did as he was told, wondering the moment it hit the ground if it would go off. It didn't.

"Hold your arms out, get on your knees, and lay down. Now!"

He stuck his arms out, and the rest became a bit unclear. If Ainle Lorcan dropped to his knees, he didn't remember, having fainted and collapsing before he had the chance to do it voluntarily.

Chapter 3

Fat Timmy was starting to get stressed, his red cheeks getting redder with this Grundy thing. He was supposed to have called hours ago. He could even feel his long hair, neatly pulled back in a ponytail, being infused with anxious gray every minute Grundy didn't call.

Timmy was not really fat, but he was big. A six foot tall Norwegian whose grandparents had immigrated to Canada before his father was born. He paced the living room, wondering if Grundy would come through, or if he would have to do something about it. Once you front twenty grand of inventory, you can't let anyone slack or others will try to take advantage. If they sense a point of weakness, it's all but over. Not once had Grundy flaked in the years they had been doing business. A day or two late here and there, but not this long. Either something had happened, or the asshole had decided to bite the hand that fed him. Timmy understood what it was like to sell on the streets, from first-hand experience. It wasn't easy. It was dangerous, with the possibility of the customer stabbing you in the back, or the cops breathing down your neck. There was no loyalty, fewer friends, and the only ones you could trust were the ones with cash. With demand for the product on the rise, this had been Grundy's big chance to move up, and if Grundy moved up, Timmy moved up.

He stared out the window, not in anticipation of Grundy showing up, but contemplating showing up at Grundy's. The TV babbled in the background, some insidious talk show where a slovenly woman didn't know which of the three men sitting across from her was the father of her toddler.

During their last exchange, Timmy provided the cocaine, a cool new untraceable smartphone, and a chance for all of them to make some real cash. If Grundy fucked up, then Timmy knew he was deep in the shit, not just in the supplier community, but mainly with his provider. He kind of had no choice. He'd give Grundy a few more hours, and if nothing happened, then he was going to be really pissed. And Grundy would definitely pay, one way or the other.

He needed to blow off steam while he waited. He stepped outside and climbed on his Harley, a big heavy beast of silver and black. Timmy fired her up and watched the gauges settle down. The chugging rhythm didn't do much to contain his building stress that was slowly trying to evolve into anger. He released the clutch and the big machine rolled up the street, smooth and solid. Timmy checked his shoulder and pulled out into traffic. Up ahead was an off ramp, so he signaled right and powered up onto the long curving access route. His speed picked up nicely and the air pushed cool and moist against his face as he accelerated up to highway speed. The fresh air helped clear his head, allowing him to consider the many possibilities of how he should deal with Grundy.

He grinned and squinted his eyes as he hit the throttle. The big machine roared into the morning. A low mist hung on the slopes of the coastal mountains as he rumbled around commuters in their smart cars and SUVs, their coffees and cell phones their only companions. He would take the long way there.

*   *   *

One could say he had been in the family business since he was able hang onto to the back of his father's Harley. Home for Tim seemed to be split between the house on the outskirts of town and the saloon filled with primarily bikers and hookers. A "real" job was never a consideration. Hell, school was an obstacle. Sometimes, Donny would take his son, Tim on errands with him, which usually consisted of going to a small house in a poor neighborhood, picking up a package and dropping it of at a nice big house in a fancy neighborhood. While Timmy could sense the tension, it had never been dangerous -- or if it was, Donny never let on. He eventually became a middleman, picking up cocaine from a guy in the Vancouver harbor and pot from the growers in the hills. He set up what he thought was a reliable Asian family to help with distribution, but it didn't take long for them to start grumbling about price, until they began short-changing him.

Donny told his son they had to pay, one way or the other. And that's when Tim stole his first car.

It wasn't just about money. There was a power struggle, both with the drug suppliers as a whole, and within the Asian families that had split off into gangs, resulting in violence in neighborhoods and pool halls for territory, forcing the bikers to lay a little lower than usual as things played themselves out.

But, when an Asian gang refused to pay the agreed price for a delivery, it was time for issues to be resolved. It was time to get what was owed, not just for the present, but future business as well. It was a beautiful spring afternoon, one of those rare blue-sky days. Donny slowly drove his big old Harley down the peaceful tree-lined street, with Timmy hanging on the back. At the end of the block, Donny made a big slow u-turn and pulled over in the shade. They waited.

It was a simple system. The dial-a-dopers would park in front of the house, leave the car running, go inside and get the package. The big men of the organization rarely got caught. If one was picked up by the cops, it was usually one of the young guys. But for the most part, their little cars were quick and speedy and got them in and out fast enough.

As they sat in the shade, a small, red Datsun 240z with all the tricks drove up. Nice sporty rims, low profile tires, a souped-up engine that hummed and whined with a downshift as it coasted to a rest in front of the neat house.

Donny signaled Timmy, and they emerged from the shadows, casually strolling towards the parked car. The driver, oblivious to them, got out, tossed a cigarette onto the asphalt and walked up to the red door, opening it without knocking, and disappearing inside.

The car was left running. Only a fool would try to steal it, especially with a buddy in the passenger seat. Donny whispered, "You get into the driver's side and take this little piece of shit car to the boys. I'll take care of the little dick in the passenger side."

Timmy watched nervously as his dad tapped the window of the Datsun. The window rolled down and a scowling Vietnamese kid looked up and spat: "What you want?"

"Dude," Donny said, hissing like a snake. "I'm taking your car."

The kid scoffed. "Get outta here, old man."

Donny reached into the window, grabbed the kid by his clean pink polo shirt and yanked him out the open window. With a heavy grunt, the big man slammed the kid head-first onto the sidewalk, the body instantly going limp.

"All yours, son."

Timmy stared wide-eyed and amazed at his dad for a moment, then scurried over to the car and jumped into the driver's seat. It smelled of leather and cigarettes. He put the car in gear, popped the clutch and sped down the street and out of the neighborhood. It was only a minute later Timmy saw his dad in the rearview mirror.

At the bar, the boys explained that although he had stolen the car, there was no way he could keep it. It was the cash they needed, not some little red car that was probably already stolen. Timmy rode along as one of the boys took the little car to a chop shop where it was sold, no questions asked. There was really no money in cars. Cars were work and too many ways things could go wrong. They were highly visible, easily tracked, and took up space. Drugs, on the other hand, were small, cost very little in comparison, could be sold for a lot more money than they cost, and there were always customers who needed the product. That night was when he met Grundy, a wannabe hanging around the saloon, buying small bags of pot, taking a small sample for himself and then re-selling the rest to street kids. Timmy came across him out behind the old saloon while sharing a joint with a group of guys. Apparently, Grundy knew something of Timmy, pulling him aside and suggesting Timmy could sell stuff to him since Grundy knew kids who would buy. It made sense. Timmy only had to deal to one guy. He could stay away from all the whiny street kids who called him whenever they ran out. Grundy became his go-to guy as his connections were always asking for more. When weed turned to coke, a good relationship became even better.

Despite their history, business was business. Friends don't take advantage of friends, he thought as he turned down the street to Grundy's apartment.

Chapter 4

Grace drove Ainle home from the hospital that night, nothing life-threatening enough to keep him there. It was after 10 PM, and he was glad to be home.

A voice mail left on Grace's phone by an anonymous school official -- probably Brad Burns, the sneaky little man who enforced the rules but didn't follow them -- said he was on medical leave for the rest of the semester, at reduced pay. Neither was really acceptable to Ainle, but he figured a little time off would help him sort it out. Grace walked into the bedroom, a mix of relief and concern on her pretty face. "Hey," he said.

"I'm so glad you're okay." She climbed on the bed and drew close. She smelled sweet and felt warm. "So what happened?" she asked in a voice that was hesitant, as if she didn't really want to know. "Where did this woman come from? What did she want? You have a black eye -- how did that happen?"

He quickly debated what to say, and how much detail to give her. After 13 years of marriage, he knew she wanted the truth, but not necessarily the whole truth.

"Some girl with a gun came into my class. I have no idea where she came from, just burst in and crashed into me. Literally, head first. I think that's where the black eye came from."

She was silent a while, probably trying to picture this.

"So, then she shot you?"

"Well . . ." He frowned as if he were trying to remember. Actually, he was trying to decide what parts to leave out. ". . . Yeah. I guess the gun just went off."

"What was she doing with a gun?"

"You got me." He shifted slightly, careful not to use his hand. "She did say something odd. 'It's not my gun.'"

"Then whose was it?"

"She never said."

"Oh, before I forget, Charles packed up your stuff in the classroom so you wouldn't have to go back."

"Ahh, good. I should give him a call tomorrow." He sat up. "I should get my cell phone out of there. Where is it?"

Grace popped up. "I'll get it. You just rest."

He watched her leave, and eased himself back onto the pillow. He was tired. Being shot can take the wind out of your sails.

She returned holding a small box, setting it on the end of the bed. She pulled out a couple of books, then a small leather backpack. "What's this?"

"I don't know. What is it?"

"Is it yours?"

"No, I would hope I have better taste than that. It looks like it's from the eighties, maybe out of a time capsule."

She set it on the bed and unzipped it, peeking in.

"It must be that's girl's," he said, just before her jaw dropped open. "What?" he asked.

She pulled out a small bundle of cash, folded and wrapped with a red rubber band.

"What the --" Ainle said.

Grace flipped through the bills. "They're all twenties."

"Unreal. That's like a thousand bucks." He pulled the bag closer with his good hand and fished inside, bringing out another wad.

"We should call the police."

"Yeah, we should, but . . ." He paused, starting to put a few of the pieces together. It was drug money. He set the money down and fished around in the pack some more. Out came baggies of white powder.

"Ainle," Grace said, half in amazement, half as a warning. Then she pulled the bag toward her and reached in, pulling out a phone.

"Can you turn it on?"

"Here, you do it. You're the techno guy."

Ainle took it in his good hand, held down the power switch, and waited. It eventually lit up. He maneuvered through the system and eventually found what he was looking for in the settings. *Grundy's Phone.*

"Anything interesting?" she asked, pulling out another small bundle of money.

"Not as interesting as what you're finding. But I think I know the owner of the phone."

"Not the girl?"

"She didn't look like a 'Grundy' to me. Unless she was Mrs. Grundy."

Another bigger bundle of money made an appearance. "Maybe she left him."

"Oh, she definitely left someone. You don't barge into a school with drugs, a gun and money and not be running away from something."

Then he felt another piece click. The police cars. The woman with the hands over her mouth. The ambulance.

Yeah, she was running, alright.

"Well, we'll take this to the police station first thing in the morning," Grace said, stuffing the items back inside the backpack.

"I think I need a doctor," he said, setting the phone on the nightstand.

"Why? Are you okay? Is something wrong?" She stopped what she was doing and took a good look at him. "Maybe you have a fever."

"Oh, I'm hot alright." He gave her a slow smirk.

She closed her eyes, took a deep breath and shook her head.

"I think I need an examination."

Still shaking her head, she smiled. "I thought you were tired."

"Tired, not dead. I'm only half crucified," he grinned and waved his injured hand.

Chapter 5

Tim brought his bike to a stop half a block from Grundy's apartment. Even in the gloom of the night, he could see the crime scene tape was up, and the forensics van looked like it was just loading up the last of the investigation gear. The feeling that something had happened to Grundy was now verified – although what had happened still was not clear. He took off his gloves, pulled out his phone, and started the "locate friend" application.

It took it a minute to do its search. Tim frowned at the glowing screen. Here he was at Grundy's place, but Grundy was clear across town.

He mapped out the best route to the location, with the phone telling him it would take 18 minutes without traffic. He considered phoning Grundy, but that was not how they did business. Grundy phoned him, and he had yet to do that.

As Tim turned his bike around, he thought it might be better to have some company with him when he found Grundy.

Tim was close to losing his cool, matching the chilly air of the night. He was out a lot of money, and now he had to race around town to collect it. He needed the cash to pay off his supplier, take care of a few other bills, and, of course, pay rent. It was a never-ending series of loans and paybacks -- as long as you made your paybacks everything was cool. Even his suppliers owed somebody. When one of the members of the chain did not keep their part of the bargain, everything got tense, debts had to be collected, serious consequences could result.

*　　*　　*

Tim pulled up to Rocket's house and parked his bike in front of the worn-looking garage, a.k.a. Rocket's workshop. The single level home included a heavy-duty front door and reinforced windows with roll shutters that told the average passerby the house was tornado-proofed. No one would have noticed if Vancouver was susceptible to tornadoes.

"Yo, big boy," Tim called. "I need beer."

Rocket pushed open the door and replied, "I got some in the ice box, help yourself. And get one for me while you're there."

"Looks like you already got one."

"Can never have too many. It's how I keep my weight down."

"You call two-forty-five down?"

"Two-forty, Sunshine, and you're moving too slow."

Tim tossed him a can before popping open his own. "So what do you need me for this time?" Rocket said.

Tim cocked his head, considering a reply. But he was right. He only visited Rocket when he needed help.

"I need your two-forty-five to make my small problem into a big problem for somebody else."

"Two-forty, and I'll be glad to help."

Tim smiled. Of course he would. Rocket didn't mind getting dirty. He kinda liked it.

So, he lifted his can, and chugged most of it. He belched heartily, then started his story. It didn't take long.

"So, Grundy owes you a bunch of dough, you owe the Asians, and the Asians still have a bug up their ass that you borrowed a car. That was, like, fucking twenty years ago!"

"I wish they got over themselves. I've made them enough money to buy a fucking car dealership."

"So what's Grundy doing in a picket fence neighborhood? He's a scummy, back alley dude."

"Definitely a fish out of water in that neck of the woods."

"Do you want to go over there and check it out? I could use a ride to clear my head." He downed the rest of his beer. "All this fucking talk is wearing me out."

"Then let's hit the road -- I'll buy the next round."

Chapter 6

He laid there, hand aching. If the pain killers did anything, he couldn't feel it. He glanced at the clock. 2:30. He had to stop doing that. It didn't help. At least Grace was out like a light.

He edged himself from of the warm bed and plodded out of the dark bedroom, down the hall, and into the kitchen. The blue light of the stove clock -- 2:31 -- and the red dot of the coffee machine helped him to find his direction. He turned on the light and felt inside the island in the middle of the kitchen, behind the pots, and pulled out the Lagavulin.

He stared at the whisky for several seconds, considering. Aged 17 years, it said. He set the bottle on the counter, held the neck with his good hand, and uncorked the scotch with his teeth. Then he found a glass and poured a nice splash. He went to the living room and stared out the window. The first taste was a delicate burn in his mouth.

The girl, the gun, the money. The drugs. Had to make one worry.

Another taste of the Lagavulin, and things seemed a little less worrisome. By the time the drink was almost gone, the thought of keeping at least one of the wads of cash was becoming a pretty good idea. After all, who would know?

Grace for one, but that would work itself out once some of the bills went away, or even a nice little trip to some place sunny and warm. It wasn't as if it was a huge sum of money. And they sure could use a little help with the house payments, the car and the credit cards.

A second glass of scotch made it a done deal. Half of the money returned to the authorities and half for the victim. If that that bullet had gone through his head, then Grace's world would have been destroyed, not to mention his. He wanted to keep all the money, but that was not going to fly with Grace. Half was going to be tricky enough.

A third glass of scotch, and his hand was hardly throbbing at all, and a bundle of cash had made its way into the cupboard where the scotch bottle had been.

California. Or maybe Greece.

Ainle poured one more scotch, and thought *Sometimes, things just work out.*

He needed to go lie down.

*   *   *

The dreams were not pleasant. Whether it was the scotch or the trauma -- most likely, both -- it was worse than lying awake and feeling his hand throb.

There was the replay of the beating. Being raised in a hockey town, and not being a hockey player, and having a strange name, often brought on an afterschool beating. Back in those days, bullying wasn't an awful social issue -- it was a way of life. You just lived with the beatings. He fell into a kind of fantasy world as a way to escape. Bruce Lee had become a hero, and his movies gave him a feeling of possibility.

It wasn't until he was married and out of college before he found a Kenpo Karate school just down the street. The yells and thuds he heard walking in brought chills. It was like home.

The nightmares cooled. His breathing leveled off.

Other than being over a liquor store, everything about the dojo, the "place of the way," the school just felt right. There was Japanese script painted on the walls with neat English translations printed below: "Body, mind and spirit." He yearned for that. Philosophical quotations by some man called Edmond Parker were written on doorways and walls in the main entrance, adding to the feeling.

The only part that seemed odd was the instructor -- not a Japanese Sensei as Ainle expected, but a white guy in his mid-30's with reddish-gray hair. He was tall, lean and fit, but the image didn't mesh with the vision in his head. At least he ran a tight class, inspecting the pairs of students performing arm locks and takedowns, making small adjustments and sometimes demonstrating the technique himself, once flipping the poor student and taking him to the mat hard and fast.

The student scrambled up, and the pair bowed slightly, saying "Thank you, Sir."

During a break, the man walked up to him.

"Welcome to Kenpo, I'm Mr. Gorman." He bowed.

Ainle returned the bow, although he had never done it before, and felt a little silly.

The senior students of the Kenpo School were younger than Ainle, and were standoffish at first, but either he began to fit in, or they accepted him. Ainle enjoyed it so much, he encouraged Grace to join, and although she was one of only two females, she became as enthusiastic as he was. The intricacies of the foot movements combined with the timing of hand placements continually had them thinking and analyzing every element of the art. They not only learned and trained in class, but read and absorbed what they could at home. And while the art form wasn't about kicking and punching and flipping an attacker for fun, Ainle enjoyed the fact that the wristlocks, the elbow strikes, and the eye gouges could really do some damage.

39

Ten years later, he realized what he had learned so far was just enough to get himself beat up, injured, or even killed. Over the years, martial art training had become more than just a hobby for Ainle and Grace. It became a significant component of their marriage and lifestyle.

After the school fell on hard times -- whether it was a lack of students to bring in the cash flow, or skyrocketing rent that caused too much financial pain -- the Kenpo closed and the couple transitioned to a TJK school, a combination of tae kwon do and jujitsu. They tried a Ninjitsu school, but only for a disastrous two weeks, where the students turned out to be society's fringe members. Long black coats on hot days so they could hide their throwing stars seemed absurd. While TJK lacked the academic level of Kenpo, it introduced them to a wonderful world of improvised weapons, conflict avoidance techniques, and soon, Filipino stick fighting.

In his light sleep, Ainle's eyes rolled in his head, and his arms twitched. He thought of the bullies growing up, and how their heads would snap back as he placed a well-deserved kick to their jaw.

If only it had really been like that.

Chapter 7

Kat felt like she was burning from the inside. She lay curled up on the narrow cot, sweating and moaning. She clutched her knees to her chest and closed her eyes tight in an effort to stave off the agony that wracked her body in waves. Twelve hours in the holding cell drove her craving for her fix to a gut churning, blinding pain.

She no longer noticed the hard cold floor or the bright yellow lights. She just wanted to curl up and die.

The police had seen it all before. The night shift was letting her sweat in hope she would say something about the dead guy in the apartment across from the school, but she was in no shape to do any talking. Not yet, anyway. They were not 100% sure she had anything to do with the apartment shooting, but being in the school put her close enough to be suspected.

41

The Tactical Unit's commanding officer, Joseph Brayton, told the processing officer, "That idiot teacher really screwed things up. His prints and DNA are fucking everywhere. One of my boys nearly popped the dumb ass. Good thing he fainted. All we can nail the girl for is running when we said stop."

Detective Donell, a grizzled fifteen-year man, stood nearby, listening, taking mental notes for the investigation. He smiled at the thought of a fainting, gun-toting teacher. He peeked in the holding cell. The idiot deserved to get shot in the hand. He's lucky he didn't catch one in the head.

They had very little evidence on her. Looking her over, it was possible she was underage and the Youth Services people might swoop in once they got wind of her presence.

"Yep, I can see this little beauty walking," he said to the window.

"What's that?" Roscoe, the supervisor, looked up from his computer.

"Ahh, nothing. I'm getting tired. If she says anything can you give me a call? I've got paperwork to do."

"Will do," said Roscoe, turning back to his own stack of papers.

Chapter 8

They ended up not leaving right away. The beer beckoned.
But once they got on their bikes and rumbled through the deserted
city streets, the night air was cool and helped clear their heads.
Walk-up apartments and old houses turned into new homes with
double garages, manicured parks and big shade trees. It was a
foreign land to them, a place where they did not belong. If anyone
was awake, they'd stick out like sore thumbs.

A left at the 7-Eleven, humming past an elementary school,
another left and they slowed to a chugging crawl. According to the
GPS on Timmy's phone, they were in the right neighborhood. They
pulled to the end of the cul-de-sac, killing their engines. Tim
checked the phone again.

"Which house?" Rocket asked.

"The glowing blob is over three houses," he said, knowing the detector offered an approximate location, based on triangulation with nearby cell towers. "It means Grundy's phone is here, but doesn't mean he is."

"Give him a call, see what happens."

*   *   *

In his slumber, he could hear Bruce Lee's cell phone ringing. He opened his eyes just before Bruce laid waste to most of Ainle's 7th grade class, girls included.

Grace's sleepy voice came from up out of the lump next to him. "Are you gonna get that?" He rolled his head and saw the glowing screen of the Grundy Phone. He picked it up.

"Hello?"

"Grundy?"

"No."

"Where's Grundy?"

"Who?" He got out of bed, now fully awake.

"Where's my money?"

"What money?" He walked to the doorway and down the hall.

"You got his phone, you got his money. His phone is my phone, and his money is my money."

"You have the wrong number," he said in the kitchen.

"We're outside your house. There's a blue Mazda with a flat tire parked in front."

Ainle paused, looking toward the living room. His heart was pounding. He took a deep breath and walked to the side of the front window, carefully peering out.

Two big men stood by the curb. One raised his hand as if to say Hi, the other had a phone to his ear.

"I'm calling the police," Ainle said.

"Just place the money and the phone outside and you will never see us again."

"I said I'm going to call the police."

"Sure, go for it. It's a free country. We'll leave, they'll come -- but, at some point, they'll leave. And we'll be back. We won't be so polite next time."

Ainle hung up and dialed 911.

* * *

"The fucker hung up on me!"

"That's rude Timmy. Rude, rude, rude, rude, *rude*."

"Let's head back to your place. The fool is calling the cops."

* * *

"Hey sweetie, what's going on?"

45

He looked up as Grace walked in, fastening her robe. "A couple of guys showed up. They called the phone and said they wanted their money."

She stood, blinking, trying to wake up and comprehend what he just said. "How did they know where it was?"

"I think they could track the phone using another phone. I called the police and they said they would send a car around. I guess it's a busy night."

"We should give them all that stuff when they get here."

"I don't like sitting here waiting. Those guys might come back."

"Then let's go to the police station."

He considered it, then nodded. "I'll call us a cab."

"A cab? Why?"

"Well, it appears our car has a flat tire."

"A -- " Grace stopped. A crease of worry appeared between her eyes. "This sounds dangerous."

"I hope not, but, yeah, it does."

*   *   *

The boys turned at the end of the street, headed down about halfway, then Tim signaled to Rocket to pull over.

"What's up," Rocket said after cutting the motor.

"Let's watch and see what happens. I'm thinking he's not calling the cops -- he's packing up and gonna blow town with my twenty grand."

"Didn't you say Grundy had a gun? If this guy has the phone and the money, wouldn't he have the gun too?"

Tim rubbed his forehead. Stupid greedy asshole. The only thing worse than a stupid greedy asshole was a stupid greedy asshole with a gun.

He stared down the street for several minutes, thinking.

He didn't know what happened to Grundy, but it wasn't good. He'd have to expect the worst. So, if Grundy was dead, then who the hell were they dealing with here?

And then the thought came to him: *What happened to Kat?*

Although she was, technically, his second cousin, she was also a dumb-ass bitch. It was bad enough he accidentally introduced her to Grundy, a man with twenty years on her, but, for all Tim knew, she was dead too.

Who is this fucking guy with Grundy's phone and money? he thought as he watched a taxi come down the street in the gloom of the night and then turn the corner, heading towards a house where a blue Mazda sat out front with a Rocket-induced flat tire.

Chapter 9

"North Side Police Station, please," Ainle said.

The middle-eastern-looking cab driver stared at them suspiciously in the rearview mirror. "Yes, sir," he said.

"Why didn't you give them the stuff?" Grace said, whispering.

"They flattened the car tire and it kind of pissed me off."

"You smell like scotch," she said. "I hope the police don't think you're drunk."

*   *   *

Tim watched the cab turn the corner, his anger in full bloom.

"Let's catch up to them and pull the injured buddy thing. You willing to lay your bike down?"

"No problem."

Their engines came to life, and the two big Harley's sped off in pursuit of the taxi. In less than a minute, the bikes were behind the cab.

*   *   *

The lights reflected in the rear-view mirror of the taxi. The brightness not only startled an already jumpy Grace and Ainle, but the driver as well.

"Why you going to the police?" the man asked in his thick accent.

"We have to drop off something we found."

As they approached a red traffic light, the lights of the motorcycles pulled up close behind the cab. Both Grace and Ainle turned around to see two large men sitting on large bikes.

"Friends of yours?" asked the driver. The light turned green, and the cab started down the long, curved road, the motorcycles following, then suddenly zooming around and bolting ahead. The three all seemed to breathe a sigh of relief as they disappeared around the bend.

As the taxi rounded the corner, something had gone terribly wrong. One of the bikes was on its side by the curb; the other bike was parked further down the road. A big guy with a moustache was flailing his arms wildly. The other rider was on his back and motionless.

"Oh my God," Grace said as the cab came to a stop.

Ainle leaned forward. "No, keep going."

"Honey, they need help," Grace said.

"I must help, I must," the driver said, putting the car in park.

Ainle didn't want to do it, but he got out of the car with the driver. "Stay here," he said to his wife. The men hurried toward the rider on the ground, who was gasping for air in raspy choking gulps.

"I'll call nine one one," the driver said, opening his cell phone.

A muzzle flash and a crack of a handgun round going off stopped Ainle in his tracks. The driver crumpled to the ground, his phone clattering to the asphalt.

From the car, Grace screamed.

"Freeze, shit head, and gimme my fucking shit." The large biker walked towards Ainle.

Ainle new he should do something or say something, but he couldn't move or even think.

"Gimme my fucking shit, you asshole," the biker said as his injured friend sat up, smiling.

Ainle's first impulse was to run, but he knew he would die, a bullet in his back. Even if the guy missed and Ainle got away, Grace would be sitting there, helpless.

Grace stepped out of the car and moved to help the injured cab driver.

Ainle turned his head and snapped at her, "Grace, give him the bag."

She nodded numbly, returned to the cab and pulled out the pack. Then she lobbed the pack towards the biker.

"Take it and get out of our lives," Ainle yelled.

Grace's throw wasn't very good, landing closer to Ainle than either of the bikers.

But what bugged Ainle the most was that it was the second time in less than 24 hours he was confronted with a gun. Police officers don't see this much action in a year. But his panic was rising, and the need to protect his wife was overcoming him.

The biker with the gun was still a good distance away, as the other stood to his full ominous height, then began moving towards Ainle and the bag.

"Grace!" Ainle yelled, not taking his eyes off the gun. "Get back in the car!"

The fake-injured biker stopped in front of the bag and kneeled down, unzipping it. He rifled around inside, and came up with a brick of cash.

"Yo, there's only ten grand here," the man said.

Ainle watched the guy with the gun turn his expression from mostly blank to pretty damn angry. If this were a cartoon, the color red would float up from his neck to his hairline, and steam would shoot out of his ears.

The two bikers reacted simultaneously -- the one with the gun moving purposefully toward Ainle, gun leveled at him; the other pulled a knife out of his back pocket and headed for the cab.

This was it. Freeze and die, or fight and maybe have a chance.

He raised his arms in a defensive stance, knowing his right hand would be of no use, but they wouldn't know that.

As the man approached, bringing the barrel of the gun up against his forehead, Ainle's good hand flashed up and slashed from right to left. At the same time, he stepped forward with his right leg, swinging his right elbow in a tight arc to deliver a horizontal strike that caught the gunman square on the hinge of his jaw. The biker crumpled to the pavement.

Ainle turned towards the cab, seeing the other man had stopped, knife in hand, seeing his buddy was down.

"Stay where you are," Ainle said, sounding more threatening than he felt.

The man glared at him, then began to charge the distance towards Ainle.

The cab suddenly lurched to life, speeding forward and hitting the man from behind, sending him bouncing onto the hood before rolling across the windshield and off to the right, landing on the back of his head, the rest of him smacking the ground better than any takedown Ainle could have executed. Grace stopped the car, and other than the softly purring engine, an eerie quiet settled around them.

"Help me," moaned the cab driver. "Help me, please."

Ainle ran to the man and kneeled down beside him. Blood stained his abdomen, and was pooling on the pavement.

Ainle took in the rest of the scene. Three down, at least one bleeding.

"Call an ambulance, call nine one one!" Ainle yelled.

The driver's hand touched Ainle's arm, "No, take me to my cousin, please. His wife is a doctor, no police."

This was all wrong. Ainle looked into the pleading eyes of the man. "You need a hospital."

"No, she is close. Please."

He frowned, feeling precious time slipping away.

"Grace! Get over here, help me."

Like a zombie, she obeyed, walking toward him stiffly, as if in shock.

"Help me put him in the car, we'll take him to his relative's."

"No. We have to call the police. This is stupid, Ainle."

"We don't have time!" he said.

They struggled, half-lifted, half-dragged the man to the cab, Ainle managing to lay him on the backseat.

Grace was already behind the wheel, so Ainle jumped into the passenger seat. He turned to the man in the back.

"Where are we going?"

Chapter 10

Ainle stumbled as he clambered out of the taxi. They were in an industrial area, full of flat-topped buildings and warehouses. The driver had sputtered an address, so he went up to the door, getting ready to pull on the handle when it popped open, nearly hitting him. A heavyset Mediterranean man with tired, dark eyes filled the doorway. He looked out at the scene, seeing Grace sitting behind the wheel of the car.

"Why are you driving our taxi?"

"The driver, he's hurt and asked us to bring him here. He said his cousin was a doctor. Please, he needs help."

The man suddenly came to life and hurried toward the cab, opening the rear door and leaning in. Ainle was right behind him.

"Saied, what happened?"

*   *   *

"That bitch fucking ran me over!" Rocket said, still lying flat on his back.

His head felt as if it exploded, his arm was numb, but he could move his fingers. He started to turn his head, but the pain told him to knock it off. He closed his eyes, grit his teeth, and tried again, more slowly.

He saw Tim lying on his back one leg bent underneath as if he were a ballerina that had fallen over. "Tim, you dead?'

No answer.

As Rocket gingerly got off the pavement, he wobbled a little, and almost fell over again. The second attempt was better, and he took a step towards his buddy. He stared for several seconds, looking to see if he was alive. If not, he would have to decide whether to pull him out off the road, or just get on his bike and get the fuck out of here.

Then he saw Tim's chest move. Rocket kicked at his leg. "Buddy, get up. We got to get out of here."

Tim's head turned to the side, and then he moaned and tried to sit up, flopped back down and rolled onto his stomach.

55

"Yeah, I know how that feels," Rocket said.

Tim crawled onto his knees and puked. Rocket stood for a minute, making sure he was done before helping him to his feet, both of them a little unsteady. They held onto each other like a couple of drunks after a bender.

"Dude, we gotta go."

"Fuck yeah," Tim said. "I need a drink."

Chapter 11

The two men in the small white van watched as a woman got out of the cab and hurried into the door of the warehouse while two men pulled a third out of the back of the taxi.

Darrell Kushner took photos while Mike Chin scrambled to take notes.

"Well, I wasn't expecting that," Chin said.

The pair had been conducting surveillance on the warehouse for two weeks, and despite considerable activity of both people and vehicles, this was the first time a body had been carted around.

"Looks like things are picking up," Kushner said, snapping a couple more photos. Once all the people had disappeared into the warehouse, the men sat back and waited for what might happen next.

"Come this way. My name is Abdullah. You have helped my cousin and for this I thank you. Please tell me what has caused this terrible thing?"

Once inside, another man had come forward and took Saied from Ainle. They then vanished into a side room with the injured man. Grace and Ainle were left standing there, taking in the view.

It looked like a warehouse from the outside, but the interior had been completely renovated, with several rooms built like some kind of windowless offices. Ornate lanterns provided both decoration and dim light, and there was the aroma of garlic and spices.

Towards the back of the main area was a round table surrounded by four men playing cards. If Ainle hadn't known better, he might have thought he had accidentally taken some of the drugs from the pack Grace was carrying.

They followed Abdullah into an office with a huge cherry wood desk and an expensive looking brown leather couch against one wall. Abdullah sat in a high-back chair behind the desk, and with a wave of one hand he gestured to Ainle and Grace to sit in two chairs. "Can I offer you some coffee?" Abdullah asked. "My sister makes the best coffee."

"Yes, please," Grace said.

Abdullah nodded, and Ainle looked to see a man standing in the doorway before he turned in search of coffee. "Please, tell me what happened," the man behind the desk said.

The man returned with a pot of coffee and two cups, pouring the dark liquid into each before leaving again.

"He likes my sister, but he does not make enough money, yet," Abdullah said with a look that was difficult to decipher. "I am sorry. I am listening now."

Ainle took a deep breath, considering what and how much to say. It was hard to tell part of the story without telling the rest.

Sensing his hesitancy, Abdullah said: "You are in trouble. I understand. You do not want to be in more trouble -- I understand this as well. But I do not know if you rescued Saied, or are the ones who injured him. I need to know whether I can help you . . . or something else."

Since all this started, Ainle felt he hadn't been making the best decisions. Now he had walked both him and his wife into another awkward corner without an easy way out. *In for a penny, in for a pound,* he thought.

So, he told the story, told it all, leaving out only the small detail of the money he stowed away behind the pots, next to the whisky. And the baggies of white powder. No sense in making it sound worse than it already was.

When Ainle was finished, Abdullah stared at him, nodding slowly. "So you think you have the money of these men?"

"Probably."

"And you still want to go to the police?"

Ainle shrugged. "Saied has been shot. I knocked out the man who shot him, and my wife ran over the other guy. I've got money that doesn't belong to me and is probably the result of some criminal activity. I mean, why *not* contact the police?"

"I don't think that is a good idea," Abdullah said. "We need to talk a little before you can return to your life."

Ainle didn't like the sound of that.

"You have helped my family and I can help you," Abdullah said, "but you must help me by not getting the authorities involved. They will ask many questions and I do not need any more police with my family. Where I grew up we never trusted the police. We solved our own concerns, and this has allowed me to have a strong business. And, God willing, a strong business for many more generations."

"But this is Canada," Ainle said. "It's different here."

"But we all have price. Look at you. For ten thousand dollars, look what you have done. Ten thousand, to me, that is nothing. Sometimes I see that every day. So, together we will work this out. But please, no police."

Abdullah paused, waiting for Ainle to reply.

After a few moments, Ainle said: "Let's assume we skip the police. Then what do we do?"

"You leave, maybe take a little holiday, go someplace warm. Spend the money. These motorcycle people will get busy with other business and forget about you. I, on the other hand, will not forget about you. You have helped me and more importantly you have helped my family. I will have Bashir take you home so you can collect what you need to. He will keep watch. All you have to do is go away and stay out of sight for a while, and everything will be normal again." He picked up a business card and wrote on the back. "Here is my personal number. If you ever need anything, just call me. I am in your debt."

"I don't know," Ainle said, doubtful. "It's . . . I don't know."

"Frightening? Yes, I'm sure it is. But will you feel safe at home?"

Ainle understood the reasoning, even agreed with it, but his gut was voting against it. On the other hand, he had to admit, he had no better idea.

Abdullah looked somberly to Ainle. "Go Montreal or Quebec City. These are beautiful places, and nobody will know you."

*   *   *

Grace and Ainle walked up the drive of their home, thanking Bashir for the ride. He nodded and said "I'll be here."

The routine of the last ten years had changed in the last twenty-four hours. Ainle had come across too many strange and mysterious people, and although he would have liked nothing better than climbing into bed, or lying on the couch zoning out in

61

front of the TV, he had a lot to consider.

He closed the door behind them, locking it. "I'm going to get in the shower," he said.

"Yes, please," Grace said, in pretty good spirits, considering. "You no smell so good."

He would have tried a zippy comeback, but he couldn't think of anything at the moment.

He went in the bedroom, stripped, threw his clothes in the bottom of the closet with the other dirty ones, and headed for the bathroom.

"Woo woo," Grace hooted from the living room.

Again, a playful reply didn't come to mind.

Instead, the police were in his thoughts. While he held them in high regards, he also understood the ramifications of reporting finding a bag of money and drugs. The police may believe him . . . or maybe not. A high school teacher with coke and several grand in cash would not look good, regardless of the story. It could impact his career, even if they believed him. Brad Burns, the school administrator, could use it as an excuse to get Ainle out, or even transfer him to another school. He had done worse to better teachers.

He got the shower nice and steamy, and got in.

If the police didn't buy his story . . . he might not be able to get a job anywhere after they arrested and prosecuted him for being a drug dealer.

He had to carefully work around his wounded hand -- an awkward proposition -- so a little thing like shampooing was a new challenge.

The Biker Dudes scared the hell out of him. The police may throw him in the clink, but the two hulks would go much further. They'd not just be out for blood.

Maybe Abdullah was right. It was the most pleasant of the possibilities.

*　　*　　*

Rocket was laid back on the old leather recliner, his body starting to stiffen-up. His back ached and he was having trouble turning his head left and right.

Tim stretched out on the big green couch, and although his jaw was not broken, it felt like it was.

They had graduated from beer to Crown Royal, which was nearly empty.

"How we gonna get it back?" Rocket asked after another sip. While he was hard on anything in a can, he was almost prissy when it came to the Royal.

"Easy, we kill him and his wife, search their house, find our money, then burn their fucking house down."

Not long after, they passed out where they lay. A half hour later, the cab driver's absconded cell phone buzzed on the coffee table. No one heard it. A few minutes later, Tim's went off,

63

blaring "Sweet Home Alabama" -- not a place he had ever actually been to, but it was $0.79 and it beat the hell of anything by Madonna. It, too, was not heard and went unanswered.

Chapter 12

Kat slammed the phone down. She was soaked in sweat and still shaking, although it was a little better.

The two officers exchanged glances, having seen it all before.

"You can try again later," the one with the nametag "Roscoe" said. "You sure you have no information for us?"

Kat scowled at them.

She was escorted back to her holding cell.

*   *   *

Tim awoke gasping, almost choking. Sleep apnea had been with him for years, and it was how he usually woke up.

Rocket was snoring with a steady rumble.

Tim got into a sitting position and picked up his phone.

Voice mail, said the alert.

He picked up the cab driver's phone.

Missed call.

He listened to the voice mail, a message from Kat saying *I'm in jail, help me.*

He didn't bother with the other phone -- "missed call" meant no message.

He used his phone to dial a number. A high-pitched Asian voice answered.

"Fat Timmy, what you want?"

"Hey Elton," he said, knowing Benjamin did not like the nickname.

"You owe me and you did not come. I had some nice music for you, but I sold it to the other guy. Now you need to wait for the next album, but you still owe me money."

"Yeah, my guy got himself in a little situation. I need a couple of days and I'll make it good for you," he said, trying to sound sincere.

"You have no choice, you and me have a good business here. Come for tea in a couple of days, we'll listen to some music. If you can't get the money, bring the girl. We call it even." Benjamin hung up the phone. There was no negotiation.

Stupid perv. Although he wasn't a fan of Kat's, he wasn't going to pimp her out. Besides, she was locked up.

Although he could get her out if he wanted to.

He didn't think Kat had turned 18 yet, which still made her a juvie. They'd let her out to the custody of a guardian before charges were filed and a court date set.

He kicked the chair Rocket was in. "Hey, want some coffee?"

"Hey, fuck . . . What?"

"Coffee," he said slowly.

"Yeah, man."

Tim went into the kitchen and started the routine.

He could go pick Kat up, but he and the police didn't see eye-to-eye. They might make a connection that he was Kat's supplier, even though he wasn't. At least not technically. He figured he was already on their radar, he didn't need to become a real target.

The coffee burbled.

He had kind of promised Kat's folks he'd keep an eye on her since they lived in Saskatoon. They didn't really want to have anything to do with her either, but still loved her and didn't want her dead or something. The girl was a self-centered whiner. Although she was well-acquainted with the word *take*, its friend *give* wasn't in her vocabulary. When she needed you, she was all over you. When you needed her, she disappeared like a fart in the night.

Benjamin, a.k.a. Elton, was always good to his word. To a fault. Kat had become a liability, and if selling her to pay the bills had to be done, so be it. But first, he had to spring Kat out of jail.

He poured two mugs of coffee and headed back to the living room. Rocket was now fully conscious, but a bit catatonic.

"You still have that lady friend? Alex? And will she do us a favor?"

Rocket looked at him as if he had just been run over by a car. "Sure. What do you need?"

"I need her to pick up Kat and pay her bail. Is she good for that?"

"Probably. But we'd probably have to go by the club and order a few private dances, if you're up for it."

"I'm always up for naked chicks dancing for me."

Rocket reached into his back pocket and pulled out his cell phone. "Aw, man. It's fucking broken."

"Use the house phone, Einstein," Tim said, handing Rocket his mug.

*   *   *

Grace came out of the bedroom, freshly showered, and Ainle knew she had been thinking about their situation. He recognized the furrowed brow.

He had a writing pad in front of him.

"What's that?"

"I thought we should figure out our options."

The furrowed brow grew deeper. "Do you think we could do it?" she asked. "I mean, really do it?

"Sweetie, there aren't that many choices. You have two weeks, right? We could go to Europe, or the States, but we'd need to get passports, exchange currencies, all that. Not with Montreal."

"Those bikers won't forget the money, I don't care what Abdullah said." There was a bit of fear in her eyes.

"I don't mean to scare you, but even if we gave them what they're asking for, I doubt they'll just walk away. Not after this morning."

Grace placed both hands over her face, and stayed that way for several moments.

He wanted to keep talking, making lame explanations about how Montreal would give them a nice little vacation, try some high-end wine, she could even practice her French. But even in his head, it sounded like a little boy trying to explain the health benefits of an ice cream cone.

Then Grace lowered her hands and nodded. "Let's do this. You buy the tickets, I'll call the school and make arrangements." She sighed. "You should do it before I change my mind or have a nervous breakdown."

Chapter 13

After some negotiations and the reality of the over-crowded holding cells, Kat was granted a No-Deposit bail, informed to stay away from illegal activities and told to report to the courts for a hearing in two months to the day. Having gone nearly 48 hours without drugs, Kat was finally able to put together more cogent thought. While still not feeling very good, she felt lucky no one had connected her to Grundy. She practically skipped out of the station, happy at not only being free, but seeing Alex, who was like a big sister with fewer rules.

"Hey Kitty Kat, long time no see," Alex said, hugging her for a moment before sniffing. "P.U. Let's get you out of here and cleaned up."

"I'd love that!"

The conversation in the Honda started off light and friendly, but turned more serious. "You fucked up," Alex said, holding Kat's hand between gear shifts. "It doesn't matter what you did, or how you did it, but you fucked up."

"Yeah, well, I had no choice."

"Bullshit," Alex said, gently. "You always have a fucking choice, even if your heart and brain tell you something else."

"I had to run, I had to go," Kat said, trying not to whine. "I just made a wrong turn."

"Hell yeah you did. You acted without thinking. I don't even know what the fuck you did, but I know that."

Kat sat quietly, feeling relieved in a way that Alex was calling her out for what she did, but not judging why she did it.

"If you want to tell me, fine," Alex said. "If you don't, fine. I'm probably better off not knowing because it'll probably scare the shit out of me. But whatever, you've got to be less impulsive. One of these days, I might be coming to pick you up at the morgue." She glanced at Kat. "Don't make me go through that."

Soon, they pulled into the Vixens lot, Alex leading Kat to the changing rooms. She pointed her in the direction of the showers, and when Kat came back, Alex was slipping on black stiletto heels over black stockings. She also wore a black sparkly top and a black ballerina skirt -- it all made her pale white skin seem almost glowing. Kat thought it was an amazing look for the tall, thin woman.

Tim and Rocket showed up just after 7, and looked out of sorts. Tim sported a nasty bruise along his jaw, while Rocket limped.

"You guys get in a fight?" Alex asked, smirking.

"You should see the other guys," Tim said, unconvincingly. He smacked a wad of bills onto the table. "Here you go. Thanks for helping."

"No, it ain't working that way," Alex said. "I need you to slip those in the right place in front of the other customers, and maybe I'll make some profit off this mess." She handed it back, then led them to the main hall.

Alex stopped in the doorway and waved at a slim blonde girl in a skimpy bikini who was selling beer from a tub full of ice. The girl brought over four bottles, then went back to her station.

"These are on the house," Alex said. "Or at least on me."

She pointed her bottle at an empty table.

"Make yourself comfortable, I'll be out soon."

All the chairs around the stage were full, college boys on an evening out, older men trying not look as pitiful as they felt and risk taking party girls all filled the front row a few truckers and the regulars.

The trio took their seats, and soon, the beers became whiskeys.

* * *

72

Ainle lay in bed, listening. Everything made him nervous. The little creaks of the house kept him on edge, always making him hold his breath for a moment, waiting for another sound that indicated someone was sneaking in. But it didn't happen.

Grace's regular, long, slow breathing didn't happen for a long time, which told him she stayed awake a lot longer than usual.

She vacillated all evening, first saying she didn't want to leave, then suggesting they leave right then.

They both jumped from the knock at the door. It turned out to be Bashir asking to use the restroom. Grace also offered him dinner, which he declined at first. Then he had second thoughts, taking a plate back out to his car.

"What if we just hung out at the airport?" she asked.

"Do you really want to do that? It's like twelve hours in uncomfortable chairs."

She sighed heavily. He hugged her, and he could feel her relax.

Now, he was the one that could have used the hug, who needed to relax. It would come, at least not tonight.

*   *   *

Alex wrapped herself in a blanket and stepped off the stage as the men and boys hooted and whistled. She headed for the table off to the side.

"Anybody for a private dance in the back room?" she said, her skin glowing and sparkling from sweat.

"I gave you most of it when you were shaking your tushy," Tim said. He slipped the rest of his money to Rocket. "Why don't you two head off and have a good time."

Rocket practically flew out of his seat, then stood there like a nervous schoolboy.

"Hold on there, big boy," Alex said. "I'll take care of you in a minute." She turned to Tim and Kat. "You two okay?"

"We be good," Tim said.

"Alrighty. Be back soon."

A tall redhead started to dance on the stage and Kat and Tim watched the sensual movements begin. Tim leaned over to Kat and whispered, "You might want to start dancing to pay back the money you owe me."

Kat's face was blank, pretending she didn't hear him."

"Where's Grundy?"

"Dead."

He paused. "How?"

"Shot."

"Who did it?"

"Me."

"Shit. Where's the money?"

"Lost."

"Lost? What the fuck does that mean?"

"It means I don't have it."

"Jesus Kat, I'm out twenty thousand. I owe ten to the Asians and they have a nasty way of collecting." He paused, letting his steam dissipate. "What are you going to do?"

She didn't answer.

Tim sat back and watched the girl on the stage and took a long drink from his beer. "So, here it is. You owe me twenty thousand dollars and the police have no idea you shot Grundy. At least not yet. If you are in jail, those Asians are going to come hunting for me, and that's going to be messy. They want the money in a couple of days and that's not going to happen unless you pull at least ten G's out of your ass."

The girl onstage gyrated in an unnatural but quite appealing way. Tim took another long drink, almost finishing the beer.

"Lucky for you, you have a pretty nice ass, and that's how we solve this little problem."

Kat shot him a look that would have stopped a lesser man.

"Don't look so surprised, but you can't hang around this city. You need to move somewhere else, leave all your stuff in that shit apartment and we'll get you working out East. The police will figure out what you did to Grundy. They're not as stupid as they look. You think that, that's when you get busted."

"Why can't I just stay with you?"

"Because you owe me twenty thousand. It's business. People die for a ten-dollar rock. Twenty thousand, baby you're screwed."

"But I don't know anybody out East."

"You don't know anybody here. You killed Grundy. I can't know you. You gotta go."

"But what do I do for work?"

"Dance, of course. I think I can talk to Alex. I think she's looking for something fresh. She can teach you. And if you need to pick up some cash on the side, well you are a pretty young thing. You'll make it up somehow. Just be creative."

"I don't want to go."

"Okay, pay me my twenty thousand dollars, and you can go your own way."

Kat just sat there, quiet. It had sunk in. "A great dancer can make fifteen hundred a week. That's six G's a month."

"But what if I don't do it?" There was a rebellious whine to her voice.

He knew her fear of being alone, abandoned. "I'll walk out of here with Rocket and Alex and you are on your own." Tim paused, counting to three. "You know I care about you. I know you just had a small set back, we all have them. I'm having one with the Asians. I owe them. It's just a shame they are not as understanding as I am." Tim placed his hand on Kat's. "Together we can solve this. And I mean you, me, Alex and Rocket. Even my family out East will help. I can make this work for all of us. There's good money out East. Good money, good clubs, good hooch. Six months or a year and you will have people working for you. Alex will help you, she already told me she will."

Tim watched Kat's shoulders relax, sensed her acceptance. She would do what was needed. She didn't need to know he had already planned to sell her for ten thousand. Now she was going to work for the Asians and send money back until she paid him his twenty.

Tim sat back, sighed, finished his beer, sipped his whiskey and smiled.

*   *   *

Rocket returned from his private dance with Alex, a big smile on his face.

"Good?" Tim asked.

"Better than good. I think my back is all better." He looked around. "Where's Kat?"

"John."

"Is she good to go?"

"She's halfway there already."

"Seriously? Just like that?"

"I am the master," Tim said, picking up his fresh beer and taking a hit.

"What are we gonna do about our friend in the 'burbs'?"

"Pay him a visit tomorrow. Get my money, plus make some dough off Kat working back East, I'll be a happy man."

Rocket clinked his beer with Tim's. "So, what are you gonna do to the guy? You haven't laid anyone out in a while."

"I haven't laid what?"

Rocket, who had just taken a big gulp of beer, sprayed it as a laugh erupted from him, which made Tim laugh as well. But without the Budweiser mist.

"Aw man, you just made me waste good beer!" he said, still laughing.

"Yeah, but it improved the carpet!"

They both guffawed loudly, making heads turn.

"Hey, man, you should go back there -- Alex is waiting for you. You don't want her falling asleep."

"Yeah, I bet during your time in there, you had to wake her up a couple times!"

"Hell, no. She was bouncing off the walls!"

"Well, I better get in there and bring her back to consciousness." Tim stood and hitched up his pants. "Time to show her a real man."

"When I see him, I'll send him back."

Whether it was the beer or the whiskey, it was the first time Tim didn't have a comeback. He stood there for a few moments, then turned and headed to the private room.

Chapter 14

Ainle sipped his morning coffee, feeling a little nervous. He had twenty thousand dollars in his luggage. Grace thought it was ten thousand. He had never really broken the law in his life, and wasn't sure he was breaking the law now. It wasn't his, but he didn't steal it. It was just there. But he still felt nervous. And lying to his wife made it feel worse. The phone shrilled, and he jumped, spilling some coffee on the counter.

He jumped up and grabbed the receiver. "Hello?" he said, throwing a dishtowel on the spill.

"Mr. Ainle? It's Abdullah. I just wanted to check that Bashir got you home okay? And tell you that Saied is going to be fine. Although he was not going to die, he thinks he was and we'll just let him keep thinking that. Have you decided where you are going to go?"

"I'm glad to hear Saied is going to be okay. Bashir was a gentleman and an excellent driver. And yes, we have decided to go to Montreal. My wife speaks French, no border crossings and that kind of stuff. To us it's like going to Europe."

"Yes, Montreal is a beautiful city. I have family there and I will tell them you will be there. My family has restaurants and some even work in the harbor. If you need anything my family will help, all you have to do is ask. Perhaps tickets to a show, or a nice meal."

"Hey Abdullah, that's nice, but it's not necessary."

"Yes it is. You saved my cousin. You honored the request and kept the police out of it. I am in your debt. Call me if you need anything when you are away, or when you get back, my friend. Write this number down -- it is my direct number. Keep it safe."

Ainle wrote it down. "Thank you Abdullah, this means a lot to me. I will keep your number just in case."

"Have a good trip. Call me when you return." And the phone connection ended.

"Just in case of what?" Grace said from behind him. "Who was that?"

"It was Abdullah the taxi guy. He has family in Montreal and said if we need anything we could call him. Saied is okay, and the entire taxi family believes they owe us."

"Well, after all the craziness, I just want to get out of here, find a nice, quiet place, and get some sleep."

"Then we should get going. You all packed?"

"Yeah. More like overpacked. Hey, you know what I found online? There's half a dozen Kenpo schools in Montreal."

He held up his hand. "Would love to, but with this, all I can do is watch."

"Yeah, I'm sure you'll milk that for as long as you can." She smirked at him. "I'll clean the spill with my good hand, and you go talk to the neighbors, see if they'll water the plants."

"I better get going. We need to leave in forty-five minutes, and Barry can talk my ear off."

*   *   *

The little white van down the street from the warehouse sat idle as Darrel took off his headset and gave a snoring Mike a poke in the ear with his pen.

"What the fuck?"

"Sleeping beauty, things are starting to happen, and wipe that drool off your cheek."

"Talk to me Darrel," Mike said as he wiped the sleep out of his eyes sensing from his partners tone that things were serious.

"Well, here's the scoop. The young couple from last night are going to Montreal and we need to tag along. This could be our first big break since the start of the summer."

Mike sighed and stretched. "Has it been that long? Nearly six months on this one? Okay, I'll start the calls and see if we can get travel authority, or are we going to have to pass this one off to the locals out there?"

"Shit, let's hope not. I don't trust the folks out there, too many holes in their force. All of it made by dirty money."

"Where did you say we're going?"

"Montreal."

Mike and Darrell looked at each other and a moment of realization settled in like warm blanket on an autumn morning.

"Montreal," Mike nodded. "That makes sense."

* * *

Kat woke next to Alex, and, for the first time in weeks -- months -- felt safe. Tim bellowed something that sounded like *"Woman, make us some food!"* It was so caveman-like, she giggled.

"What a prick," the lump next to her said.

"What would he do if we weren't here?" Kat asked.

Alex rolled over and pushed the hair out of her face. "He probably says that anyway, just nobody does anything. Then he goes to Burger King."

Kat sat up on her elbows and whispered: "What if we sneak out?"

Alex turned her head and blinked at Kat. "It's okay. Montreal is beautiful."

82

"Sure it is."

"New city, new start. To me it's like a promotion. Come on, let's make the fatties some food."

Kat smiled a thin smile. "Okay, but why am I scared?"

"Something new, different, a life full of new strangers. But hey, we'll be room-mates. It's going to be fine." She rolled to the edge of the bed. "Come, before Yogi and Boo-Boo get grumpy."

*   *   *

Rocket pulled himself off the couch, drawn by the smell of coffee and bacon. And the need to piss. The achiness and stiffness from his neck and back were worse, if anything, but he was getting used to it. After standing in front of the toilet for what seemed like an hour, he came out to find Tim glowering by the window.

"What's the plan today?"

"A busy day, Rocket. We got a lot to do. Need to call Elton, let him know the deal, make arrangements for a resupply, then go visit our friends with the Mazda."

"Well, then, we should get ourselves some food and get our asses moving."

*   *   *

They pulled away from their home, and while Grace seemed to gaze at it longingly, Ainle was watching for any sign of the bikers. He realized that if they came back -- and they probably would -- they might not be on motorcycles. He felt the need to check every car they passed, the ones behind them, even parked ones.

"Did you bring the . . . backpack?" Grace asked.

"Yes, but I took out the flour," he said, carefully, knowing the driver might be listening.

"Flour? What . . . oh, that. Yeah."

"I should have destroyed it. It's probably spoiled by now."

"And the phone?"

"Stowed away in the bedroom. I took out the battery."

"And the . . . papers."

"Yes," he said, glancing at the driver, who was Jamaican or Bahamian or from somewhere in the Caribbean. He seemed more interested in texting on his cell phone. "All the paper."

"I'm not sure we should use it."

"I know, but there's not much of a choice."

"What did you tell Barry?"

"That we're going away so I can heal, get my head together. Getting shot messes with your head."

"Did you tell them where we are going?" "Just the city," he said, purposely vague in case Mr. Cab Driver was taking notes.

"Did you tell him the name of the hotel?"

"Yeah. He has my cell number in case they need to reach us."

"Can we change hotels when we get there? Just to, you know, be safe?"

"We could, if it will make you feel better, but those biker guys are small time -- not members of the Hells Angels or something. I doubt these bozos could find their big toe because they're too busy looking for strip clubs. As long as we keep you out of those, we'll be fine."

"Oh stop it. It was only one time." Graces cheeks reddened a little.

He grinned at her "You did have fun."

"Yeah, well, I did it for the exercise. Those girls are extremely athletic."

"Mm hmm," he hummed.

They fell into silence, Ainle playing through certain scenarios in his mind -- like what if the bikers show up at the terminal? Are on the plane? Meet them at the gate at Montreal-Trudeau airport? Knock on their hotel room door? Everything played out in different ways, and as he considered each, he found himself relaxing. It was like a proactive approach to his fear, rather than passive worrying.

His main goal was to protect Grace. That was a given. But lurking in the background was two weeks from now -- what happened when they got home? Was two weeks away enough? How long would it take those guys to give up?

When they entered the airport entrance, he pulled out enough cash to cover the fare and a tip, and felt his anxiety ratchet up a few notches.

Chapter 15

Tim set his coffee down then looked over the table at Rocket. "You ready?"

"Fuck yeah," Rocket said. Then a pause. "For what?"

"I'm gonna call Elton, make a deal. Get that settled, then we'll go bust a head."

Rocket looked around to make sure Kat wasn't within earshot. The girls were off in the bedroom getting ready for their big adventure. "You sure you wanna give Kat up for ten G's?"

"She gave me no choice."

"That's harsh." Rocket looked at his empty coffee mug.

"Yep, it's her or me. No fucking way I'm taking a bullet for her. She screwed up, she pays."

"It's still harsh."

Benjamin Wong sat at his gigantic desk, looking over spreadsheets. Basically, counting his money. He had to keep on top of it to make sure everything was coming in as it was supposed to. He had a beautiful house, a dedicated wife, two sons who worked the family business and three cars. A cream-colored Bentley Brookland for Sunday and Dim Sum, a jet black BMW X 6 for road trips, and a black Nissan 350z with full modifications (but the sons always drove that one.) He kept the cars in good shape at his auto body shop where he also funneled his proceeds from the drugs and prostitution. It was a good set up.

Keeping the money clean was the most difficult part. Big houses and fancy cars were difficult to explain to the taxman, but that's why he had high-priced lawyers and accountants. He lit a cigarette. As a man who supplied people their vices, this was his only one. He never touched the drugs, or the women, but he never judged those that did. They were his livelihood. The drugs were very lucrative, but the women were just starting to turn a profit -- especially the ones he sent to Southeast Asia. Those were just starting to click. If he got in good with the Eastern Family, it could turn into a quarter million profit, easy.

He still had to work out the routes to get the girls there. The Eastern family had the connections, but also took most of the profit. Plus custom agents, security personnel, forgers, even Interpol had taken money to allow the transportation of human flesh. It all required more money than he could imagine. The Eastern family knew the schedules of the employees, where they lived, where their families lived and, most importantly, their weaknesses. With that leverage, they would do what you wanted. Having a piece of that action was a nice dream, and everybody needed a dream.

His phone rang, and he looked at the screen.

"Hello," he said, pretending to not know who was calling.

"Elton, it's Tim. I think I have a solution to our little situation."

"Good to hear it, Fat Timmy," he teased back. "Are you going to visit me and check my music collection? Perhaps I can get one of my sons to install a stereo system on that bike of yours?"

"One of these days, one of these days. I'll see you in an hour."

"Make it two hours, I'm busy." He hung up. He did not need the extra hour -- he just liked to keep things on his terms.

* * *

"Did he hang up on you again?"

"Always does."

"Want me to come with you?"

"No. Stay with the girls and make sure they don't take off. I'll be back in three or four hours and then we'll go check out that Mazda."

"Then we'll celebrate."

"Fuck yeah."

*　　*　　*

Benjamin opened the office door and allowed Tim to enter first. As always, tea was prepared.

Tim sat in low leather chair at a round table more suited to a lawyer's office.

They went through the routine. Tim waited for Benjamin to pour the tea. Tim never really cared for it, but it was part of doing business. Benjamin made a big deal out of the pouring, then carefully handing over the cup like it was liquid gold.

"May you always have good health, and good fortune," Benjamin said.

"Cheers," Tim said, taking an obligatory sip.

"So, what is this plan you have that you need to come all the way here to present?"

"I owe you ten thousand dollars, so I've come to clear my debt. Not with money, but something better."

"Sounds intriguing. Tell me more."

"We talked about the girl, Kat. She is worth twenty grand, so I figure you can have her, and if you add in a kilo, and we can call it even."

Benjamin looked thoughtful. "She is a beautiful woman, a desirable commodity. But not worth twenty."

"She is young and can make you much more than that," Tim said.

Benjamin appeared thoughtful. "I will give you five for her and you will only owe me five, plus I will front you one kilo."

"Fifteen and one kilo."

"Eight and no kilo."

"Ten and a kilo."

Benjamin was silent for a long time. Tim knew he got what he wanted. He hated the dance, but it paid off.

"Done my friend, done. Ten, and I'll front you half a kilo, and another half when you deliver the goods to the family in Montreal."

"Okay, ten. Front me a kilo, and another kilo on delivery."

"No, half a kilo in Montreal, and I'll cover your tickets and hotel. I'll arrange it -- you just have to pick up the tickets at the airline desk. But be careful. My cousin Lin likes to talk."

"I can handle that. Deal."

They shook hands, a moment of mutual respect. Tim felt a big weight off his wide shoulders. Benjamin had always been fair, and he never felt there was any doubt, but he could never be too careful. During one of these negotiations a few years ago, there were three young gun-toting Asian men standing in the room. Even that time, Benjamin gave him what he wanted, but Tim was sweating bullets.

"How do you like the tea?" Benjamin asked.

"It's fine tea," Tim said, smiling, more out of relief than the love of tea.

*   *   *

Tim fired up the hog, disquieting the peaceful, upscale neighborhood. He moved down the driveway, and cruised down the pleasant, green-lined streets. His heart was light and his stomach was empty. They needed to move to the next step. The coke would sell in two weeks and he would have another twenty grand. He would unload the liability that Kat represented, plus a chance to get out of town. After what they were going to do this afternoon, getting out of town would be essential.

Once out of the neighborhood, he pulled off to the side of the road and pulled out his cell phone.

"Hey, how'd it go?"

"It's all good. How are the girls?"

"Sleeping."

"Good. They'll need it. Meet me at the diner, we'll get some lunch."

Chapter16

Grace and Ainle arrived at the departure gate two hours early, walked through security without any problems, and found a nice place to have lunch. Ainle knew Grace was not relaxed, he could feel the tension in her hand as they sat at the restaurant. Hell, he might have been more tense, but he couldn't let on.

"You okay?" Ainle asked, hoping to get her to talk, to get it out. "What's the problem?"

"Where's the money?"

"A bunch is in my wallet, literally a bunch. It's putting a dent in my butt. And the rest is in two envelopes, flat on the bottom of my carry bag."

She nodded, but didn't look satisfied.

"Is it alright, the hotel thing?" he asked.

"Yes."

"I thought you liked the Delta Centre Ville?"

"I do."

"It will be a great place to stay. It has that nice boutique in the lobby, the restaurant, the lounge."

"What if they come looking for us?" She put her hands to the side of her head and pulled her blonde hair back and tied it absently.

She was distracted, afraid. He needed to comfort her, even if she didn't want it.

"We can change hotels. I can go online find a nice place and stay some place nobody knows. We can be like spies in one of those espionage books. Or that French film you like with Alain Delon. The one with the Japanese title."

"You like it, not me," she corrected him. "But if we change hotels I'll feel a little better."

"Alright, we'll change hotels."

He saw her relax, she put her hands on the table and he held them.

"Thank you," she said softly.

The waitress approached. "Are you ready to order?"

*   *   *

"Well, " Mike said as he put his phone away. "It looks like we've got sharesies."

"What?" Darrel sometimes became frustrated with his partners tendency to make up words.

"You know what I mean. We get the travel vouchers and we're good to go, but we have to hook up with the local police. After all, it's their patch and we are their guests. It's what the boss said."

"Yeah, no big surprise there. Just once I would love to follow someone and not let the locals know. I'll bet you all the mobsters in Montreal already know we're on our way."

"I hope not. I'm in no mood for dying in the land of the French."

"Who are the contacts out there?" Darrell asked as he put the van in gear and slowly cruised out of the warehouse district and went East towards the airport.

"Two guys called, Jacques and Francis."

"Are you serious? What are they going to be wearing? Berets and little moustaches?"

"You know it. You had better buy yourself one at the airport."

"What do I need two for..."

*   *   *

The lunch had been greasy and filling, and the ride back to Rocket's place refreshing. Their bikes humming smoothly as they cruised past construction sites and office buildings.

They put the bikes in the garage, and Tim dismounted, enjoying both the look and smell of the room.

The garage was an art gallery of engine repair. The floor was next to spotless, the benches clean and organized, and the walls held an assortment of tools that appeared to have never been used. But Rocket was working on bikes nearly every day. The workshop contained all the gear necessary to tear a bike down to the frame and then put it back so that it looked like a completely different bike.

Rocket punched a button on the stereo and rock music began to bounce around the room. Tim smiled at the sound and stood against one of the benches that surrounded the shop, trying to guess the song. "Okay, who is this?"

"Man, this is Ginger Baker," Rocket said with a mix of astonishment and pride.

"Very nice." Tim took a seat on a stool. "I need to stash this kilo. You got a place?"

"Sure," he said, rolling back his tool chest, revealing a safe built into the floor. "Stuff it in here."

It was four feet long and two feet wide. The locking mechanism extremely complex, almost bank-worthy. The lid opened with a hydraulic hiss and Tim pulled the kilo out of his saddlebag and placed it into the corner of the safe, beside a long, flat carry case.

"When was the last time you used that rifle?" Tim asked.

"Went to the range the other day, before you came over. Do you think we'll need it?"

"No, I think torching the place is the way to go with this one."

"I've got some containers on that shelf there, and some fuel over there." Rocket pointed to a bench with a fume hood at the back of the shop.

"You ever get a silencer for that rig?" Tim asked, pointing at the gun again.

"A sound suppressor, my friend. Get with the lingo."

Half an hour later, supplies packed for their little trip to the suburbs, both men were feeling pumped. Tim wanted his money. He might have gotten a break from Elton, but the cash was very much needed. It was as if nothing else existed for him, only the need to get back what was rightfully his.

Tim knew Rocket loved this kind of work. He loved wrecking things as much as fixing his bikes. He would let Rocket get his rocks off and have some fun.

He also knew when he was finished packing his saddlebags that none of the supplies were coming back. While Rocket felt the excitement of a professional athlete about to step onto to the field of play -- eager, heart pounding, eyes-wide and bright, ready to go -- Tim was more calculating and considering all the possibilities -- the dangers, the pitfalls, the downsides.

The bikes fired up, they roared with raw power. The clutches were released and gears were engaged. The machines rolled onto the street, banked left and accelerated into the early afternoon sun.

Inside the house, Kat rolled over and hugged Alex, "This is so much better than jail."

*   *   *

The flight to Montreal was long and tedious, but Ainle had been able to research an alternative hotel prior to their departure.

"How about we stay at the Hilton?"

"Sounds expensive."

"We have this extra cash. Plus I'll feel better when we spend it."

"Me too."

"You'll like this place, it's just up the road from the Delta, so you can still hit that boutique if you want to. We can have our big adventure." Ainle was trying too hard to make Grace feel relaxed.

"It's more like 'a nice voyage'."

"And it will be," he said, trying to reassure her.

The weight of the money was starting to make him second-guess his choice, but he knew it was too late to do anything. The idea of spending the money seemed like the best plan for getting rid of his feelings of uncertainty.

*   *   *

The two officers from the Service de police de la Ville de Montreal or SPMV sipped airport coffee and scanned the arrivals area of the Pierre Elliot Trudeau Airport. Detective Francis Goupil passed the faxed photograph over to his shorter and older partner, Detective Jacques Laforge. Goupil hated the fax system, everybody in the office saw what was up and sometimes he was not sure if he could trust his fellow officers as much as he used to as a young cadet. There had been so many problems with the bikers in the 90's, the mafia that never went away and now the new drug-lords. Cash money was being tossed around like confetti at a wedding. The big money was such a lure. He had even thought about it himself, who wouldn't think about an extra thousand dollars a week. But then some low life son of a bitch owned you. Francis looked at his distorted reflection in a fashion advertisement and said, "Nobody owns Goupil."

"Yo, Francis," Laforge said from a few meters away. "Stop talking to yourself, looks like we have friends."

Goupil turned and smiled at being caught in a self talk. "Let's see where they take us, Jacques."

Both officers loved this part of their job. The unpredictability of subjects who had no idea they were being followed.

"Francis, I'll get the car, you do the eyes."

It was a well practiced routine. Laforge loved to drive and fancied himself a Formula One quality driver. Goupil, years ago discovered he had an uncanny ability to become invisible in plain sight and loved the game of the hunt. A game he usually excelled at.

"Okay, get your ears on," Goupil said as he tapped the tiny ear-bud in his ear.

Laforge nodded and disappeared into the moving mass of travelers on his way to get their car.

It was easy for Detective Goupil to follow the man and woman. The woman did all the talking and man carried their bags.

Goupil keyed his mic, "Looks like they're going to the limo service. Pretty blonde woman in a gray windbreaker and a tall male in a tan jacket. I'll meet you in the front."

"Got it."

* * *

Ainle hoisted the bags and collected Grace who was staring back at the arrivals gate. "Come on sweetie, lets take a limo or towne-car, not a taxi. I've had enough of those for a lifetime." He smiled and tried to make his troubled wife feel a little easier.

They moved slowly towards the airport exit and something caught Ainle's eye. Was is it the woman with the little yappy dog or the short haired man who seemed to turn suddenly when they moved his direction?

"Who's he talking to?" Ainle said as he leaned in towards Grace who was looking at an information sign.

"Stop," she pleaded. "You're freaking me out. It's just some guy on a cell phone. Everybody has them these days." She tried to tease him back, but felt worried at the thought that somebody might know where they were.

"Sorry babe. I'll keep my paranoia in check." Ainle decided to try and make a mental note of the short brown hair and that the man only seemed to be about five feet six or seven. About the same height as Grace. He turned to get one last look at the short haired man, but he was no longer there. The little dog still barked, but a mother and child stood where the short haired man had been. It was as if he had never been there at all.

Ainle chastised himself for being so paranoid and directed Grace to the limo line-up but couldn't shake the feeling that somebody somewhere was watching them.

Chapter 17

The boys slowly drove their bikes past the house and took a long look at the cute little one family home. Flower baskets hung from the veranda and the curtains were closed. The house had the feel of nobody home.

They drove to the end of the cul-de-sac and casually rumbled into the alleyway that separated the suburban block system. They turned their bikes to the right and rode down a back alley past the fenced back yards of three houses and pulled up side by side behind a single car garage and shut down their engines.

"I get the feeling they're gone," said Tim.

"Nice garage back here. I can get in through that gate if you want. Looks like it's a storage area for old wood and that sort of junk. Could be a good starting point."

"Let's go to the front and see who's home. If they are out, we'll ask the neighbors. We'll do the 'out of town brother and buddy on a road trip' thing, and see who talks. You want to be my brother, Rocket?"

"You bet. Just let me work my charm on the housewives. I might even get lucky."

"Maybe even a daughter for you, Big Timmy."

"That could work. We need someone to replace Kat."

They restarted the bikes and drove around to the front of the house and parked their bikes at the front path of Grace and Ainle's house. Tim put on his best fake smile and walked to the front door.

He rang the doorbell.

Silence.

Good, he thought. *No dogs.*

He rang the doorbell a second time.

Nothing.

On to the next.

*   *   *

Rocket climbed off his bike, and went to the house immediately to the right. The place had dead flowers and a messy lawn. Children's toys littered the front porch.

Rocket rang the bell, children's voices called out, then a woman's voice yelled and the children became silent.

"Bonjour, hello?" an attractive but tired-looking African woman said through the half-open door.

Rocket turned his smile on. "I'm here to visit my brother," he said, pointing to the house next door. "Do you know why he's not home?"

But the African lady just shook her head, spoke quickly in French, then closed the door.

Rocket waved politely and walked back to the bikes where Tim was waiting.

"I think she likes me," said Rocket.

"Yeah, you're getting married."

Rocket blushed. "I'll try across the road."

He walked up the driveway to a small neat porch with a bench for flowers and a red door. He rang the doorbell and waited. An older Chinese lady came to the door and opened it slightly.

Rocket flashed his smile.

"Hi there, I'm here to see if you know where my brother is. He lives over there." Rocket pointed across the street.

"Who?" "My brother"

"Who's your brother?"

"Over there." Rocket tried his smile a second time and pointed to where Tim was standing. Tim gave a little wave.

"Come back tonight when my husband is home, he might know." And she closed the door.

"What was that?" Tim said.

"I don't think she believed me."

"Wow, struck out twice," Tim said.

"Too much man for them, I guess."

"Well, try that one over there. Maybe she'll be into plus-sized dudes."

Rocket walked up the steps to a nicely kept, small white house with a brown veranda and matching chairs in one corner. He rang the bell and wondered what life must be like in such a conservative world. Boring. It all looked so innocent, but he knew everyone had secrets.

A blonde woman opened the door and again he tried his charm. "Good afternoon, I was supposed to stop in and visit my brother, he seems to be out. He injured his hand, and I wanted to check on him. Would you know if he is out or if he will be back later?"

"Oh dear," she said. "I don't know." She was hesitant, and Rocket thought he detected a slight accent.

"Are you Polish?" he asked. "My friend's family are from Warsaw." He lied as he pointed over to Tim who smiled and waved.

"Yes, my family is Polish," she said, eyes widening slightly, "but we are not from the big city, a smaller town in the south."

"Oh it's beautiful there, I've seen the pictures when having dinner with my friend."

In the back of his mind, he was impressed with the way females bought his lies.

"Did my brother say anything about when he would be back?" He smiled gently.

She paused a moment, thinking. It wasn't clear if she wanted to say anything.

"Well, it's going to be about two weeks. They went to Montreal. Grace is a French teacher -- did you know that? And Ainle was shot in the hand in that school shooting. It is a terrible thing what some kids are doing these days."

Rocket shook his head as if disgusted. "Yes, and it's a shame. Well, I tried his cell phone, so maybe he's on the plane and can't answer." He smiled again. "Thank you, you have been so helpful."

He turned as if to leave, then stopped.

"I was wondering, did he say where they would be staying? I know my brother, he always likes to stay in the same hotels when he finds a nice one." He smiled his best soft, gentle smile.

"The Delta Centre Ville," she said.

"Well, again, thank you so much," Rocket smiled and waved. "Enjoy your afternoon."

"Thank you. You too." She backed into the house, closed and locked her door.

"Got it?" Tim asked as Rocket approached.

"Got it. He's in Montreal for a couple weeks."

"Of all the places, eh. You know where in Montreal?"

"Sure do."

"You want to go to Montreal?"

"Sounds like fun. I haven't been with the Frenchies in a few years. It will be nice to get out of town."

Tim was grinning. "It would be fun to run into them there."

Rocket rubbed his big hands together.

Tim paused and looked around the quiet neighborhood. The day was warm, the sky blue and cloudless.

"That fucker stole my money, hit me in the face with a cheap shot. Then his bitch wife runs you over with the fucking cab. "Now he's on a holiday and I'm paying!"

"It ain't right, man, it ain't right."

Tim took a deep breath.

"Let's go burn something down."

*　　*　　*

The boys fired up their bikes, slowly and smoothly cruising around to the back of the house.

A tan colored six-foot high fence ran the twenty-five foot width of the property.

They killed their motors and dismounted.

"I wish I knew this fucker's name. I'd write it in the dirt with my piss."

"Ainle."

"What?"

"His name is Ainle."

Tim frowned, confused, "What kind of stupid fucking name is that?"

"I don't know, it's what the Polack woman told me. Ainle and Grace."

"Sounds like a stupid-ass TV show."

He returned his attention to the matter at hand. A garage started where the fence ended and Tim went to the electronic security lock, trying a couple of number combinations. 1-2-3-4, no luck. 4-3-2-1, nothing. 0-0-0-0, zip. He could be here all day.

"What's the address here?"

"Uh . . ." Rocket looked around and saw numbers tacked on the upper eave of the garage. "Three-six-oh-four."

Tim punched that in, and the door groaned and began to roll up. Tim walked inside and stood in the middle of the garage, and surveying the messy interior. "Does that door over there lead to the house?"

Rocket walked over and opened it. "Yep. We should find a heater or furnace. If we start it in here, it won't look like an accident."

"I don't fucking care about that. Let them know. They need to know."

"Okay."

Rocket started to pour the gasoline. He poured from the side of the garage, over some of the cardboard boxes, toward the washing/drying machines, to the door leading into the kitchen.

"Let's light this candle."

Rocket held his zippo to an old rag, watching it catch fire, and dropping it to start the gasoline trail.

They went out and sat on their bikes for an exhilarating moment as the flame burned orange and blue, crawling along the floor towards the kitchen door. Tim casually started his bike, and rode out of the alley, and banking to the right and onto the street with a grinning Rocket pulling up the rear.

Behind them, smoke began to rise into the air. At first, it looked like someone using their fireplace. But as the flames devoured the boxes, then the door, and started consuming the wall, the thick black smoke began making itself more prominent. Tim and Rocket watched from a good distance, and the emergency response vehicles roaring down the street told them they did the job, and did it right.

Chapter 18

Grace held Ainle's arm in hers and tried to take in the roof top oasis of the Hilton Bonaventure. "This is amazing. Did you know this was here?"

"I had no idea, Grace. We could spend the entire time just up here."

It was two-and-a-half acres of green space at the centerpiece of the rooftop. All the rooms formed an unusual geometric shape that surrounded the grass, trees and a small river that meandered from one end to the other.

"Oh, sweetie, can we afford this?"

"Of course. We have more than enough cash."

Grace let go of his arm and took another look at the roof top garden. "I feel kind of guilty."

Ainle walked over to the stream, kneeled down, and put his hand in the cold, fast-moving water.

"It's like this place. It's not who I am. This little, river is not real. It's nice, like the money. It's a nice thing to have, but it's not real. It's not who we are."

She kneeled beside him. "I know it's not who we are. But it makes me wonder who we are." She paused, still troubled. "So, what's next?"

"Well, we are here. Let's just spend some of the money, have some fun. Then, we'll come back here, share a cheap bottle of wine and make out." He smiled.

Grace wrapped her arms around him. "I love only you," she whispered. "Je t'aime."

Ainle could feel her tears. "I love you too, Grace." And for several moments, they held each other. The roof top garden might have been an oasis, but the weather was changing, and clouds moved through the cityscape as the wind picked up from the St. Lawrence river and wound its way through the buildings of old Montreal, forced upward by the tall structures. It was cool and swirling as it passed through the roof top garden.

Ainle felt Grace shiver. "Come on, let's go in and check the room."

"Yeah, looks like rain," Grace said looking up at the quickly-changing clouds.

The room was nice. One king-sized bed and windows with an uninspiring view.

"Well babe," Ainle said standing at the window, hands on his hips. "Nice view of the train station. I read this train station dates back to before world war one."

"That's nice," Grace said, not impressed. "Let's go out for a nice dinner."

"I'm ready, just need to get a jacket."

*   *   *

Part of old Montreal's charm is in the stone. Gray limestone slabs formed the outer walls of many structures. In places, it is stained black from years of diesel exhaust spewing through the narrow streets. The tightly-packed buildings resembled a mix of a French village and 1800's London. Banking institutions, churches, tiny boutique hotels and cobble stone streets hosting maple syrup tourist traps and below-street-level bistros. The warm, yellow glow of the early evening shoplights gave an inviting and peaceful welcome in the cool autumn evening.

"Want to try down here?" Ainle asked as he stood peering down a stone stairwell.

"I need a new coat," Grace said. "It's cold here at night."

"Okay, let's have a snack first, then we can go looking."

La Crème-de-la Crème was like so many bistros in the Old City. Upstairs were apartments for students and artists. The doorway, where Grace and Ainle stood, gave rear access that went down below the street, but the door on the other side of the building opened onto street level where on the chilly evening, tables with umbrellas sat empty. Music and the aroma of garlic came up the stairs to meet them. Grace breathed in deep and exhaled. Ainle was looking down the narrow street.

"Wow, what an amazing smell," she said. "Let's eat and warm up, then go looking at jackets. You should really get one too. You need a new coat. Dress as nice as the other men in Montreal."

Two girls walked past arm in arm, talking quickly and laughing together.

Ainle watched them, feeling an uneasy disquiet come over him. Then he caught himself. "You're right, people do dress nice," he observed.

"They smell great," Grace said, watching the girls.

Ainle turned to look at her. "That's weird Grace."

"Why? One of them has really nice perfume."

"You have an amazing nose. And, it's also kind of hot that you think those girls smell nice."

"Relax, it's nothing special. In fact, I can't believe that you didn't catch that. It was a fresh citrus aroma, like summer in France."

"I liked their boots. You'd look hot in a pair like those."

"Yeah, but they'd probably kill my feet. I'm not as young as you wish I were."

"I bet you'd find something you'd like."

"I guess we do have a little extra money, and I don't have any shoes like that. I'll let you buy me some after we eat." Grace stood on her toes and gave Ainle a soft kiss.

"Do you want to eat here?" Ainle asked. "Does this place suit your nose?"

Grace smiled and made a show of breathing in deep and then making a small groan of pleasure, knowing it would tease Ainle. "This place smells great. Garlic, coffee, wet stone and --" She sniffed. "-- maybe a little moldy."

"So, do you want to skip it or go in?"

"I'm hungry."

Ainle led Grace down the stairs and into the long, narrow bistro. On the left was a bar with brass beer taps and sparkling wine glasses. Small tables for two or four lined the wall across from the bar. A tall, slim barman nodded as they entered and he pointed to a table by the window that looked out onto the street.

"This place is great," said Ainle as he placed his hand onto the solid rock that made the wall by the window.

"I'd like a beer, please," Ainle said to the waiter.

"Red wine," said Grace.

The waiter smiled and nodded, then disappeared.

The place had several diners, but was not packed. The ambiance was comfortable and friendly. Ainle looked around to see who was around them.

"Okay, here's an idea." He leaned in toward his wife. "If we get separated and we need a place to meet, let's make this our rendezvous point."

"Separated? What do you mean?"

"Well, you know how when we go shopping together, and I . . ."

"Wander off, bored with me looking at clothes and shoes?"

"Yeah, that. So, maybe I'll wander here, have a beer, read a book, chill out. We just meet up here."

"Don't watch too many French girls," she teased.

"I only have eyes for you. I just saw the boots and thought they would look great on you."

The waiter appeared with their drinks, then made a quick retreat.

"Drink your beer, Romeo."

"Cheers, sweetie," he said as they touched glasses. "I think it's time to try some tasty food. Does it still smell amazing?"

"Almost as amazing as those girls," she said, wiggling her eyebrows.

Ainle sat back and smiled. "You are a bad girl."

"You wish."

*   *   *

Francis took a long draw on his cigarette paused and exhaled a beautiful blue cloud of toxic smoke. He had an excellent view from across the road of the young couple who were having a nice lunch in Crème de la Crème. All he knew was that he and Jacques had to keep an eye on them until the cowboys from the west got out to Montreal and relieved them. It was a classic piss-off to be called off the job they had been doing just to keep an eye on a couple of tourists from the west. But when it came down to it, the day was warm and the pretty girls were wearing the last of their summer clothes, things could be worse.

The small ear-bud speaker beeped once in his ear and Jacques spoke slow and steady. "My friend, all I have to look at are pretty girls and fat Americans, how are your eyes?"

Francis paused and said, "I can see them both and it looks like we will be here for a little while. They are getting themselves lunch."

"Good, if you can see them, then I'll get myself a snack. Let me know if they leave."

"Remember, no poutine for you, you're starting to look like one of those fat Americans, and hey, don't shoot anybody."

"It was either me or him, partner, you'd of done the same."

* * *

Ainle pushed his hand through his hair, and stared out the window and across the road. The guy at the bus stop had missed three buses. He just sat there smoking. A strange feeling of being watched briefly clenched a knot in his belly.

"What's up sweetie?" Grace asked.

"Nothing, really."

"Are you watching the guy at the bus stop?"

"I am. Is he one of Abdulla's friends? He does not look like a biker."

"We should pay and go. I don't like the way you look, I'm concerned that we didn't really get away from our problems."

"Yeah, lets go spend that money and get back to the hotel."

*   *   *

Francis keyed his mic and spoke quickly, "Looks like they're on the move, Jacques. Going your way."

"Okay, got it. Let's see where they go." Detective Jacques Laforge dumped his half empty coffee into a garbage bin and leaned back into the shadow of an old curio shop.

The young couple came up out of the bistro, looked left and then right, whispered to each other and walked slowly off to his right.

"They're going East on St. Paul, my friend."

"Okay," Goupil replied. " I'll follow from down here on Rue de la Commune. Let me know when you need a switch."

"Will do, let's go for 30 minute switches."

*   *   *

By the time the fire department got the blaze under control, the house was destroyed.

The Captain had been directing his men and taking notes. One of the guys approached. He was covered in sweat and his jacket looked too big for him.

"Captain."

"What's up, Sullivan?"

"It looks to me like it might have started in the garage. I think this could be arson."

"And what makes you say that, my young Jedi?"

Nervous to appear a fool, Sullivan said, "Looks like a fire trail across the floor and up the door. Plus, there appears to be a gas can melted onto the floor by the door."

Not to discourage the young man -- even though those clues would have been noticed by a Boy Scout with bad eyesight -- he patted him on the shoulder. "Give me a tour, Sully, and then I'll get the Arson boys on the job."

The young man smiled proudly, and turned, leading his Captain into what looked to be a crime scene.

*   *   *

"That was a good day's work, Rocket," Tim said as he passed over an ice cold beer.

"A good fire always makes me thirsty."

"You're always thirsty, dude."

They stood at the busy bar of the Vixens club, taking in the sights and sounds. A tall, slim red-head -- apparently, a true red-head -- was collecting her articles of clothing off the stage and both Tim and Rocket were admiring her athletic movements and healthy skin tone. The rest of her looked pretty good too. Tim turned towards the bartender, waving him over, then nodding at the stage.

"Hey, Sammy. Who's the red-head?"

Sammy was an older guy, always wore dapper clothes, with white shirts buttoned all the way to the neck. His quick beady eyes missed nothing, and his dark hair was slicked back, looking oily and greasy like his skin. Tim knew, though, that bartenders like Sammy knew everything about everyone, even if it was the first time he'd laid eyes on them.

"She's new, I think from out East. I heard she got into a little trouble with a guy and showed up here. Today's her first day."

Tim slipped a twenty on the bar. "Do you think she might like to make a little money?"

"I can ask."

"Find out if she's cool. I'm not looking for a single mom going to cosmetic school. I need a girl who can take over for Kat."

"Yeah, I heard Alex was going out East and was taking someone with her. The sooner Kat gets out of town, the better. I heard from a guy they might be trying to connect her to Grundy. The dead do talk, you know."

"Thanks for the info." Tim slid over another twenty. "You're a good intel guy."

Sammy smiled, making the money disappear. "Your daddy was good to me in the old days." Sammy looked away, then turned back to Tim. "Excuse me, I've got some impatient ladies who need my expertise." He headed towards the far end of the bar, working on filling new drink orders.

Tim became pensive, feeling the need to get his plan sorted out.

"What do you think of Sammy?" Tim asked.

"What do you mean?"

"Could he be our new Grundy?"

Rocket shook his head, uncertain. "I don't know. I wouldn't say he's clean, but I've never seen him do anything sleazy. I trust him, but I don't know if he'd go for it. And the red-head's too new to know if we can trust her."

"You're right there. But we can charm her, flash the cash, and hey, if she wants to make some serious coin, we're here for her."

"It could work," Rocket said. "What about the girls? How do you want to move them out East? Car, bus, train or plane?"

Tim took a long drink. "Bus is out, we could lose them on the way -- and I don't want to drive. I'll go stir-crazy. "

"That leaves plane or train -- like that John Candy movie," Rocket said, trying to lighten Tim's mood.

"The plane has security and would be six hours of travel time. Six hours ain't bad, I could handle that, but security could be trouble. But we're not crossing the border, so security should not be extreme. The train is two-and-a-half or three days and that's got to be boring as hell. I might fucking kill someone just to stay awake. What's your choice?"

"Plane," he said instantly. "Shorter travel time, plus you said Elton was going to get the tickets and hotel. We do the pre-check in at the kiosks. All we need are ID's, and they only eyeball them. It's not like going to the States where they do background checks. The plane is my choice."

Tim took another long drink and clinked his glass against Rocket's. "We'll have a great time in Montreal -- and maybe we'll bump into the scumbags that ripped us off."

"Yeah, that would be a plus -- a chance to bump some heads. And right now, the way things are with Kat killing Grundy, shooting that guy, losing the drugs and money, getting arrested, that cab driver getting shot, plus the house fire, I don't think we should hang here. Besides," Rocket said, smiling, "there's those places with the meat sandwiches, and those fine French girls, you don't need to ask me twice."

Tim nodded to Rocket then leaned over the bar and yelled: "Yo, Sammy! When do you get a break?"

"Ten minutes." Sammy called back.

"How about you and Red meet us in the back? I've got an idea I'd like to bounce off you."

Sammy gave Tim a thumbs-up and smiled.

* * *

The back room had old chairs and couches, an ancient worn coffee table and a door solid enough to turn the music of the club into a low, dull thud.

Sammy and the red-head sat on one couch, Rocket and Tim on the two single chairs on either side. They both tried to look relaxed and not imposing. The buzz from the beers helped.

"Okay, I have an opening in the family business and Sammy, I think you're ready to step up. What do you think about getting a promotion?"

Sammy's shifty eyes went from Tim to Rocket and back again. "Is this Grundy's old job?"

"Yes, it is."

Sammy didn't react at first, then smiled. "Sounds interesting."

"And you need an apprentice. That's where you come in, Red," he said, looking the woman in the eye and not at her extensive assets. "Are you cool with making big money?"

"My name is Jasmine," she said, matter-of-factly.

Tim sensed some confidence there, but not a lot. If she were all that full of herself, she'd turn him down outright. But the kind of false confidence he was reading meant she had something to prove.

"Jasmine," Tim said, with a slight smile. "Beautiful name. This is a job that can bring you, Sammy and me large amounts of money in a very short time. My other girl is getting a promotion and moving back East. I know Sammy is ready."

Tim glanced over to Sammy, who smiled and nodded his approval.

"But this job requires two, and I think you'd be perfect. Are you in?"

"Why do you think I'm perfect?" she asked. "We only just met."

Tim shrugged. "I don't know, call it good instincts."

"Is it my looks? 'Cause if it is, I can do just fine here."

"Your looks are part of it, sure, but I sense some smarts, some fire for something better."

Jasmine stared at Tim for several moments. "How much money?"

Without hesitating, Tim said: "Double, triple you could make here on a good night, with a lot less work."

She absorbed this, and Tim knew she was on board. "I'm not hooking. I don't do that."

"Sammy is your boss," Tim said. "Sammy works for me and Rocket, you are the apprentice. He ain't no pimp -- ask anyone here. When Sammy gets promoted, you get Sammy's job. It's a great business model. We all make money together."

"Just to be clear," she said, "we're talking drugs here, right?"

Rocket shook his head. "We don't like to say that kind of thing out loud. We sell music."

"And a little advice, since I've been in the music business a while," Tim said. "Do not sample or use the product. I've had associates in the past that fuck up their lives over it, and they're not singing anymore, if you know what I mean."

"Besides," Rocket added, "we don't like missing any inventory."

"She's cool," Sammy said, jumping in. He looked at her for reassurance.

"I can count on you, both of you?" Tim asked. "Rocket is going to set you up with the resource and contact information. I've got to arrange some travel plans, a little business to expand the company."

He stood and held out his hand to Sammy. "Deal?"

Sammy took it and shook. "Absolutely. Deal."

Then Tim turned to Jasmine. "Deal?"

She smiled coyly, then held out a nicely manicured hand. "Deal."

"Welcome aboard," Tim said, shaking her dainty hand.

Chapter 19

"Are you ready to head back or would you like to go for a coffee?"

"Let's go back to the hotel." Grace looked at her collection of bags and boxes. They had walked into the boutique half an hour before closing and Grace made excellent use of the time. "Can you pay the girl?"

Ainle gave her a wry smile, took out a fold of cash and handed it over. She gave him his change, and thanked them for coming to her shop.

With a large bag in each hand Ainle and Grace walked out into the early evening. The air was fresh and cool and people bustled past. Ainle hailed a taxi, and then he saw him.

It had to be the guy from the airport.

A taxi hissed to a stop in front of them and Ainle stepped back a little from the curb and lightly bumped into Grace. He took a second look across the street and the guy was gone. Two girls were locking their bicycles and smiling to each other.

"Stop staring at the girls, sweetie," Grace teased.

Ainle took a deep breath and they piled into the taxi for the short ride to the hotel.

"*Merçi*," Grace said to the driver when they arrived at the hotel. Ainle paid the fare as a uniformed doorman opened the doors to the hotel. White marble stairs and a deep blue water wall welcomed them, providing an additional calm.

Carrying most of the bags, Ainle elbowed the elevator button, and the doors opened immediately. They got inside the empty car and, as the door began to swish closed, a large fleshy hand reached in, and the door retracted back open. Three large Asian men and two young girls jammed themselves into the elevator.

Grace looked at Ainle and then at the Asian gentlemen. Ainle knew what she was thinking. It had to be the expensive suits. She was window shopping, wanting him to get something just like theirs. Tomorrow was going to be spent in a men's store. And why not, he thought. The suits were extremely quite nice. Ainle glanced at the girls, both white and pretty, and he then looked over to Grace.

She noticed it too.

The short skirts and tight tops made them appear to be party girls, but they looked like they were sixteen -- definitely not older than twenty. They were an odd group, two suburban high school chicks and three jumbo older Asians -- not that much older, but old enough to know better than to be with jail bait.

Ainle understood Grace's concern, but he resumed his pensive stare at the changing numbers as the elevator approached their floor.

They stopped, and everyone disembarked -- the Asian men first, the girls second, followed by Grace and Ainle. Ainle whispered for Grace to slow down, let the other party get well ahead of them. They watched the five walk down the corridor and turn to the right and out of view.

"Come on, let's see where they are going," Ainle suggested, heading toward the hallway.

Grace scurried along behind him, trying to keep her bags under control, and caught up to him standing at the end of the corridor.

"They went in there," he nodded to two large double doors.

"Okay, and..."

"Two young girls, three Asian men in fancy suits and a luxury suite at an expensive hotel? Something is wrong. Those girls must be escorts or strippers."

"Maybe, but so? There's nothing illegal about being a stripper."

"Come on, Grace, you saw their age."

"Yes, but it could be the girls are singers and they are being promoted for a Japanese or Korean tour."

Ainle sighed. "That's possible, but not likely."

"Come on, Mr. Secret Agent, let's go party in our own room. You make the martinis and I'll show you what I bought." Grace walked down the corridor in a kind of bump-and-grind. She looked back over her shoulder, blonde hair across her head and eyes. "Want to see those boots I bought?"

Ainle could see the mischief in her eyes, and he smiled.

"Martinis, here we come!"

*　　*　　*

Ainle stood at the bar mixing the drinks. "Hey Grace, I can't stop thinking about those young girls and those older men. Something felt wrong." Finished with the martinis, Ainle set them on the coffee table.

"I know," Grace called from the washroom. "So tell me, what do you think of my purchase?"

She entered the room wearing a sleeveless, tight fitting grey dress that went to her knees and hugged her body. The grey leather boots reached up as far as the hem of the dress.

"Wow," Ainle said. "That's hot. You're right -- what Asians? What girls? I love those boots."

"I chose the ones with the flat heels -- the high heels looked too much like the style of a streetwalker to me."

"Come here, baby, and keep your boots on."

*   *   *

Grace was covered is sweat as she slowly climbed off Ainle. She stood at the foot of the bed still breathing hard, wearing only her long boots and tying her hair back into a pony tail.

"Wow," she said. "So how much do you like my boots?"

"Wow," Ainle said, almost panting. "I love them."

"I need a shower," and she left to wash up. One boot, then the next, flew out of the washroom and landed and tumbled at the foot of the bed.

*   *   *

The airport was relatively quiet and not too busy. The four of them boarded the red-eye flight like one big dysfunctional family. The tired and bored security people saw them as a couple of strippers and a pair of big oil field workers. All four passed through security without incident.

Kat was having her first plane ride and was wide-eyed and pensive. Alex was tired and grumpy. Rocket was like a little kid with his magazine and candy. And Tim was constantly watching, trying to make sure that Kat or Alex didn't screw things up.

Six hours later, the party arrived in Montreal at 7am. This airport was alive with business traffic as they stood by the carousel waiting for the luggage. Rocket was watching the crowds of travelers as if he were trying to spot the one who didn't belong.

"I'll call Elton's cousin," Tim said. "He has a cousin everywhere. Then we'll take a cab, collect the money and stuff. Hang out for a while, maybe a week, then unload the stuff. We get a whack of cash and head back. By then Sammy should have sold all the stuff and we just made ourselves fifty grand for a week's work. And if we bump into our suburban friends, maybe we get another twenty thousand back. Business is looking good." He pulled out his cell phone and made his call, getting the address, and the four of them took a shuttle to downtown Montreal.

Elton had booked them a room at one of his favorite hotels, The Queen Elizabeth. It was in an excellent location, only minutes from the Bonaventure train station and just a few minutes from Old Montreal. A little bit to the north and East was the university area and all the college bars. Just beyond there, Chinatown was only ten minutes south. Fifteen minutes East of the hotel -- and on the periphery of Chinatown -- were strip clubs and army surplus stores with low rent apartments upstairs. It was an area where tourists walk through quickly while on their way to the relative safety of somewhere else. The St. Laurence seaway and the harbor's chic café's and bistros were only another fifteen to twenty minutes south. It was an excellent base camp for both business and pleasure.

The hotel entrance was classic early 1900's ornate extravagance blended with high tech flat screens and computer terminals. The giant arching entryway appeared golden in the morning light. A massive lobby welcomed them as a bellhop collected their bags and placed them on a brass-railed trolley.

Elton had done his part of the bargain: The room was an executive suite, with three bedrooms -- one each for Tim and Rocket, and one for the girls to share.

"I got to crash, folks," Tim said. "Order some food if you guys are hungry, but don't leave the room."

"I'll babysit the ladies, bro. Then, we'll sample the delights of this fine town." Rocket said as he fired up the TV, and the girls disappeared into their room.

*   *   *

Still in a sleep-daze, Tim stumbled to a window and stared out at the cityscape.

It was mid-day, and time to get the business going. He had connections from the old days that now lived out here. A couple of the boys had been from Vancouver, came out for some "business", been arrested, did their time and then stayed in Montreal and Quebec. Tim's old buddies were as close as like Tim and Rocket -- independent, making good money and staying out of the big gang radar, like The Angels, who ran both cities. There was a philosophy for the independents. They believed being part of a major motorcycle gang was no different than working for an oil company or a banking institution. Tim and his close circle of friends were the last of the free men. No patches, no big organization, no boss.

Tim saw his reflection in the window, he realized his belly had become bigger over the last few years, but that was the price of doing excellent business. Food and drink were plentiful.

"Yo, Rocket, let's go find the boys from the old days."

"Sounds good, I need some air," Rocket said as he sat up and rubbed the sleep from his eyes. "Are we going to the El Matador tonight?"

"Yes we are. It's one of Elton's places -- or at least one of his cousin's places, something like that. We'll go there, drop the girls off and then snoop around some of the hotels."

"Like cops, looking for a couple of bank robbers."

"Just like that."

"Right on, I need a shower first."

* * *

The officers tracked the tourists through the streets the way they would hunt a wild animal. Jacques followed from well back, maintaining a steady pace while relaying movement details up to

Francis who followed from the front. The two officers saw each other at nearly the same time.

As Francis walked over, he studied his partner putting his phone away.

"Who you talking to?" Francis asked. He had developed a mild curiosity about his partner over the last couple of months. He was looking good lately, nice shoes and now that new Dodge Charger.

"You first," Jacques stalled.

"The cowboys from the west have arrived. They want a briefing. Who you talking to?"

"Hey you want to make a little extra money?"

"How?"

"Working a little after hours security for a high-roller party out in the acreages. Good cash, lots of ladies and hey, easy money."

"Are you serious? Sorry, that's your gig, man. Caro would throw me out if I was to spend a Friday night watching the girls."

"That's the price you pay for marrying an Irish girl."

"You should be careful with that high roller shit."

"Don't worry about me, you're the old one that stays home on a Friday night."

"Careful my friend, I don't want you to get compromised. Is it the Italian's this time?" Francis asked, curious about where the money was coming from.

"No, this is a party for real money. I think it's a going away party for people from Hong Kong."

"That is big money. Maybe you should take some pictures, you never know who you'll meet. You keep the dirty money to yourself. Maybe the cowboys will join you."

"It's not dirty money," Jacques said a little quicker than he had wanted.

Francis looked to his partner and wondered if the gangs now owned him. It was a sinking feeling for a police officer to suspect that his partner was no longer clean. Francis looked up at the wall of the Hilton hotel and tried to push away his growing mood of dread.

"It's easy money, Francis."

"No such thing," Francis said more to himself than to Jacques.

*   *   *

Grace came out of shower, a towel around her head and wearing a white fluffy robe. She had enjoyed sleeping most of the day away. "I'm hungry, what about you?"

Ainle was looking through a tourist magazine on What To Do In Montreal. "Yeah, I'm starved," he said. "How about a coffee and croissant, then check out this Kenpo school. It's in one of those old walk-up row houses over towards the University."

"Let's eat first."

*   *   *

"Girls," Tim called out, "order some breakfast and bill it to the room."

"Alrighty," one of them said. It sounded like Alex.

Tim smiled at this. The room was being paid for by Elton, or one of his mysterious cousins. They might as well enjoy themselves.

Rocket came out of his room ready to go people hunting. He was dressed casual: baggy black jeans, oversized black button up shirt and long black leather jacket.

"You look like a giant ninja," Tim said.

"Ninja's are deadly," Rocket said. He got into a low, karate-chop pose.

"Yeah, that looks dangerous," Tim said, smiling. "What's with those girls? They sure sleep a lot."

"Yeah, they're not really the 'go getter' kind of people. That's why they work for us."

"Or Elton."

Tim got into his baggy blue jeans and gray sweater.

"Let's get a bite to eat and then start at the Delta Hotel. We can go from there. But after lunch we need to meet the Asian guys at El Matador. I'm sure the place is different from the old days. Remember when the Latinos used to own it? They had all those storage rooms in the basement for the booze and cigarettes. And they caught you down there getting it on with that Spanish girl."

"Jeez, that was a nasty night." Rocket paused to remember. "She was a sweet little thing. Her brother was none too pleased with me." He shook his head. "That was a long time ago. Booze and smokes -- that was a mistake. The First Nations took over the smokes and what were they thinking with the booze? Did they think it was 1920's prohibition?"

"Do you remember that trip when we rode our bikes out here, picked up the stuff and sold it all the way back?"

"Sure do. Damn, that was over fifteen years ago. What a good ride. I'd like to do that again, eh?"

"Okay, we'll set it up for next summer. Let's get some grub and see how the boys have changed. We sure have."

*   *   *

Grace and Ainle sat in the window of a small bistro. Grace was watching the busy foot traffic of St. Catherine Street as Ainle talked on the phone. The lunch rush had passed and the sun cast long shadows down the quiet street. The lattes were excellent and they smiled at each other over the top of the frothy sweet drinks.

Ainle set his phone down on the table. "It's set, we can take the train at one, get there for a two-thirty private lesson."

Grace swirled the coffee drink in her glass, smirking. "I think it's your turn to shop. I think you need a new suit."

"Really?" Ainle said, smiling. "I don't know . . . I might out-class you. Everyone will be looking at me," he protested mildly.

"I'm willing to take that chance."

"Okay, don't say I didn't tell you so."

"I'll wear those boots all night if you look at a nice suit for me."

He pretended to think about this. "Deal. But I don't think you'll enjoy sleeping in your shoes all night."

"Who said anything about sleeping?"

Ainle's face turned as red as a stoplight.

* * *

"They sure eat enough," Jacques spoke into his mic as he sat in his 2010 Earth-brown, Dodge Charger.

"Just let me know what's happening. I'm almost finished at the hotel."

Francis was completing the last of his work with the hotel concierge, and discovered a small anomaly. The guest had paid a week in advance in cash, something extremely rare in the world of credit cards. And with a little friendly persuasion Francis had been able to get their names, Ainle and Grace Larcon.

The paying in cash had piqued his detective curiosity, but at the same time he couldn't wait for the surveillance team from Vancouver. He had his own work to do, plus he couldn't stop feeling that he and Jacques were on a punishment detail. He had

137

his own work to do and maybe working a partner rotation.

The speaker in his ear beeped once.

"Hey partner," Jacques said."It looks like they're getting ready to move."

"On my way, I'm just waiting for the elevator."

*   *   *

Tim and Rocket walked out onto St. Catherine street and were enthused by the vibrancy of the street. They walked several blocks East then turned left at Boulevard St. Laurent. They found themselves a quiet bistro in the university district and each ordered a black coffee. They were anxious to check out El Matador and set up the exchange, but Tim didn't want to rush. The exchange of human flesh for cocaine was almost as intoxicating as the drug itself -- not that Tim cared for the powder all that much. He didn't like sniffing the stuff up his nose.

Tim and Rocket left the café and they went back down Boulevard St. Laurent, across St. Catherine Street and out of the University district towards Old Montreal -- which used to be a smugglers haven. It was at a crossroads. On the south side of St. Catherine's, Boulevard St. Laurent was one of those dynamic city areas plagued with a variety of socio-economic changes. The boulevard leads the traveler towards the El Matador, Chinatown, and the harbor. Thirty minutes south of the University district, the stylish clothes shops and bistros of north St. Laurent fade away.

Chic is replaced with less fashionable shops like military surplus stores with their cheap knives and used camouflage jackets, and head shops for buying crack pipes and rolling papers, all of it framed by abandoned lots. Then, where the tents and cardboard shelters end, strip clubs and massage parlors sprout like canker sores.

The El Matador was a tall beacon of neon sandwiched between a pawn store on one side, and a porn shop on the other. Once upon a time, El Matador was a dance club where the community of the 1950's came for a Latin experience. The late 60's brought a change, and hippies shunning money -- only seeking love -- meant El Matador fell to ruin.

The 70's brought a revival as it became a tacky disco haven. The Latino crowd returned with dreams of dancing as an escape. Even when business was slow, the nearby harbor made illegal alcohol and cigarette sales a business opportunity that led the club to becoming an after-hours party place. When every other place was closed for the night, you could go to El Matador for drinks and more. Illegal alcohol was in abundance, and the dealers and the prostitutes began to set up shop, creating a late night hook-up joint. The place changed forever when the dance floor and disco became a strip stage, and as the owners changed, the cigarettes changed from tobacco to marijuana, and the booze lost favor for cocaine and more. It was both the cocaine and the "more" that brought people like Tim and Rocket. The El Matador was a key hub for incoming and outgoing products. Nothing was produced, but almost anything could be purchased, if you had the money.

With such a variety of illegal products available, there was always a gathering of interesting and unusual customers. Business was good and security tight.

There was a team of new security guys trying to earn trust. The more trust you earned the deeper inside you got. Inside at the coat check, the security wore suits and looked respectable. They were body builders and MMA athletes looking to make money for training. The basement was high-tech and the people had literally gone through security school training. The products that were protected in the basement required a special detail. These were the long-term members and all had earned the trust of their bosses and knew large sums of money came their way when problems were dealt with cleanly. Mr. Jackson was in charge of keeping the extensive basement clean.

The basement was a warren of closed shops that were leftover from Montreal's underground city. Though the city's below-street-level shops were still a vibrant corporate enterprise, as with many giant ideas, small pockets did not make growth. Success of the underground city stayed in the business and university areas. Train stations and chain stores grew around the high traffic areas, but the outer edges fell into disuse. Planned subway stations were never built, and legitimate business never arrived. Many of the abandoned shops worked as storage for El Matador, but some were renovated into smaller private bars, rooms for sleeping, a variety of gambling dens and even a few theme-related rooms with beds for the inevitable private parties.

Tim and Rocket stood across the street and looked up at the tall blue and red El Matador neon sign -- a giant image of a matador poised to insert a sword into the neck of the charging bull. The place looked low rent from the outside. They spotted the outside security before any of them took notice of the pair. A wiry guy in an oversized basketball shirt and baggy jeans hanging way too low was heading their way.

"Did we look that obvious when we were young?" Rocket said.

Tim walked in the direction of the stick figure in clothes. "Good afternoon," he said. "Mr. Wong sent us with a delivery and a pick up. Is Mr. Lin working today?"

"Mr. Lin works every day. Who are you?" Skinny said, sounding and looking grumpy.

"I'm Tim and this is Rocket. I'd appreciate it if you'd tell your boss we're here. He's expecting us."

"Just wait here." Skinny tried to sound ominous, but just came across as shifty. He walked inside, then stuck his head out the door in less than thirty seconds, waving them in.

*   *   *

Grace and Ainle found the Kenpo School in a nice area of the university district. Master Thomas was a tall man with

141

shoulder length gray hair who met them at the door to the dojo. The training area was a refurbished, red brick, old walk-up row house. Massive maple trees lined the street and were in full bloom in anticipation to of the autumn color change. The training area inside the house was clean and fresh, and high windows opened to let both good light and cool air to enter. Mirrored walls reflected the light giving the room a bright, vibrant feel.

Grace inhaled deeply. "Hmm, smells nice in here."

"Thank you," Master Thomas said. "My wife keeps the place organized." His movements were smooth and controlled, a relaxed man in a state of inner peace. "Please change and meet in the training room and we shall see how Mr. Gorman has trained you."

"You know Mr. Gorman?" Ainle asked.

"Years ago we competed, he is an excellent kenpoist. So, now I have high expectations for you." He smiled thinly. "Meet me in the dojo in 10 minutes."

* * *

Jacques put the Dodge in park and leaned back into the leather seats. "How do you like her?"

"She's a nice ride," Francis said trying to determine how to talk to his partner about his after hour work, but his phone beeped. "Oui, bonjour, "he answered.

After a short conversation he clicked off his phone and Jacques looked over from the drivers seat, a quizzical look on his face.

"The cowboys?" Jacques asked.

"They're on their way. Should be about an hour and then we can dump these English Muffins and get back to our own work. Like, security guard for gangsters." Francis looked over and saw the anger redden his partners cheeks.

"Watch it, Officer Goupil, you are walking on thin ice."

"Don't fuck with me, partner."

"Maybe you should check the back of this building and make sure the English don't leave by the back door."

"My pleasure," and Goupil got out of the car and closed the door harder than he intended. "Fuck," he said to the empty street and stuffed his hands in his pockets and went down the street to find a back alley.

Officer Jacques took out his phone and dialed, a wheezy voice answered "What took you so long?" the man on the other end of the line asked.

"He's not in, but I am, you still need me for Friday?"

"Of course," and the line went dead.

*   *   *

The club was empty and musty and, with the lights on, looked a little worn down. A dance stage dominated the big room, with chairs and tables surrounding it, and three bars that accented three walls. Tim and Rocket followed Skinny past the back bar and down a flight of stairs into a basement complex. Here, the air was noticeably cooler and damper. They went down a hallway and were led to an office door with a small brass sign that read "Private." Inside, Mr. Lin's office was sparse. There were calendars with highlighted dates on the walls. A few black filing cabinets, an industrial shredder and desk peaked out from under stacked papers.

"Welcome," Mr. Lin said politely as he hung up his phone. He was on the small, thin and short side. "You have a delivery for me, and I a delivery for you. Your delivery is where?"

"We just wanted to make sure we had the correct address," Tim said. The lie came easily. "It's been a long while since I was here last. The basement seems different.."

"My cousin did not tell you about the renovations we have done? This basement has always been here. The corridors go way back to the underground city. The old cigarette and alcohol smugglers used these halls to stay underground all the way to the harbor. You should see some of the old artifacts we have found. But now, many of those tunnels are closed -- poor construction, you know." He paused. "Anyway, thank you for the girls. You must stay with us tonight. I will show you some of the other improvements. There are many rooms down here. We have poker, roulette, dancing, and more. When you return tonight, we'll have a 'get-to-know-you' party. There is always money to be made with our western cousins. Return tonight, sometime after 8pm, and we will get the business out of the way. Then, we can relax, have drinks, girls and fun." Mr. Lin gave a huge smile. To Tim, it looked sinister.

"We'll see you tonight, thanks for everything," Tim said, smiling back.

*   *   *

Grace and Ainle were exhausted. The workout was more than just physical -- it was emotional and intellectual. The hand techniques were quick and solid, their mental focus had to be sharp or else Master Thomas would say after Ainle walked into a strike: "You were hit because your mind is elsewhere. Control yourself, control your mind, control your emotions, or you could end up dead. Remember, Kenpo is not just exercise. Sometimes it is all you have. And sometimes it is all there is. Now, focus."

Ainle and Grace thanked Master Thomas at the door, and they stepped out onto the lush street of a warm Montreal afternoon. The trees cast shadows across the sidewalk, parked cars and locked bicycles. Grace breathed in deep and tasted the humid afternoon air, "That was great. Back to the hotel and eat?"

"Let's take a little side-trip, and go down here," Ainle said, pointing to the East side of the street. "The university district is

145

that way. Maybe we can get a snack and a glass of ice cold beer."

"I'll have a water."

*   *   *

Back at the Queen Elizabeth Hotel, the girls were enjoying a massage. Two masseurs kneaded their bodies, rubbing and squeezing and caressing, and Alex and Kat were in a state of ecstasy. They had, so far, enjoyed everything about Montreal, and now they never wanted to leave. It was like the Hollywood starlet life they had dreamed of as little girls.

The suite door rattled and Tim and Rocket walked in.

"Looking good girls," Tim said, taking out two fifty dollar bills and telling the masseurs to pack it up early. "The girls have to get dressed, were going to a party."

"Party?" Alex asked, as she rolled over letting the towel fall to the floor.

"Yeah, whose party?" Kat said, sitting up, her towel falling to her waist.

Rocket let out a low grunt as he stared at the two naked girls.

"You girls will fit in fine at the party," Tim said. "It's at your new dance club. The place is famous and you'll have a chance to make a lot of extra money."

Rocket walked up to them and let his hand slide across both their backs, emitting another growl. "You girls better get dressed before I forget myself," he said. "Make sure you wear something small and tight. Show off those bodies."

Alex slid off the massage table, took Kat's hand, and pulled her towards their room. They stopped in the doorway holding their towels in one hand, with Alex letting her hair fall across her eyes, they posed in their best sultry stances. Alex asked softly, "Is this going to make us extra money?"

"Yes it will," Tim said. He looked at Rocket, who was gawking as if he'd never seen a naked woman before, much less Alex and Kat in the buff. "Yes it will."

Chapter 20

The Republic was an eclectic bistro that looked more like it should be in Prague or Budapest than in Montreal. University students sat in red velvet booths and worked on laptops and huddled over unfinished papers as Ainle and Grace finished their late lunch. Both were getting stiff from the workout.

"Let's head back to the hotel and have a shower," Ainle said as he set his empty coffee onto the dark wood table. "Do you want to go through Chinatown on the way back? It's just on the other side of St. Catherine's street."

"Yeah. Maybe we can get a gift for my mom," Grace said.

They left the Bistro and began the walk south on Boulevard St. Laurent. As they crossed St. Catherine Street, the university flair changed considerably. The buildings were older and not well maintained. Some had plywood sheets over broken and forgotten windows. A homeless tent village filled a space where a building used to be and decidedly un-chic stores replaced the pleasant bistros and shops a few blocks north.

"This is not Chinatown," said Grace, weaving her arm around Ainle's. "Are you sure this is the right way?"

"I think it is. It should be only a few blocks ahead. Let's go a couple more blocks, then if things get worse we'll just go back."

"It looks like it might be getting better," she said. "The surplus stores are being replaced with strip bars."

"Would you like to apply for a job? I could be your manager."

She punched his upper arm with her free hand. "You perv."

"What? You could make a lot of money."

"Thanks, I think, for the compliment, but there aren't enough showers in the world."

"Well, then maybe you could do private shows, and I'll be your exclusive customer."

"Maybe. But only if you apply me with appropriate amounts of wine."

"Okay. In the meantime, I really would like a beer. Do any of these bars seem decent enough to you?"

"Not really," she said. "They look like they range from 'dive' to 'worse dive.' Unless you're looking to get beat up and maybe pick up a disease from a stool that hasn't been cleaned in a decade, I'd pass."

They walked past the narrow entrance to a bar with neon lights flashing GIRLS ALL DAY GIRLS ALL NIGHT.

"Can you smell that?" she asked.

"Urine and cigarettes. Reminds me of a couple of college frat houses."

"You belonged to a fraternity?"

He shook his head. "I didn't say I went inside."

"Hey buddy, spare some change?"

They both jumped at the voice.

It was a figure in the shadows of a doorway. Ainle saw he was just a kid, no more than 18, but ragged and street-worn. He held out a hand so dirty, Ainle thought at first he was wearing a glove.

"No, sorry. All tapped out," Ainle said.

"In those clothes?" the kid said from behind them. "You're fucking kidding me."

Grace pulled on Ainle's arm and led them across the street to give them some distance.

"Okay," Ainle said, "we'll walk to the end of the block and if things don't get better we'll go back the way we came."

"No," she said. "I don't want to go back. We just need to get out of here."

"Yeah, this area would be a bad place to be after dark." Ainle nodded his head toward a building ahead with a large neon sign. "That looks better than most, but I can't tell if it's a strip bar or a night club."

"I don't know. If it had gladiators, then maybe you could get me in there. But bull fighters?"

"Okay, good to know. I'll cross the matador costume off my list." His eyes scanned further up the street. "I think we're through the worst. I see Chinese restaurants and thrift shops ahead. Let's find something your mom would like. Maybe an Elvis clock, or one of those cats that waves in the window."

"What would she do with two?" Grace said, smirking. "I wonder if any of these places sells breastplates and swords. I bet you'd look great as Spartacus in a little leather skirt."

Ainle laughed. "I'll wear a leather skirt if you will."

"In public?"

He looked down at her, trying to see if she were joking. "With underwear, or commando?"

"What do you think?"

* * *

Francis had been watching Ainle and Grace while Jacques went to pick up the officers from the west. He'd found the young couple easy to observe and it was apparent they had no idea they were being watched or how to avoid observation. They seemed like tourists. He had stood in the window of a flower shop across from the Republic as they sat in the big front window drinking coffees. Now, they were walking down the street and into a nasty

151

neighborhood. It was like they were a couple of idiots. They even looked like tourists who had made a wrong turn. He just hoped he didn't have to rescue them from some crack-head who saw easy money.

Easy money. What's with all the easy money?

The familiar beep in his ear sounded as his phone rang, "Speaking of easy money," he said to himself as he clicked his phone.

"Francis, I have the cowboys. Where are you?"

"I am down by the El Matador," Francis paused while he waited for Jacques to respond. "Hello, Jacques? Are you there? Did I lose the connection?"

"No, no," Jacques responded, gathering himself. "Really? You are at the El Matador? Why are you there?"

"It's where the tourists are. These two are just tourists, I think they're going to head back to the hotel. Let's meet there and hand off this baby sitting job and get back to our own work."

"Good plan my friend. See you soon."

*   *   *

Alex stepped out of the room wearing a pink corset, short black skirt and heels; Kat was in a white halter-top and black skirt and heels. If the guys had any imagination, they wouldn't need it.

"Ladies, you look great," Tim said, and whistled.

Rocket nodded dumbly. "You girls look sweet."

152

"What's this party going to be like?" asked Kat, looking like she was a little out of her element.

"It's going to be fun, don't worry. There'll be big spenders and even a few major moneymen from Asia and overseas. There will be great music, lots of drink and a few treats for excitement. Have a drink, girls," said Tim, motioning towards the bar. "When we get to the party I'll introduce you to Mr. Lin. Rocket and I have a little business to take care of, then we'll party." Tim raised his beer.

"So how long will we work there?" Alex asked. "Where will we stay? I know we can't stay here forever."

"Mr. Lin has a place all set up. It's cool. You get paid, you work and you come back west this time next year. All your bills will be paid. Sound good?"

Tim knew it was unlikely he would really see these girls again. Business was business, and Kat had lost him twenty grand. If things hadn't gone differently, that loss could have cost him his life.

He did feel a touch of regret at leaving Alex behind, but somebody had to look after Kat. Was he getting soft in his tough life? Maybe, but sometimes, tough choices had to be made.

*   *   *

They entered the hotel room and Grace pointed at the phone. The message light was flashing.

"Does anyone know we're here?"

"Probably the hotel telling us they have a special wine-and-dine in the restaurant, or there's some band playing in the lounge."

She picked up the phone and pressed the voice mail button.

"What is it?" he asked as her face changed to something like horror.

She hung up the phone. "There's been a fire. The house is gone, burned down. Destroyed."

"What? How -- There . . . There must be some kind of mistake."

Grace started to cry. "No, it's all gone. Everything. We . . . We have to go back. Ainle, we have to go back!"

"We can't, honey. This . . ." He paused, collecting the right words. "They did this."

"The bikers? They burned down our house?"

He nodded somberly. "It had to be them. Did the message say anything about arson?"

Grace sniffed. "No, just something about filing an insurance claim."

Ainle tried not to think about all the stuff that was lost, tried to concentrate on what they needed to do, what they *should* do.

"We need to stay low," he said. "Those guys got their revenge. They'll move on."

"Are you sure?" she said, managing to sound both doubtful and hopeful at the same time.

"We'll just need to find a place to stay while insurance sorts things out."

"I don' t -- no, won't stay with my mother," Grace said.

"What about your sister?"

"I suppose we could, if we want to slowly go insane."

"Okay, well we don't have to make a decision right this minute." He paused, standing awkwardly, not sure what to do. "I need a drink."

Grace wiped her face with the back of her hand. "Yes, maybe a dozen. Why don't you make us a couple, and I'll call the insurance company?"

"We're out. I'll go get some."

Grace slouched on the couch and stared off into space.

"Everything gone," she said.

*   *   *

Down on the street the early evening air was still warm, or maybe it was the gray baggy sweater he was wearing. The underground mall in the train station had a collection of coffee shops, bakeries and liquor stores that he would normally enjoy browsing. Now he was on a mission. He found a well-stocked adult beverages establishment and chose an expensive bottle of Swedish Vodka and a two litre bottle of club soda. After the cash purchase, he ventured back through the mall and up onto the street.

155

He looked up at their hotel and thought about their home, gone in a fire.

The sooner the money was gone, the better he thought he would feel. But on the other hand, they now needed the money to survive for a few more weeks until things could be sorted out.

Ainle crossed the road and entered the hotel, went to the elevator and pushed the button. When the doors opened, out stepped the three Asian men, all dressed in different, but still expensive-looking suits.

They pushed past Ainle like he was not there.

"Have a nice day," Ainle mumbled.

Back in the room Grace was on the phone with the insurance company. She finished the call, hung up and sat there with a look of exasperation.

"You were right. It was arson," she said.

"Do they know who?"

"No, but they know it wasn't us, so insurance will take over all the details from here. When we get back, they'll have a hotel for a few days until we find a place to stay." She sighed. "Pour me a drink, then let's go out. I need a walk."

"I need to get drunk."

Again, Grace broke into tears. "It's like they stole all our stuff -- pictures, diplomas, music, everything."

"Hey," Ainle said softly as he put his arms around her and held her close. "We're okay. Look at it this way. We finally got rid of that old, ugly table."

The joke didn't seem to work, so he took a different tact.

"We can start fresh. We have this money, so let's spend it and see how much fun we can have."

"Thank you," Grace said through tears that were starting to subside. "Do you really think those bikers will give up?"

"Well, you did run one over with a taxi."

She smacked him on the chest with an open palm. "That's not helping."

"Look, they got their revenge, true. But they don't know we're here. They will not bother us again."

"What about when we go back?"

He shrugged. "Maybe we don't. Maybe we go live somewhere else."

"Where?"

"Wherever. We could even look around here."

Then something else occurred to him.

"What about Abdullah and the taxi people? They said they would help us if we needed. Maybe they rent apartments or have a condo."

Grace frowned. "Really? We offend two bikers, you beat up one and I run over the other, we're on holiday with their stolen money, and now you want to make arrangements with those taxi people which one of the bikers shot? I don't know, but it seems we crossed a line somewhere and I don't know if I like this side of it."

"Speaking of crossing a line, I saw those three Asian guys leaving the elevator when I was coming back. They were dressed all fancy, but the girls weren't with them."

"Yeah, throw them into the mix, and I'm not feeling very good or safe. We have to figure out something."

"Okay, but not now. Tonight, we drink."

*   *   *

The exchange had gone well. The Frenchies were glad to hand over the surveillance to the Cowboys and Mike had got himself a nice rental mini-van. He parked it with a good view of the main entrance while Darrel had jumped out to follow Ainle into the nearby market. Mike was happy with the French surveillance team, they had the names, some good photos and even better, one of them had been able to get a listening device into the room's phone. Not only would it transmit phone conversations, but if the conversation was close enough to the phone it would pick that up as well.

Darrel climbed back into the van with a couple of plastic bags containing bottles of water and sandwiches and said, "Looks like there's some sort of party going on. He just bought a bottle of Vodka, looks like they're planning a little party."

"Well get this, their house just burned down. I got the message from dispatch when you were at that mall. It might even be arson, but it's too soon to tell."

"This is crazy! There's something going on here, I can feel it."

"Hey, check out the dudes coming out of the hotel." Mike interrupted his partner. "Get the camera going, why are they familiar?"

As Darrel took his first pictures and then began to zoom in to get detailed shots he said, "Hey, what's with the two French guys. Something's up there."

"No kidding, Ol' Jacques seemed a little stressed."

"And that Francis was clearly pissed about something. We need to keep them in the dark."

"I hear you partner, that's a loud and clear."

Chapter 21

Tim, Rocket, Alex and Kat sat in Mr. Lin's, with Lin unable to keep his eyes off the ladies. Or, more accurately, their breasts. Their legs and, occasionally, their faces also got attention.

Tim realized they weren't going to get very much done with two distractions in the room.

"Girls," Tim said. "Go visit the party and have some fun. Let us finish the business here so we don't bore you"

"Okay, boys," Alex said, knowing who her audience was, and playing it up. "Kat and I are going to play." She pointed at each man, one at a time. "Don't miss us too much." Then she leaned towards Mr. Lin and whispered, "We'll be back."

Mr. Lin watched as the girls left, taking a long look at their asses. He smiled, taking off his glasses and cleaning the lenses as if they had fogged up.

"They will fit in nicely," he said, seeming a bit flushed.

"I thought you might like them," Tim said. "Now about our kilo . . ."

Lin pulled a small bag off the floor and set it on the desk. "Here it is," he said. "Do not sell it all in one place." Then he offered a half-laugh/half-snort.

Tim frowned. He didn't like the feeling he was getting.

"Okay," he said. "The girls still need to get packed up, so we'll take them with us tonight, and bring them back tomorrow."

"That is excellent. Tonight, let them be seen by the customers and tomorrow I will put them to work. I have several guests from overseas who will find those ladies delectable." He gave a wheezing high-pitch laugh, and Tim and Rocket looked at each other Then they smiled politely and stood.

"Thank you, Mr. Lin. We have enjoyed doing business with you."

Lin nodded, with an eerie smile on his face.

"Yes, get a drink," Lin said, "and I will take you for a tour of the underground city. You will like it. Over the years, it has gone from being a path for smugglers to shops and so much more. But my friends, it is still an interesting place for smugglers and . . . garbage disposal." Again, the wheezing laugh punctuated the statement.

Rocket saw the girls. They were easy to spot, out on the dance floor moving together with determined sensuousness, like nobody else was in the club. They drew plenty of attention from the hungry eyes of the men.

"So Tim, what's with the girls? It's like a lesbian thing they got going on."

"I don't know, maybe they switched teams."

Tim stepped up to the bar and ordered a couple of beers. He was quiet for a minute, and waited for the bottles to arrive and the bartender disappeared before he said anything.

"You know, there's something not right about this guy or this place."

"Yeah," Rocket said, nodding. "There's a vibe here that gives me the creeps. Especially when he laughed, that was just plain nasty."

"It reminds me of those Columbians from years ago. They were bad folks."

"Yeah," Rocket agreed. "That wasn't a good scene."

Tim guzzled his beer. "We need to do this business and move on."

"What about the girls?"

"It's done. They're here, we're here, and money is money. There's no going back."

"Yeah, but I bet you were thinking of pulling something over on this place."

"Gave it some thought, but it's their territory. I'm not ready to die for some chick that ripped me off for twenty grand. Not yet." He tilted his head slightly. "Put on a grin, brother, here comes Mr. Giggles."

Lin approached with two solidly built bodyguards.

"Your girls are putting on a wonderful show," he said.

The three looked out to the dance floor, watching Kat and Alex with their arms around each other's shoulders, their heads almost touching as their hips swayed and rolled to the slow, electronic music.

"Those girls will bring me plenty of money," Lin smiled. "Let me show you our underground city. There might be opportunities for you to make more money and even spend some time in one of our little shops."

*   *   *

Ainle and Grace had been bar hopping for hours. Both were feeling the influence of assorted drinks and Grace had a slight weave in her walk as they passed through the front doors of the Le Titanic, an Irish style pub with stereotypical Republic of Ireland flags contrasted with informational posters in French. A large dark wood bar framed the back wall where pretty girls wearing short kilts and white shirts would bring drink trays to loud groups at tall tables.

"Have a seat anywhere, love," said one of the girls as she passed with a tray of empties.

They chose a table by a window with a street view of Boulevard St. Laurent. University students and tourists milled past on their way to a party and more drinking.

"I like this area. It's nice being around a university crowd," Grace said after their drinks arrived -- a dark beer for Ainle and a vodka and soda for Grace. "It's so vibrant."

"I miss those days," said Ainle. "Life was so simple then."

"It sure seemed like more fun back then, but you know we were so broke there's no way we could have afforded a place like this," Grace raised her glass. "So, cheers." They touched their glasses together, looked each other in the eyes and took a drink.

Voices in the corner of the bar grew louder as two young university boys squared off, chest to chest. Two bouncers jumped in and pulled the boys apart. One was escorted out the back and the other out the front door. Front door boy put up a fight and as a result was tossed out and into a group of passing men in expensive suits. Front door boy made the mistake of a drunken threat to one of the gentlemen and, in a lightening flash of movement, a powerful arm grabbed the boy by the throat and shoved him up against a light post in front of the window where Grace and Ainle were sitting.

"Jeez, that's one of the guys from the elevator," Ainle said.

"It is!"

"Looks like that drunk guy insulted the wrong suits."

One of the suits, a tall lean Asian man, leaned over and talked to his friend who was holding the drunk by the throat, nodded an agreement then released the kid. The university boy staggered away, hunched over, one hand holding his bruised throat.

"Hey, let's see where they are going," Ainle said as he pulled out a twenty and laid it on the table. "Drink up."

"What? Are you serious? Why follow some drunk kid who'll probably just pee on a tree."

"No, the Asian guys. Let's see what they do. We're on an adventure, so let's act on it. You can be my Secret Agent side-kick."

"You're drunk."

"Maybe. But this place is too much of a fake Irish pub, anyway. It's making me grumpy."

"No, the beer is making you grumpy."

"Come on, let's *do* something." He stood up.

"Okay, let's do this, Mr. Bond. But if we see a cool place for a drink, we'll do the Secret Agent thing have a martini."

They headed out of the din of the bar and onto the comparative quiet of the evening street. A heavy gray cloud had rolled in from the St. Laurence and, like a lid on a pot, preserved the afternoon heat. A cool day had become a warm, humid evening.

Ainle pointed. "They're over there, heading south."

Grace took Ainle's arm in hers and they walked in pursuit.

"Why are we doing this?" Grace asked.

Ahead, the trio stopped.

Playing the role of spy, Ainle tugged Grace into the light of a shop window and stopped. Bright lights illuminated their faces as kitchen aids and home décor supplies served as a backdrop. "I'm curious. These guys are up to something. Those girls they were with weren't their assistants. Something seems off. I want to find out what they're up to. And we needed to clear our heads. What better than a little adventure?"

He peeked his head out of the doorway and took a look down the street.

"They're crossing the street up there. Let's go."

*   *   *

"What the fuck!" Mike said.

"Are you serious?" Darrel was staring across the road at the aftermath of the scuffle. Those are the Asian guys from the hotel and now this husband and wife are going to follow them. Is this for real?"

"Well, partner. Let's join this gong show."

*   *   *

At the back of the bar was a heavy door that opened to a stairway that went down below the bar. Tim looked down, and an eerie feeling came over him.

Lin led the way, Tim and Rocket following. At the bottom of the stairs, a wide hallway opened in front of them. A hallway to the left, another straight ahead, and a third to the right.

"Look what we have built. This is how we move some of our money. Money comes in from the girls, and the products, and we reinvest into construction. It is a wonderful way to stimulate the economy." Mr. Lin was sounding more like a politician than a businessman of the underground.

Tim was impressed with the size of the complex. It was more like a mall than a drug and prostitution den. There were flat screen TV's, promoting weekly drink specials, images of the girls who danced at the club faded in and out while hidden speakers played techno-music at a soft level.

"Mr. Lin, what are some of the stuff you've got going on down here," Tim said.

"Yes, it is very interesting. These rooms on the left and right are for cards and dice. If you like poker, you can play here for as long as you like. As long as you have money, that is." And he laughed that squeaky, wheezy laugh again.

The three men walked past a few doors on each side and came to something like an intersection.

"To the left," Mr. Lin pointed, "is where we keep our drinks and food supplies. There is a street access down that way. To the right, that can lead us all the way to the harbor, but it is not fully developed yet. There are water leaks and a few hazards, so we'll stay out of there. Straight ahead is our developing shopping district."

At various points on the ceiling and walls, surveillance cameras captured everything, at every angle.

"This place sure has changed since we were here last," Rocket said, keeping his head down as if to not be seen on camera.

"When was that?" asked Mr. Lin.

"Oh, ten or fifteen years ago," Rocket said.

"Follow me gentlemen. We have many shops down here."

They came upon an open door, and Mr. Lin held his hand out like the perfect host, letting Tim and Rocket walk past a young security man who nodded quickly in acknowledgement of the tour. Inside, men were gathered around a roulette wheel. A well-dressed young Asian man was calling for last bets, while a long-legged blonde girl wearing a vibrant green top and short white skirt took drink orders. Mr. Lin talked briefly with the roulette master who sent the girl over with a selection of drinks.

"Gentlemen," said Mr. Lin, "please. On the house."

The guys grabbed a beer.

"You see," Mr. Lin was smiling and acting like a conscientious host, "our girls, after they dance, can work in the shops. The tips are excellent."

The girl gave a practiced smile and walked away.

"So, you see, Alex and Kat will be able to make some excellent money on the side. It's a paradise down here. Let us continue the tour," said Lin as he led the men out of the room and down the corridor, now followed by an extra security detail.

They passed several unassuming doors and paused at an area with heavy double-doors on both the left and the right.

"On this side," Lin said, gesturing to the left, "we have supplies and resources. Mr. Rocket, do you like to shoot?"

"I sure do."

"While you are here you can get a little target practice. We have a large indoor range. It is, in fact, one of our legitimate businesses. The Red Dragon shooting range is completely legal -- but down here, we have access to the less-than-legal weapons. For a price of course." And he added that wheezing laugh.

"Cool," Rocket said. "If I need a rifle, I'll come to you first." He pointed to the right. "Hey, what's down there?"

"Girls," Lin said, slightly lasciviously. "We have girls for gentlemen who have . . . unusual tastes."

Tim had a furrowed brow, but Rocket was more than curious.

Rocket put his arm around Mr. Lin's shoulder and said, "Take me shopping."

"What would you like?"

"Oh, I don't know. Something foreign."

"Follow me," said Lin, leading them off down the hall.

The light shifted from bright to a much lower and softer tone. Along the walls, there were more doors, on the right and on the left.

"Red door or blue?" Lin asked.

"Let's choose blue," said Rocket.

Lin opened the door and the scent of cheap Jasmine perfume greeted them. On the left was a large blue sectional couch. Three Asian girls dressed in assorted lingerie sat waiting. They looked like they were about to appear in a lingerie fashion shoot. Each girl was slim, had long dark hair, and were expressionless.

"These girls will do anything you like. I mean anything." Mr. Lin smiled. "Your desire is their duty."

Rocket nodded. "Are they from Taiwan?"

"No, girls are from Cambodia. Their families owe money and as payment, the family lends us their assets."

"They look young," Rocket said as he glanced at Tim.

"We can go younger, if you want to pay extra." Lin became serious. "You can bring us more girls the next time you visit and you will get paid even more."

Rocket and Tim understood prostitution, guns and drugs. But they had a code. A distorted code, but a code that still had lines. One of those lines they didn't cross was kids. Selling women could put them away, dealing drugs could put them away even longer, but pimping out kids was practically a life sentence.

"I'll keep that in mind," Rocket said. To Tim, he looked troubled, finally catching up with how Tim had been feeling.

Lin turned to Tim to gauge his reaction.

"I prefer older women,"

"We can do that too," Lin said, kind of winking.

"Let's return to the bar," Tim said.

"Okay, my friends, one more room. This you will see is a very important room. Follow me."

Mr. Lin led them out of the blue room.

Tim was feeling a little nauseous. There was a lot he thought he could take, but the levels of depravity down here were things he had not considered.

Mr. Lin stopped at another solid door and opened it. This room was stark, almost empty. In the middle was a table with leather straps for ankles and wrists. There was a drain hole in the middle of the floor and a hose attached to the tiled wall. A tall gray metal closet stood alone against the far wall.

"What's this? A torture chamber?" Rocket asked.

"Yes it is." Lin was somber. Dead serious. He turned to Rocket and looked him in the eyes without blinking. "If anyone crosses me, this is where they come to die."

"Nice to know." Rocket met Lin's cold gaze. "We're just here to make money."

Tim interrupted the staring match. "We're cool. Let's get another drink. Mine's empty."

"Yes," Lin said. "Enough talk of such things. Let's party."

*　　*　　*

"I need a drink," Ainle muttered. They had followed the three men for several blocks until they entered a place called El Matador. It looked like a strip club.

"I'm not going in there."

"I don't think I want to either," Ainle said.

The club had a steady flow of traffic in and out the entrance, and cars were bumper to bumper on the street as they crawled past the blue and red neon sign.

Ainle said, "Okay, let's head down the street and into Chinatown."

"Is this where those girls came from?" Grace asked.

"Maybe. We should have a drink at the hotel bar. We can keep watch on the elevator and see when those Asian guys show up."

"Well, that sounds like a better idea than being in a scummy part of town and following Asian gangsters around," Grace shivered.

The wind had shifted, developing an autumn chill as it came off the St. Lawrence Seaway.

Ainle held Grace close. "Come on, let's go back."

They waited a few moments, huddled together and warming up before they prepared to scurry off down the street and disappear into Montreal's Chinatown.

Chapter 22

Mr. Lin led his party back through the maze of underground corridors and up into the main bar. He escorted them to a large, slightly elevated private table with a view of the entire bar area. Drinks arrived quickly. Alex and Kat made an appearance, coming over to join the group.

"Come on, girls," Tim said. "Party's over. We need to get back to the hotel and collect your gear."

The girls appeared uncertain, but they obeyed and headed to the front doors, followed by Tim and Rocket. They stepped out of the club and into the wind that swirled around them as a taxi pulled up.

Kat followed Alex into the back seat of the cab, with Rocket right behind. Tim climbed into the front seat.

Tim turned back to the three in the backseat, about to say something, when he saw Kat staring, eyes huge and mouth wide open, like she had seen a ghost.

He followed Kat's gaze across the street to a young couple who were just turning away and walking, hunched together, moving towards Chinatown.

"What's up?" he asked.

"It's the guy from the school."

"What school?"

"The one I got arrested in. It's the teacher guy."

"Cabbie, go around the block," Tim ordered.

Rocket leaned forward as the cab made a turn to the left. "How the hell does that work?"

"Cosmic justice, my friend. The powers that be have placed that schmuck in our reach for us to do something about it. This might be a very interesting meeting, if we can connect with our friend and his honey," Tim paused for a moment as he looked for the couple. "He's got twenty grand of our money and I want it back."

By the time the cab had made its loop around the block, the man and woman had disappeared into the narrow streets of Chinatown.

"Pull over here, we'll walk," Tim told the cabbie as he fished out money for the short fare.

*   *   *

Grace pointed at a little sidewalk bar that offered mussels as their specialty. "Ainle, let's go in here."

"I didn't know you liked mussels."

"I don't, I'm just too cold."

Ainle paused, looking around for maybe a better place. Hopefully one with alcohol.

He saw a cab pull up to the curb down the street, and people getting out. He thought for a moment of going to the curb, waving and shouting to get the taxi's attention. A quick and easy way back to the hotel. He actually raised his hand and opened his mouth when he realized some of those people looked vaguely familiar.

Then it came to him.

Ainle took Grace by the hand. "Let's get inside. I think I saw that girl who was in my school, the one who shot me." He left out that the two big men with her and the other woman looked like the bikers.

They hurried in and took a seat by the window.

"Ainle," Grace said. "She might see you."

"It would be better if I can keep an eye on them."

"Them?"

"Would you like a drink?" the waitress asked.

"I'll have a vodka and club soda," said Grace. "Make it a double."

"I'll have the same," said Ainle.

There were a few other couples in the quiet bar. The drinks arrived promptly.

"Would you like something to eat?" ventured the waitress.

"Um, we'll look over the menu," Grace said, trying to smile. She took her drink and downed it. "And two more of these."

The waitress offered a thin smile, taking away the empty glass.

Ainle was staring out the window.

"What did you mean 'them'?"

"She was with others."

"Are you sure it was her?"

"I'm not one hundred percent sure, but seventy-five percent sure."

"Who is she with?"

"A couple of guys and a woman."

"What would she be doing here?"

He shook his head as if he didn't know, while connecting the dots in his head. She had the drugs and money. Then the bikers showed up looking for it. Their house burned down.

Maybe Barry or Gabriela had told the bikers where Ainle and Grace had gone. Now they're all in Montreal.

"*Merçi*," Ainle said to the waitress as she brought the fresh drinks.

"Okay, now what?"

Ainle was thinking. If he was right, he had to come up with something.

"Do you remember S.A.T. and S.E.T.?" he said before taking a drink.

She blinked at him, confused. "Are you serious?"

"Strategic Awareness Tactics, and Strategic Environmental Tactics."

"Yes . . . And?"

"And we just have to be vigilant."

"Thanks, that makes it better." Grace finished her drink and waved at the waitress for more.

"We need to be aware of where we are and who is around. Like this place, this is a good spot to watch the area. We can see the entire plaza, see people coming from every side. Here, we are safe."

The waitress arrived with the drinks. "Have you decided on anything yet, or should I give you a few more minutes?"

"Excuse me," Grace asked the waitress. "Is there another entrance to your bar?"

"Only the back door, out through the kitchen."

"Thank you, Marie-Claire," Grace said, reading the woman's nametag. "Can we have the check just in case we have to leave?"

* * *

"Listen girls," Tim was surveying the area, trying to get a feel for the place. "Here," he gave Alex some cash from his pocket. "Go in there and get a bite, stay warm, and Rocket and I will hook up with you in twenty or thirty minutes."

Alex snatched the money and the girls scrambled across the street and into a bar that specialized in mussels.

* * *

Ainle picked up a menu to shield his face from view of the girls. Grace sat stiffly, not daring to move. Both were afraid to breathe. He peeked around the edge of the mini-booklet and watched the girls scurry into the bar, and take a table back by the warmth of the kitchen. Fortunately, the girl who shot him -- what was her name? Did she ever tell him? -- sat with her back mostly to him.

Ainle's wheels of thought were spinning furiously. He felt his blood pressure crank up to an uncomfortable level. He leaned into Grace who was staring out the window.

"Turn away," he hissed.

He adjusted the menu to block his view of the window -- what a stupid place to sit -- and waited as the two men walked slowly down the sidewalk, and past them.

"Oh my God," Ainle whispered across the table. "That was close."

Grace slowly finished her drink trying to keep her back to the girls. "What are we going to do? We just can't sit here."

"Remember that little French Bistro from the other the other day?"

"Jesus, Ainle. They're all French Bistros."

"The one with the basement."

"Crème de la Crème?"

"If we get split up, we'll meet there."

"Split up?"

"Just in case. It won't happen, but just in case. If they're looking for us they're most likely looking for a couple. So, in an emergency it might be a way to give them the slip."

"This *is* an emergency."

"Here you go --" the waitress started.

This startled Grace, who knocked her empty glass off the table, sending it crashing onto the tile floor, breaking into a hundred pieces. The other diners looked their way to see what happened. Ainle hunched down to help pick up the glass, but also hid his face from anyone looking. Grace turned her head towards the window.

*　　*　　*

"That's the guy," Kat whispered to Alex. "That's the guy from the school who got me arrested."

Alex looked around in her purse, found her phone and dialed.

Tim answered on the first ring. *"Yeah?"*

"They are sitting in front of us, right at a window seat!"

"Thanks, we'll be right over to say hello."

Chapter 23

Ainle stood, put money on the table, and turned with Grace to leave. Out of the corner of his eye, he saw the two big figures moving past the window.

Grace grabbed Ainle's hand and squeezed. "They're coming."

"Let's get out the back," Ainle said, turning towards the kitchen.

The two women saw them coming. The one with dark hair stood up quickly, knocking her chair over. She put her hand on her hips like a traffic cop. The woman from the school got up and stomped fiercely toward Grace and Ainle.

Ainle stopped in the middle of the bar holding Grace's hand. The girl from the school stopped to the right of Ainle. The dark-haired one stood in front of Grace.

Ainle looked around. Diners watched with curiosity at the strange scene. The two bikers entered through the door, smiling.

"Let's go," Ainle said to Grace, walking directly towards the women who stood with hands on their hips. He closed the gap and shot out an open hand, stiff-arming the dark one hard in the chest with a palm heel strike. The impact drove her backwards.

She stumbled against the overturned chair, lost her balance and tumbled in a pile to the tile floor.

Somebody yelled something in French at Ainle, apparently not pleased with him striking a girl.

Ainle tugged Grace's arm, pulling her into a run as they fled down the corridor towards the kitchen and out the backdoor, into a dark alley. He saw boxes and pails of grease on either side.

"Left," Ainle said quickly, and they bolted down the narrow passage. Low light lit their path. A loud bellow came from behind them as the bikers came in pursuit.

Ainle and Grace got to the end of the street, already breathing hard. He looked back from where they came and saw the silhouette of the big men barreling towards them.

Ainle tugged on his wife again, saying, "This way, out into the plaza."

They darted to the left and into the open, where small groups of tourists milled about in the odd shaped shadows of the old stone buildings.

"This way," Ainle said between gasps of air. "Come on, let's walk and try to blend in."

"What should we do? Call the police?" She was tightly gripping Ainle's arm.

"No, let's keep moving and work our way back to the hotel."

"What if they see us?"

"They won't," Ainle said, glancing back over his shoulder, seeing the two big figures enter into the plaza back where they had just come from. "Turn here," and he tugged Grace to the right onto Rue Notre Dame.

"Why?"

"I just saw them."

"Where?"

"Back there. Keep going, we'll make the next right."

"Why not left?"

"Okay, left. Let's try to get behind them."

"What are you talking about?"

"Here, left." They walked with quick short steps across a narrow street and down towards the next corner.

*   *   *

"Down there," Tim said, setting off towards the next corner.

They had closed the gap, and when they got to the corner they watched the couple cross the street to the left.

Rocket was looking drained after the short runs. "Dude, you go down to the next street, I'll follow this way."

And Tim went on down Rue Notre Dame in the same direction as the people who had his money.

*   *   *

"Okay, left again," Ainle gasped, turning with Grace back towards the plaza. Shops were closing and the traffic was thinning as the night grew late.

*   *   *

Rocket started a fast walk in an effort to catch his breath and slow his wildly thumping heart. Though he was driven by a motivation to avenge the theft, his body had trouble keeping up. At the corner of the next building, he stopped and leaned against the concrete slabs and casually tried to peer around the buildings cornerstones. A sense of satisfaction coursed through Rocket as he watched the couple walking quickly his way, peeking over their shoulders to see who was behind them.

Rocket waited.

"Come on, there's the plaza -- we'll go back up there."

"Is that the river over there?" Grace pointed to the right.

"It is, but it's too open and we need some place to lay low. We gotta make it to the bistro? We'll be safe and get a coffee."

"But it's back the other way."

"We'll turn at the corner, there. Then we can loop back around."

Ainle knew he sounded confident, but he felt no confidence in his choice.

*   *   *

Tim held back at his corner and watched the two ahead of him walk into the trap.

When the couple turned left at Rocket's corner, he raced down the sidewalk in the direction of the plaza.

At the corner he hesitated, peering around the gray slab building, watching the young couple huddled together as they took fast little steps, looking around as they moved back up the square. They turned left again.

Rocket was in the shadowed doorway of the building and came down the steps away from the door, joining his partner.

"There they go," Tim said calmly. "Let's tag along and see where they end up."

Both men hunched their shoulders a little, put their hands in their pockets and walked slowly, but deliberately in the same direction as the couple.

*　　*　　*

The narrow, dimly lit, crowded street of people heading back home or wherever they came from gave Ainle a feeling of concealment and security.

"Okay, wait a moment. I think we lost them," he said, looking around the street. "Mr. Bond at your service."

Grace was shivering, not just from the cold. "Thank you, James. But I need to stop. I want to be in the hotel."

"Okay. Let's try this."

Ahead of them and to the right was a doorman directing potential customers into a place called the Maple Shack -- a small bar that specialized in poutine, French fries with cheese curds.

*　　*　　*

Back in a darkened alcove, Tim and Rocket stopped and watched as their prey went into a small bar.

"They're amateurs," said Tim.

"What now?"

"Why don't you go to the girls, take them back to the hotel and I'll meet you later." He sneered. "This is kind of personal."

Rocket nodded and headed back to the plaza, disappearing around the corner in search of Alex and Kat.

Tim slowly walked past the Maple Shack and peered into the doorway. The bar was packed and noisy. He could just see the man directing his wife to a seat at the back. The man held up his hand, apparently ordering two drinks.

He thought they were safe. Fools.

*   *   *

Ainle and Grace felt protected by the moving, boisterous crowd. Drinks were on their way, the bar was warm, and French techno music played.

Ainle took the seat that faced the door, but he had to lean into the aisle to actually see it. "I think this is better than a window seat.

"You think?" said Grace.

"You tired?" Ainle asked, missing the sarcasm.

"I'm exhausted. That was stressful. We have to figure this out. I'm not cut out for a life on the run. What do you want to do, Secret Agent Man? What's the plan?"

"I have no idea, but give me a minute."

Grace shook her head. "You got us into this, you need to get us out."

*   *   *

By the time Rocket returned from getting the girls and taking them to the hotel, the couple had finished two more drinks, a plate of poutine and were paying up their bill.

"Here you go," Rocket said as he strolled up to Tim, carrying two coffees.

Tim took one. "They're still in there," he said. "And here they come. It looks like they are a little under the influence. This should be easy."

"Let's follow them to the next stop and follow them a little further to see if we get a chance to stop them."

"Good plan, my man."

*   *   *

The couple walked a little unsteady out of the Maple Shack and joined the crowds of revelers heading home.

Tim and Rocket split up to opposite sides of the street and hung back, casually sipping their coffees as they followed their prey.

"Old Montreal" transitioned into "New Montreal." The rustic and stylish Victorian buildings ended and broken and abandoned buildings filled the gap between the old world and the new. Municipal lighting was caught in the transition. The streets were not yet refurbished and not yet modern, just a little darker and empty of life. Tourists and locals alike walked quickly through the two blocks of the poorly lit and broken part of the city.

The guys welcomed this as a spot to engage the young couple who had ripped them off. Rocket tossed his half-empty cup into an empty lot and, staying on their side of the street, ran up ahead in order to get in front of the man and woman.

*　　*　　*

It was the sound of running feet that alerted Ainle to something unusual. He caught a glimpse of a big man lumbering up the other side of the street. Long hair bounced on wide shoulders as the runner went up the shadowed sidewalk.

He grabbed Grace's hand. "Wait a second." He pulled her to a stop. "Let's go back to the corner. It's dark here and that guy who ran past gave me the creeps."

Grace nodded, and they turned to reverse direction, only to come face-to-face with a big, smiling biker. They turned again to run back the way they came and the big man from the other side of the street had crossed over, closing the gap.

They were trapped.

In that frozen moment of time, Ainle remembered something from an old book he read as a student.

When in an ambush, attack.

But there was one more option.

So they ran.

Ainle grabbed Grace's hand, bolting across the road towards a dark alley. In seconds they were engulfed in the blackness of a place that they did not know.

Voices behind them sounded something like "killing them dead," and this spurned them on into the blind alley.

Ainle glanced back to get perspective. He needed to know if he was going to keep going straight, or left, or right.

The bikers thumped onto the cobbled-stone road and after them. Left and right were no longer options.

Ainle looking back, hooked the curb with his leading foot and sprawled flat and awkward onto the slab of the cold, gritty alley. His injured hand sparked pain as he stumbled to get up in an attempt to keep away from the men in pursuit.

Grace stopped and doubled-back, coming to help her husband onto his feet. She pulled him up and they both looked back.

The big men stood silhouetted at the entrance of the alley, two large dark shadows with their breath clouds luminous in the air.

Ainle and Grace backed slowly down the alley, trying to keep their distance.

"Well, well," one of the men hissed. "Look who we have here."

Ainle paused, dusting himself off.

Grace pulled on his arm. "Come on," she whispered as the two big men walked closer. "The last time they had a gun and a knife. Let's get out of here."

"You owe us money!" a man yelled down the alley.

Ainle turned and whispered to Grace, "Let's get into the light and out of this alley."

And they turned and ran again, their feet pounding hard, the sound echoed off the stone buildings.

*   *   *

Tim and Rocket stood at the end of the alley watching the couple run away.

"Give me a break," Rocket said, his hands on his hips. "How much fucking running are we going to do?"

"As much as it takes till we get my money," grumbled Tim as he started off after the man and woman, who turned right at the end of the alley.

*   *   *

The alley gave them two alternatives: To the left and to the right. If Ainle had his bearing straight, the left went towards the river and darkness, and the right led to busy streets and a massive church.

"This way," Ainle heaved and gasped for air. "Let's lose them!"

*   *   *

They absorbed themselves into what was left of the milling tourists and late night couples. Tim headed out, followed by a sick-looking Rocket, and watched the couple blend into the crowd.

He stopped, allowing Rocket to catch up.

"Okay, I'll watch for that schmuck, you follow the blondie in the boots."

"Thanks, brother," Rocket replied. "I like those boots." They headed off again in search of their victims.

"Yeah, me too. Too bad they don't slow her down."

Tim and Rocket kept an eye on the pair, following from a distance.

Rocket pointed. "Look, they're going into another bar. These two are either raging drunks or crazy."

The two men came to a stop just down from the bar's entrance.

"You know what?" Rocket said, watching the entrance to the bar. "They're in a blues joint. Here we are chasing them up one street and down the next. Think about it Tim, if they hadn't punched you out, stolen your money and run me over, they seem like kinda cool folks."

"Are you serious?"

"It's like a great blues song, dude. She's hot, they like to party and they don't take any shit. Not bad qualities, really."

"Okay, whatever. Admire them all you want, but I want my money. Twenty-fucking-grand."

*   *   *

Ainle pulled Grace through the bar, having no idea where they were going. The place was dark and packed with people. Small tables for four or five people formed a semi-circle out from a low stage as a blues band played something sad. The music was loud, the crowd just as loud and vocal. A waitress came up to Ainle and pointed towards the bar.

"Only place available is at the bar," she yelled.

"Thank you," Ainle yelled back. "Is there a way out the back?"

The waitress frowned at him. "No!" And she walked away.

"That was smooth," Grace said directly into his ear.

"I gotta figure this out," he said back at her. He led her towards the bar.

"Make mine a water."

"What?"

"Water!"

"Okay, but I'm having a water!"

They got themselves a place at the bar. Ainle ordered a water and Grace held up two fingers. The bartender looked at them as if they were space aliens. Ainle had to admit ordering water in a blues bar was like asking for a hot dog at a steakhouse.

The band started playing the next song, and Ainle turned to the stage, watching a big man with an even bigger nose wearing a small hat sitting on a chair and playing a red guitar. A slim

194

twenty-something girl in a tight leopard pattern dress wrapped both hands around the silver microphone and when she sang, the audience stopped talking. She owned the audience and they were mesmerized by her power.

Ainle leaned over to Grace, "Wow."

"I know that girl is amazing, Mr. Bond," Grace said. "But we've gotta get out of here. I know how we get back to the hotel."

"How?"

"Call a cab, Einstein. Get them to meet us in front of the bar and away we go."

Ainle smiled. "Sounds like you're the brains of the operation." He waved the bartender over. "Can you call us a taxi, please?"

"Yes sir," the bartender said. At least, that's what Ainle thought he said over the din of the band.

A few minutes later the bartender came over. "The taxi will be here in ten to fifteen. Just meet them at the front and you're set."

"Thanks," Ainle said, slipping the man a twenty.

"Thank you, sir."

"Twenty for two waters? Not bad," Grace said.

They waited a couple of songs and got themselves ready to leave. They looked at each other for a few long moments, gearing themselves up for heading outside.

Ainle leaned in and said, "When we get to the hotel, we stay in the room all day. Sound good?"

195

"Sounds good, let's go."

*   *   *

"Okay," Darrel finished his coffee. The little plaza square was almost empty and he knew they had lost them.

"I think we fucked up, Mike."

"They went into that little place and now what? Did they see us? Are they really that smart?"

"No, but we missed something. We've been here for almost an hour and they're not coming out that front door. Okay, hotel? Wait for them there?"

"Yeah, might as well, pay up partner."

Chapter 24

The chill was starting to get to the boys. They were tired of standing and waiting, and were getting impatient. Their legs were sore and the thought of a hotel room with a couple of dancers was feeling like a better option than standing outside for nothing.

Rocket tilted his head. "And there she blows," he said as the couple walked out of the bar and stood at the curb. "What are they doing? Why are they just standing there?"

"Come on," Tim said, moving off the sidewalk and into the road. "They're waiting for a cab."

*　*　*

A cab honked, and Ainle looked up to see one of the bikers heading for them. In a flash, he wondered where the other was.

"Go!" Ainle said.

"What?" Grace said.

"*Go*!" Ainle yelled as the other man seized his arm and back of the neck.

Grace looked to see Ainle being pushed behind her and she balled her fist, delivering a big looping left hook to the man's temple.

The guy saw it coming and hunched his shoulders as he pushed Ainle. The punch glanced off his shoulder and connected harmlessly with the side of his head.

People stopped to watch a girl throw a big wild punch at a big, bad biker, and that's when the other raced in.

Ainle spun into his attacker's grab, and lost his footing. He fell to the ground, but broke free of the hold on him.

"Grace, run!" Ainle yelled.

Their eyes met and he saw a look of terror.

*　　*　　*

Someone reached for her, and in a panic, she ran blindly into the traffic. A mini-van screeched and laid on the horn.

She darted left behind a small car that had a storage rack on the roof, then onto the sidewalk, turning to her right in a full sprint. She flew past shops that sold jackets and shoes, then left into a dark small street, and left again into a narrow alley. Garbage bins and empty cardboard boxes lined it. An old junkie peered out of a back doorway, and she fled alone and scared into the darkness.

*　　*　　*

Rocket's plan had failed when Ainle fell to the ground. Now people were watching, some yelling in French . . . and that caused a little worry since he had no idea what they were saying. But it didn't sound pleasant. Plus, Tim was off and running after the girl in the boots.

Fuck it, he thought. *This is not going the right way.*

He took one quick look at the sprawled man on the ground, pointed a gnarled finger at him, and then took off after Tim. He ran down one street and then the next. He caught Tim at the entrance to the alleyway.

"Yo, Tim, what the fuck?"

Tim turned to look at Rocket, both men were breathing hard.

"She's in here. She went down this alley."

Together, they slowly walked into the alley. It was wide, almost a normal street except there were no streetlights, just the backs of tall limestone buildings that formed a canyon of walls, casting shadows that seemed to add to the darkness. Black iron fire escapes hovered ten feet above their heads on either side. Arched doorways and large garbage bins sat in the gloom and small weeds lay in broken clumps against one wall. A ways into the alley, Tim spotted a tall junkie hugging the stone dimness of a doorway. As the big men got close, he stepped out of his lair.

"Gimme your money."

*   *   *

Grace heard the voices from behind an industrial-sized garbage box.

She had turned down into the alley, saw the row of boxes up against the wall, and thought that with the shadows, it seemed like a good hiding place. She crouched behind them and waited to see if her pursuer ran past.

One big man stopped at the entrance, then the other joined him. She squatted down and cursed under her breath. She should have kept running.

Terror panicked her into trying to squeeze into a space between the bin and the building. The area was barely large enough for her to fit herself into, but it was out of sight, dark, almost pitch black.

"Piss off," one of the men said.

She peeked around the edge of the box.

The junkie she had passed was confronting the bikers, pulling a knife and clicking it open. He lunged at one of the men, who saw it coming and moved aside.

The junkie charged past.

The other biker side-stepped the other way and got behind the junkie, wrapping the bum's arms around him in a bear hug, pinning him at the same time. The other biker went to work, unloading a series of punches to the belly of the junkie until the knife clattered to the pavement.

Grace could hear the fleshy thuds and decided she had seen enough. She tried to crawl further behind the bin.

The junkie moaned and began to cry as the blows took their toll. The man dishing out the punishment grunted as he fatigued from the exertion. Then, for a moment, all went quiet.

"Well, this is a nice knife," the man said.

Grace prayed for them to leave the poor man alone, even though it took the attention off of her. She peeked out again and heard the high-pitched gasp of the junkie as the knife was thrust into his chest. Then she watched in horror as the knife was drawn across his throat and watched the body crumpling to the ground.

"Rocket," the man said. "This is what we do to those fuckers when we find them. We clear?"

"We clear," replied the other man.

Grace was sure her breathing was going to give her away. She heard their feet on the pavement. Her mind was saying, "Run." But her heart was saying, "No, freeze or die."

She remembered Ainle saying long ago that movement often gave animals away. She tried to control her breathing, but it didn't work. Air would not get into her lungs.

Stay calm, she told herself.

She knew they were so close, they could smell her if the alley's smell didn't overwhelm hers.

"Drag the fucking body into the shadows," one biker said to the other.

Grace felt panic again. It became her titanic battle.

Just run.

Don't run.

The urge to run was almost overwhelming, but she knew it meant her doom.

She began a self-talk to weigh her options.

I'm fast, they can't catch me. Stay, they will move on. If they knew I was here they would have got me already. You are a Kenpo warrior. You are a brown belt.

"Black belts are at this level," Mr. Gorman had said, holding his hand out. *They made the plateau. Brown belts want the*

201

next level. They've come so far. Fear the brown belt because they are hungry. Hungry to prove they have it.

The memory was almost like a meditation. Her breathing slowed, she heard but did not see the movement of the bikers heading on down the alley.

She had lost them.

She was alone and scared.

*　　*　　*

Ainle was standing outside the blues bar with a crowd milling around. He had seen Grace racing out through the traffic, one biker following, then the other. He had tried to grab the man and trip him, but missed.

After the commotion, people passed by him, not caring about what had just happened.

Ainle and Grace had made a plan to meet at the bistro if they got split up, and that was the general direction Grace had run.

He was terrified for her. It all sounded so full of bravado to split up and meet at the bistro, but now it seemed like a stupid idea. What if the place was closed? What then?

Ainle headed off in the same general direction Grace had gone. He would go to the bistro and wait, inside or out. He considered calling her phone, but as he waited for the light to change at the corner, he decided that might make things worse.

The light changed and he crossed the road, heading towards the river and the cute little bistro.

*   *   *

Grace cowered behind the garbage bin. The pavement was cold and damp. Sour garbage smell surrounded her.

She listened.

Nothing.

She inched her way to the end of the bin, hesitated, listened, slowly exhaled, and dragged herself out from behind the bin. She crouched at the end, peering around the corner in the direction the bikers had gone.

The alley was empty.

To her right, she thought she could see a shoe.

She had to check, had to see if the guy was okay, even though she knew otherwise. She felt responsible, somehow. If she had gone somewhere else he would be okay, as okay as a back alley druggie could be.

Grace scurried to the other side of the alley. She reached out and touched the foot, shaking it gently.

"Are you Okay?" she asked softly.

No answer.

Grace knew he was dead although she had never seen a dead person before, she just knew. She crawled further into the darkness where the body was dumped and put her hand on the man's chest just to make sure. Her hand felt the sticky warmth of the man's blood soaked old shirt. Emotion was no longer in her control and in the dark back alley she wept for the death a junkie.

"Hello kitten," came a voice from the shadows.

Grace's heart sank and she stopped breathing. She strangely didn't feel any fear.

"Why did you kill him?" she said, trying to choke back tears.

"He was the last straw. You and your guy pushed me over the edge. So gimme my fucking money and everyone goes home."

"I don't have it."

The other man approached. "It's time to move out."

The first man waved him off. "You come with us and then we'll call your husband. He's going to bring the money and then you can get back to your little holiday. You're going to walk with us real nice like, and you're not going to scream, because if you do, I'm going to slit that pretty little throat."

Grace looked up at the man and saw a face that terrified her. The eyes seemed to have a fiery madness above a crooked smile and gray stubble. His tongue licked his lips slowly and she felt a cold that didn't come from the weather.

She stood up and saw the other guy was being watchful, looking up and down the alley for any surprise visitors.

In a moment of desperation, she lashed out at the man in front of her with a wild punch and kick. She felt her arm and shoulder jam into something hard as she made contact. Her leg swung wildly, missing the collapsing man, who rolled away.

A crushing grip closed around her flailing arms, pinning them to her sides, and she was driven with power into the ground.

Her lungs were emptied of air as the man's mass tried to push her down through the surface of the road, her face pressed to the side, and she was staring at the worn shoes of the dead junkie.

His powerful hand clamped onto her arm and Grace gasped for air as the grip tightened into a painful, solid hold that yanked her up to her feet.

"You still got it bro," the other man said as he massaged his jaw. "That was a mighty fine tackle. We should vanish while the vanishing is still good."

They walked down the alley and out onto the street, the flagstone buildings pale in the city's light.

Grace looked into the shop windows they passed, her reflection distorted and unfamiliar.

Cars rattled on the cobblestone streets and the man increased his grip on her arm as he saw her looking at the buildings.

"Don't even think about it, sweetie. You'll be dead in the middle of your scream. Then, we'll kill your hubby just for fun."

The other man laughed. "Maybe we'll cut off his dick, for a memento."

"Asshole," Grace said, and the pain in her arm increased tenfold.

They arrived at El Matador and made their way to the back office. The music was loud and pounding, the blue and yellow lights were in full effect as two girls strutted and gyrated on the stage.

Grace and one man stood by a door while the other man went to make arrangements.

"You like what you see?" the man asked as he watched the girls on the stage.

"Why am I here?"

"Your husband has something of ours, now we have something of his."

"This is stupid."

"Yep, now we trade you for our money."

"This is kidnapping."

"So what? Your husband stole twenty G's from us."

"Twenty? Ten."

"So, he lied to you too. Wow, he's a stand-up guy."

"Says the one who's selling people."

"Hey, it's a living and the pay is better than yours."

"And yet you look like street scum. Go figure."

"You better watch out, young lady, or . . ."

Grace tuned him out, instead she was looking around the bar and thinking about why Ainle had not told her the complete truth about the money. *Why would he lie?* she thought. *He could be such an idiot.*

"Okay," the other man said as he returned. "We'll keep her here in one of the rooms downstairs."

Grace tensed and lunged, trying to run, but the man anticipated it and grabbed her by the collar of her shirt, spun her around and slammed her against the wall. The knife appeared as if out of nowhere. He leaned hard against her, placing the blade against her throat. "I'll gut you right here, kitten."

Grace closed her eyes and turned her head to move as far away as possible. She could smell beer and something sour, and she wanted to cry.

Chapter 25

Ainle arrived at Crème-de-la-Crème and was pleasantly surprised to find it open. He found a table where he could see both doors, ordered a coffee and waited for Grace to walk in. After half an hour he still had hope she was going to show up. After an hour, and he started to think she had gone to the hotel. And when the bistro closed shortly thereafter, panic and fear were mixed with guilt. He now knew everything that had gone wrong was his fault. He was solely responsible for this disaster.

Ainle sat with his head in his hands, the bistro now empty. The waiter asked him to pay his bill. He did, and walked out to the street, standing there for a long time, not wanting to go to the hotel in case she was still coming, but knowing she wasn't.

His last hope was the hotel. Maybe that's where she was, she had to be. He couldn't think of any other option, wouldn't let the other possibilities become thoughts for fear of them becoming reality.

He walked and got into the elevator at the Hilton. As the doors closed, he saw the three Asian men with two girls. Two different girls. He let the doors close not wanting to be near anyone or slow down his rush to the room.

She had to be there. She had to be.

He slid his key card in anticipation of a hug and a kiss and an explanation.

The room was empty and dark. He checked everywhere, even the closet, just in case.

He lay on the bed and curled into a ball, and prayed. He thought in the middle of his prayer, *"When was the last time you did this?"*

By morning, he was still alone and nearly every situation had gone through his head. He felt physically sick. They had always known where the other was. Always. The not knowing was something he had heard on television when a parent talked about a missing child. Now, he understood. He knew he had to call the police. It was the last and only option.

As he sat on the edge of the bed staring at the phone trying to figure out what to say, how to phrase it, what to tell Grace's parents, he could only feel his overwhelming guilt over every aspect from the moment he saw the money, until he decided to step outside and wait for the cab in the open rather than waiting inside. It was his job to protect his wife, and instead he put her in the line of killers.

The light on the phone blinked, before it rang.

"Grace?" he said into the phone, sounding desperate.

It was a man's voice, *"You wish."*

He blinked, caught off guard. "Who is this?"

"I'm the guy who you stole from."

"Bullshit. I never stole anything from you."

"You have my money and I want it back. I have your wife."

"Listen scumbag, you hurt her, I'll kill you."

"Whatever. You bring my money and you'll get your woman back. She's hot. My associate and I could have some fun with her. So, you better come meet me. I know you'll leave the cops out of this. You've been living on drug money, so you're not innocent in this little game. We going to meet?"

Grace was never going to forgive him.

"Where?"

*   *   *

"Well, fuck me blind," Darrel muttered.

"What's up?" said Mike as he woke up in the passenger seat of the van.

"The guy is back without his wife." The tone of surprise was unmistakable in his voice.

"Are you shitting me?"

"No, and the Asian guys, they just arrived too."

"Okay, they're all in on something. This is a great night."

*   *   *

Rocket hung up, looked at Tim, and smiled. "Looks good. He's going to meet us in a couple of hours."

They had escorted the woman to one of the underground rooms at El Matador, for a small fee from Mr. Lin, no questions asked.

"What's the plan?" Rocket asked.

"Well, we meet this guy, get the money and sell his wife to Lin. We can make some serious coin today."

"We don't give her back?"

"What's the point?" said Tim. "What can he do?"

"Call the cops?" Rocket said, concerned.

"That's why we meet him without the wife, then get the money and we go back west."

"Okay, brother. But this guy is unpredictable."

"Yeah, when we meet, we split up and we do it outside, in broad daylight. Come on, let's go deal with Alex and Kat. They belong to Lin today. Business is good, business is good."

*   *   *

Grace was in shock. She thought she had put up a good fight, but their size and surprise had overwhelmed her. She had thrown some punches and the way her hand hurt, she knew at least one had connected.

She was in a small, stark room. The walls were white and she sat on a small cot. A rough, old army-style blanket was all she had, so she wrapped it around her shoulders as she sat staring at the floor. She was in prison for doing nothing more than defending herself.

The heavy door rattled and opened, and the bikers walked in. They were big men and now looked even bigger. One had a swollen eye. It was a small consolation that she had damaged one of them. She wondered if he was the same one she had hit with the taxi.

The two men stood and stared at her.

"Stand up," the bigger of the two men said. "My name is Tim, but you can call me, 'Boss'."

Grace stood and stared at them, somewhat in defiance, and partially in disbelief.

"Listen sweetie," Tim said, trying to sound kind. "Your man owes me money and when I get it back, he gets you back."

And with that, they turned and walked out. The door thudded shut and the dull mechanical sound of the lock snapped into place.

She stepped over and pulled on the handle, knowing it wouldn't move, and it didn't.

*   *   *

At the Queen Elizabeth Hotel, Alex and Kat were packing up the last of their belongings and saying goodbye to the luxurious room. Both were nervous and felt that something was not right with the club called El Matador.

Alex turned to Kat, both feeling and seeing the uncomfortable state she was in, "We'll work a little, and then we can get out of this town, okay?"

"Yeah, I guess," Kat's voice was soft and empty.

"Listen, we'll have fun, make some money, then go travel. Next summer, we could go to Japan or Italy."

Dreams of escape had become their way of communicating and coping with their current lives. Change is more difficult to handle when it's not under your control.

The hotel room door swung open, and Tim walked in.

"You girls get packed and ready. We gotta do something real quick, then we'll be back to blow this joint."

Tim saw Kat's reluctance.

"I'm sorry, Kat," Tim said. "Once you get the money paid back, you can buy yourself out of this club. But you do have a chance to make some good money. You girls will do great, you're top notch dancers."

"And hey," Rocket added, "just stay out of those basement rooms."

Rocket exchanged a look with Tim that Alex picked up on. She looked over to Kat and shivered.

*   *   *

Ainle sat on the foot of his king size bed and tried to figure what he had done, and what he needed to do.

He had spent about five of the twenty thousand.

When things like this happened to people on television or in the news, calling the police was always the obvious choice. But in a real-world situation, with life and death in the balance, it was easier to question that.

Then, he had an idea.

He pulled out the paper, picked up the phone and dialed.

"Hello my friend," answered Abdullah. *"How are you and your beautiful wife doing?"*

"Not good. Not good at all."

"What is wrong? How can I help you?"

Ainle told him what had happened, keeping it brief, and trying not to cry. He succeeded, for the most part.

"I just don't know what to do," Ainle said, summing up. "What is your advice?"

"Well, I think you need to pay back the money and hope for the best. My business is small compared the motorcycle groups out there. Where you are, the gangs run all the business. You have

the motorcycle groups with all the fancy labels and they are always shooting each other for control. Then you have the new money that is sneaking itself into the market, all those South East Asians taking the role of the South Americans. It's crazy where you are. I just have a small family business compared to your new friends."

"They are not my friends."

"I know, figure of speaking. My apologies."

"No problem. I just don't want you to think I am in business with them."

"Listen, my contact is with the ships out there. It's a very nice harbor. All I can help you with is a boat ride. Just in case you need to travel a little farther, every few days I have a ship or two that come in and drop off a few things, and then moves on. If you need, let me know and you can catch a ride to one of our destinations, for a small price of course."

"Thank you for your suggestion and help, Abdullah. I don't think I will need anything like that, but I appreciate the offer."

"Okay, take care my friend." And Abdullah hung up the phone.

Ainle decided that getting on a boat and going far, far away was not really a solution. And it certainly didn't help his wife.

*　　*　　*

"Well, that's news. Shipping in and out of Montreal. So, that's one of the connections."

"Where are the ships coming from?" Mike asked.

"Patience, patience. It could be the Middle East, Africa or Europe, somewhere, anywhere. Tracking back will keep the boys in the office warm at night."

Mike and Darrell smiled.

This was a great discovery, the start of a great night.

"Mike, what are the odds the Frenchies are listening to this as well?"

"I say, one hundred percent."

*   *   *

Grace sat on the narrow cot staring at the wall, seething with anger. It was hard to believe any of this could happen, but yet, here she was.

The door lock rattled as the bolt released and the hinges squeaked as it opened. Four men stood crowded in the opening. All were Asians.

She wouldn't have recognized three of them if it wasn't for their expensive suits.

The fourth man, a needle-headed sweaty guy, seemed to be in charge. He said something in an Asian language she guessed was not Chinese.

The three suits looked at each other, nodded and stepped into the room. The needle-head smiled and laughed an eerie, wheezing sound as he closed the door.

Absolute terror embraced her and she wrapped her arms around her knees and curled up into a tight ball, staring at the locked door, wishing it to magically open.

*   *   *

Ainle was doing all he could to get everything he needed. He was meeting the bikers in an hour and he was still in the hotel room. He got the money and put it an envelope he got from the concierge, grabbed his ATM card, and raced out the door.

He exited the elevator on the ground floor and set off to the nearest bank. He still needed another five thousand dollars to even out the twenty, but he was sure they would only allow two thousand at one time. He knew he was going to have to fake the difference or figure something else out.

They were to meet out in the open on a main street. By the time Ainle had got most of the money he needed, he was running behind the schedule he had planned for himself, hoping to be at the meeting place thirty minutes before he was to confront the bikers, but now he had to hurry just to be there on time.

There was a park bench at the corner of Rue Saint Urbain and Rue Brady. He was to arrive at 11 AM and sit with the money and wait -- that was the plan. It seemed simple enough, but the way the last several days had played out, nothing was simple. They had his wife. Nothing simple about that. As Ainle turned onto Saint Urbain, the sky began to clear and the clouds of the day before began to give way to a crisp clear, blue sky. This helped Ainle feel uplifted and hopeful. He walked up the street and music echoed down toward him and he wondered where it came from.

He looked up the street and an empty park bench waited in the sun. Across the road and in the shade of a multi-level parking lot stood a chubby young Asian woman singing into a microphone while her skinny boyfriend played an electric guitar.

Ainle sat back on the bench, stretched out his legs and waited. Despite the cool day, he was sweating. It had nothing to do with the sun, or his brisk walk with thousands in an envelope. His eyes swept the scene, checking out everything and everyone, hoping to spot his bride, to see her smiling, and happy, and free.

Businessmen and women milled past on their way to lunch. Some dropped money into the open guitar case of the musician, others paused and lit cigarettes. A young couple met, hugged, kissed, and ran across the street into a café. A woman pushed a stroller with a toddler who was crying and fussing over something only known to him.

"Gimme my fucking money."

The voice came from slightly behind and to the right of him. Ainle turned to look up at the large frame of one of the bikers. How such a big guy had managed to sneak up on him baffled him, and it probably showed on his face. Then he looked around, to each side and behind the man.

"Where's Grace?" Ainle demanded, trying to sound annoyed.

"Fuck you. My money."

Ainle tried to stand, but a powerful hand was placed on his shoulder. He looked to the left and saw a big paw with tattoos across the fingers. He remembered the tattoo from the night he pried the knife out of the man's hand after Grace hit him with the taxi.

Ainle reached up and carefully removed the hand from his shoulder, standing, turning and moving nose-to-nose with the man on his right. "Where's my wife?" he demanded, allowing the anger to bleed through.

The man acted fast -- a lot faster than Ainle would have thought -- delivering a short, hard strike to Ainle's lower abdomen, knocking the wind out of him. He quickly collapsed onto the bench and tried to suck air back in.

The other man with the tattooed hand sat down beside him and put one powerful arm around Ainle's shoulders.

Passers-by kept coming and going, nobody seemed to notice anything unusual.

The man leaned in to Ainle, his breath a musky stink, "Listen, dude -- you give us the money and we will get your woman. It's really not that complicated. But you keep the money, we keep the woman. So, if you love your woman, hand over the cash, please."

Ainle's brain raced. He had what they wanted, but they didn't return the favor. Grace was not here. But if he didn't hand over the money, he might never see her again.

He reached into his new leather jacket and took out the stuffed envelope and passed it over to the man.

"Thanks," the biker said. And then he turned and walked away.

"Hey! Wait! You can't break the fucking deal! What the hell is wrong with you? *Where is my wife?"*

But the two men just kept walking away.

Fired up, full of righteous anger, Ainle chased after them, grabbed the tattoo-handed man by the shoulder and spun the big guy around. As if anticipating it, the man delivered a thundering left hook that caught Ainle square on the hinge of the jaw. His vision sparkled bright white before turning black as he crumpled to the pavement, unconscious.

Ainle lay on the wide sidewalk, blood pooling around his mouth and nose.

* * *

Mike and Darrel sat in the shadows of large tree, just up the street from the street musicians, mouths wide open in amazement.

"Did you see that?" Mike said already knowing the answer.

"Holy crap, who the hell saw that coming?

"Obviously not him, he's out cold."

"Should we help him," Darrel asked.

"No, we've got to let this play out."

Chapter 26

Tim and Rocket climbed into a taxi and disappeared into the lunch hour traffic. "That guy deserves to die," Tim muttered as the taxi drove them to the hotel.

"Why?"

"He's light," Tim held up the envelope. "There's two G's missing. Maybe more."

"Ah, whatever," said Rocket. "Let's get out of here, get out of this place and go for a ride. We've got Red and Sammy selling for us back home. I need to put some distance between El Matador, Lin and that fucked up underground palace of his. I have no problems with strippers and hookers, but that kid shit is too much for me. If I stay here much longer, I'll burn that fucking place down next."

"You need a drink."

Rocket pretended to think about this. "Yes, yes I do."

"El Matador?" Tim said, laughing.

"If I get a cocktail there, it will be a Molotov cocktail." Rocket looked out the cabs window and watched the storefronts scroll past, "Fuck man, let's just drop off the girls and go from there."

*   *   *

The girls were packed and ready to start their new jobs. Neither was too keen on the idea, and both were creeped out by Lin and his weird laugh.

"Okay girls, let's go party!" Tim said as he walked into the suite.

The girls offered small smiles, and the four of them with bags of clothes set off for El Matador. Rocket tried to make a few jokes to lighten the atmosphere, but they fell flat, and silence resumed. When they arrived at the club, Mr. Lin greeted them and directed the girls where to store their clothes and that a driver would take them to their apartment after their shift.

Being broke and in debt, the girls were ready to start making some money.

*   *   *

A passersby stopped and picked Ainle up by the arms, hoisting him to his feet.

A groggy Ainle tried to put together a coherent sentence. "Where did they go?" he asked nobody in particular.

"Who?" a heavily accented French voice said.

"The guy who hit me."

"Sit, they must be gone. Punks."

224

Ainle's head was spinning and he thought how strange it was that the street musicians were still playing.

"I have to go."

"Sit. You're bleeding. Wipe the blood away. Here." The stranger handed him a cloth handkerchief.

"Thanks," and he held the kerchief to his nose, then inspected the blood stain.

There was a lot more than he expected.

"Sorry, it's ruined."

"Keep it."

"Thanks, I have to get my wife."

"Okay, be careful."

Ainle wandered up the street and his head slowly cleared with the fresh air and the noontime sun. It was a nice day if you were on a holiday. Not such a good one if bikers had kidnapped your wife and had just punched your lights out.

He had no idea where he was going or what he should do. As he wandered, he ended up in Montreal's Chinatown. A police car slowed and the hard-eyed officer watched him.

He considered waving the officer over, but knew he couldn't. What would he tell them? It was too unbelievable -- even he still had trouble wrapping his head around it.

Ainle found himself at the corner of Boulevard St. Laurent and Lauguchitere. To the left was the scummy district and the El Matador, to the right was the harbor and more police patrols.

He turned left and walked towards the broken buildings, broken streets and the broken lives of those who lived there.

*   *   *

Grace was confused, terrified and furious. She was tired, needed the bathroom and was doing all she could to choke back tears.

The door rattled and one of the workers opened the door. He held a tray with water and a bowl of food.

"I need the washroom," Grace said.

The assistant set the tray down on the floor and signaled for Grace to follow him. Surprised, she stood shakily, and left the room, following the man to the right. A ways down the hallway, the assistant stopped, smiled a kind smile, and motioned towards a door. Grace hesitated a moment, then opened it, a sensor light flicking on as she entered.

As she headed for one of the stalls, she looked for windows, a door, some way to escape. There was nothing but walls. The washroom was cold compared to her cell -- to anyone else, it might be a room, but not to her.

Nobody knew where she was, and or why. She started to shake with fear. It was the first time in her life when she truly knew what it felt like to be alone.

She left the stall and went to the sink and washed her hands. After using the soap, she slipped the small bar into her pocket.

She thought Ainle would be pleased with her. And she had every intention of proudly telling him how strong she was . . . immediately after she kicked his ass.

Grace was thinking about one of those crazy things Ainle had been going on about like he did sometimes. Some hostage thing he had been reading about that she had only half-listened to. Where had they been? Had it been on one of their getaways in the mountains? They had been sitting on the front porch of one of those old cabins up in the Rockies of Alberta. "Rustic" the advertisement had called it, but run-down was more accurate.

She tried to push the blue sky and granite mountain image from her memory, trying to remember what he had been talking about.

Sweden, that was it. The Stockholm Syndrome.

She had to admit, she didn't always listen to his stories. She loved him, but sometimes his amateur research side-projects were not the most interesting things.

"Hey, hurry up," the worker called, poking his head in the doorway.

Now she remembered. It was that old World War II prison camp movie he talked her into watching.

"It was a prisoner's duty to escape," he had said.

But the prisoner of war stuff was not the important part. There had been something more to what he was talking about. He had a trick sometimes of tying something significant into his little stories.

She looked at herself in the mirror and looked into her own eyes as it came to her.

"Ainle," she whispered to her reflection. "Thank you."

She took a second soap bar, slipping it into another pocket.

Subversion is what it was. Appear to be weak and frail, don't appear to be a threat.

Don't let them see it coming, is what he said.

The door flew open. "Let's go!" the assistant shouted, no longer being a nice guy.

Grace flinched, realizing it was pretty easy to look scared when you really were. Now it was just a matter of waiting for an opportunity.

She bowed her head, hunched her shoulders and scurried out to the hallway, whispering, "Thank you."

Back in her cell, she sat, mouse-like, realizing something else -- that the Stockholm thing might have come true. There was the reality of losing herself -- her morals, her strength, her common sense -- in the effort to do anything for her captors in order to stay alive.

It felt like a fear unlike anything she had experienced before -- a sinking feeling, like parts of her were falling away.

Moving was almost impossible, air was difficult to find, she had to force herself to breathe in, then concentrate to breathe out. It was a fear that left her frozen, unable to move.

The door rattled and Grace was startled. It opened to show the worker again, smiling. She sensed the smile was not genuine -- or maybe it was, she didn't know -- but she felt it was not kind. He knew something she didn't, and she had a feeling she wouldn't like it.

"Come with me."

"Why?" she asked.

"We just need to evaluate your cost."

That didn't make any sense. But wanting to obey -- or, rather, not be hurt -- and holding onto the slim possibility she might be let go, Grace followed her captor out the door.

In the hallway, she realized too late she had just missed an opportunity.

He had stopped, and Grace walked past him. He was a little taller than her, slim, almost too skinny. Chinese, maybe Vietnamese, and quite young.

If the chance came again, she decided she would hit him on the back of head.

But she was in front, leading the way to who knows what.

They veered off to the left. Down the hall, a door opened and a dark room waited.

She stopped, tense and sweating.

Several soft spotlights came on. Some pointed straight down and illuminated a red-carpeted floor. Two or three others were directed to a low stage.

Her escort softly placed his palm on her back and gently pushed her forward. "It's okay," he whispered, "I'm here for you."

She knew there were others to her right -- she could feel them, smell their soapy cleanness and harsh, cheap cologne.

Grace was escorted down the narrow aisle, heard murmurs of languages she did not understand. At the end of the aisle, she climbed the two stairs onto the stage and stood to one side of the spotlight, trying to stay in the shadows. Her escort nudged her into the light and then he left the stage.

She put her hand to her forehead to shield the light, her hair felt oily and she knew she needed a shower. Voices mumbled, and she felt sick and scared.

She stood there for a couple of minutes until her escort returned and walked her off the stage, down the aisle, out the room and back to her cell.

"What was that all about?" she asked the assistant.

"You've been sold," he said with a smile.

She sat on the couch, her mouth fell open and she stared at the assistant helpless and vulnerable.

"Help me," she pleaded, "please get me out of here, I'll do anything."

"I know."

The door closed and locked. The last words of her captor, *I know*, stirred her loneliness and terror into a revulsion and hatred. Disgust was brought on by the realization that she was willing to do anything to be freed. *Anything.* She hated herself for becoming that person. It was just like that fucking movie that Ainle talked about last summer.

Someone was going to pay.

Chapter 27

The sun was setting and Ainle was walking aimlessly towards El Matador. It was his only connection to the bikers in Montreal.

After cleaning himself up in the bathroom, he bought a strong cup from a coffee shop and wrapped both hands around the paper travel mug drawing heat to keep his hands warm. From a sidewalk vendor he bought a hotdog with the works. He had no plan and stuffing food and coffee into him seemed to help settle his growing panic.

Ainle stopped at the curb and took a bite from his hotdog while holding his coffee with his other hand. From where he stood, he could look up Boulevard St. Laurent and see the large blue and red neon sign of El Matador like a beacon that drew him towards an unknown world.

He decided to wait for a little bit, then go to the police. That was the extent of his plan, for what it was worth. He still wasn't sure what the police would do, if they believed him. He knew he should have gone to the police earlier, but the theft of money, the injured cabbie back home and now all this. Things had just spiraled out of control.

He found a bench near a bus stop and sat down with a good view of the front entrance of El Matador. He finished his hotdog, crumpled the wrapper and stuffed it in his pocket and pulled his jacket close against the wind that was coming off the St. Laurence.

He supposed he could tell the police that the bikers kidnapped his wife and not bother to mention to the cops about the found money. Just skip that part. The police would probably wonder why two Hell's Angels -- or whatever they were -- would randomly kidnap a school teacher's wife for no apparent reason.

He could tell them the bikers burned down their house then followed them to Montreal and took Grace off the streets.

But there still was no *why.* The authorities always want to know *why.*

He put both hands around his coffee and waited and watched. And thought.

*   *   *

"Are you serious?" Mike asked Darrel.

233

"I think he's going to go in there."

"When you said party you were right. This guys going to end up dead. We should get involved."

"What's that old saying about God protecting drunks and fools, well this guy is both."

"This is not going to end well, plus it's getting fucking cold out here."

*　*　*

"Gentlemen," Mr. Lin said with a grin. "I believe it is time to do some business."

A short, wide gray combination safe was in one corner of the room beside a green banana plant. Lin began turning the dial and opened it. From where Tim sat, he could see stacks of money.

Lin reached in and came out with two bricks of bills. "Here you go," he said as he handed them over.

"Thanks, mate," Rocket said while Tim counted the money.

Tim nodded, satisfied.

"Thank you for your business, please come back for more. All three of those women will bring us plenty of cash. You will always be welcome at El Matador," Lin said, punctuated with his wheezing laugh.

Tim thanked Lin as well, though the words felt stupid coming out of him. He and Rocket headed out, suggesting they grab a beer first, something which Rocket would not argue with.

*   *   *

Ainle finished his coffee, put the cup in a garbage can and walked across the street. Cars passed on either side of him as he made his way up to the doors of the club. Two college boys pushed in before him and he followed them through the doors and up to the coat check girl, who had about three too many piercings in her face.

The entrance way was dark and the thud of dance music could be felt almost as much as heard. A mean looking security guy scanned the college students with a metal detector and then moved the wand over Ainle. The college boys went through the next set of doors and Ainle followed. The boys went to the bar on the right and Ainle went left towards a darker section of the bar. He found himself a table and sat down.

He felt out of place. Maybe because he was. He had no idea what to do, and it seemed even more noticeable sitting in the dark while watching a pretty, yet strange woman gyrate naked on the stage. What the hell was he doing here?

"Want a drink?" an attractive waitress with short brown hair and a tiny outfit asked him.

"A beer," Ainle answered. A second girl followed and approached him and asked Ainle if he wanted a private dance. Ainle declined and waited for his beer as the girl went to the next table and repeated her dance request.

Men cheered in appreciation of the dancing. The waitress brought Ainle's beer and as she set it down she said in a smooth French-accented voice, "Would you like some company?" She had the kind of smile that was practiced and perfected. He wondered if she spent hours in her dismal apartment performing in front of a mirror.

"No thanks," he said, then thought it might be a way to get to other parts of the bar. He added, "Maybe later. I need some food first, can I order a burger?"

"Bien sur, of course," she said, then disappeared into the gloom.

Ainle wondered what she was thinking. Was he another married businessman on a conference or something? She might feel she'd be able to get something from him once he was fed and a little bit drunk. Or a lot drunk -- although based on the watered-down beer, that might take a while. Somehow, in some weird way, it was better than walking the streets. He would just pretend he was another middle-aged guy looking to relive his younger days, days he never really had. Which was kind of true.

*   *   *

Grace was pacing back and forth in her holding cell, her anger getting towards a boiling point. She wanted to hit the first guy who walked through the door. And when the door rattled and the lock moved to open, she reacted accordingly, by curling up into a ball on the cot.

The door squeaked, and silhouetted in the doorway were the three Asians. They did not recognize her, but they seemed to be sizing her up.

She wanted to meet their gaze and stare them down, but she couldn't. So she closed her eyes and prayed they would leave.

The door squeaked shut.

The lock clicked into place.

She opened her eyes and saw her prayer had been answered. She was alone.

*   *   *

Ainle sat back as he finished his beer and looked around. Towards the back of the club was a bar with waitresses getting drinks as they chatted with bartenders and bouncers. It had been a long time since he had been in a strip club and he realized that it didn't matter where in the country you were. They all seemed the same. They all had dark corners, bright stages with men and sometimes a few women sitting around them. Girls in bikinis selling beer from mini-bathtubs full of ice, little offices for the manager often situated at some remote corner near the bar. Then he saw them. The flashing purple and yellow lights made it difficult to know for sure at first, but he knew it was them.

"Another beer?" the waitress asked.

"Yes please. What's down there?" Ainle pointed in the general area he thought he had seen the bikers.

"We have VIP rooms if you would like a private dance," she said, taking the opportunity to upsell a potential client. "We can go back there and I'll show you what we have to offer." She leaned over to show off her nicely shaped breasts barely held back by a sparkly bikini top and slowly set his beer down, smiling as she let her tongue gently touch her upper lip.

"Let me finish my beer and I think I might be interested," Ainle said, smiling.

"Okay, I'll be back soon," and the waitress smoothly moved away.

*　　*　　*

"Listen, bud," Tim said, getting agitated. "It's a kilo you owe me, not a half."

"Okay, okay. I give you half now and half in a couple of days."

"Bullshit. All now or things are gonna get seriously messed up."

Either Lin didn't understand the threat, or ignored it. "Business has been so good lately, our supplies are low. Let me see what we have. No need to get worried. Come with me and I'll give you what you need."

Tim did not like the way things were going.

"Stay sharp," Rocket said. "This guy is setting us up."

"No," Mr. Lin pleaded. "It's just an honest mistake."

"Sure," Tim said, trying not to sound sarcastic. He realized he couldn't antagonize the guy too much, considering the amount of security around the place. He reached into his pocket and felt the folding knife... just in case. "Okay, Mr. Lin. Lead on."

The three men walked around the side of the bar and through the rear doors and down into the underground complex.

*   *   *

Alex and Kat were in their final stages of preparation when Rollie, the chubby stage manager, came into the room. His suit jacket was cheap and his white shirt had a beer spill on it.

"Listen girls, I want you two to go on the stage together. It's your first show with us, and what a great way to make a big splash. Some of these guys might want to buy you for the night after the dance. And for two girls, the price doubles. We can all make money," Rollie flashed a sharp smile.

The girls looked at each other, shrugged, smiled politely at the man, and, without saying anything, walked together out of the change area. Tim, Rocket and Mr. Lin were coming down the stairs.

"Hey," Kat said. "We're going on stage. Come watch our first show."

239

"Just a little business first, then we'll be right there," Tim replied with a reassuring wink.

"You girls are looking sweet as honey," Rocket said.

"Thanks," Kat said, smiling brightly while Alex frowned and pouted as they walked past.

*   *   *

From where Ainle was sitting, he was able to watch -- but not hear -- the conversation unfold. With the music being so loud, even if he was sitting at the nearest table, he'd have to resort to lip-reading. It looked like the bikers were arguing with the Chinese guy in the crappy suit. And while that was interesting enough, it was the three Asian guys that came through the back doors that got his attention. They approached the bikers and the Chinese man, seeming to wait their turn to talk with the one in the crappy suit. With a bunch of nodding and fake smiles, the bikers and the Chinese man seemed to come to some sort of agreement, got a fresh round of new drinks, and headed for the rear doors, where they disappeared. The three Asian guys seemed perplexed and looked at each other, becoming animated in a brief conversation before also going through the doors.

The waitress returned to check on Ainle. He asked her, "Is your offer of a private dance still available?" thinking it might be his chance to see what was behind those doors.

She smiled, touched his arm lightly and said, "Of course, sweetie."

Ainle saw how pretty she really was. *What's a nice girl like you doing in a place like this?*

"It's fifty for three songs," she said. "And I don't do anything extra."

"Hey that's fine with me," he said trying to sound cooler than he felt. He wasn't sure what would happen, though he had a pretty good idea what an "extra" might be.

His heart was pounding as the waitress took his hand and led him to the back doors by the bar. A solid and miserable-looking bouncer who looked like he just finished pumping iron all day gave him a once-over inspection on his way past, making sure Ainle was just another lonely guy looking for comfort. He decided Ainle was not a troublemaker.

The bouncer nodded, and gave the woman a look that said he was looking out for her.

"This one's a pussy cat," she said to the bouncer as they passed through the doors.

*   *   *

Another bouncer put his arm out and said, "Hold it, Amber," as the two women from the mussels bar came through the doors, walked past them and strutted to the stage. Ainle turned his head and looked down, pretending to fumble for change as he held his breath as they walked by.

"Hands off the new girls," Amber said to the bouncer as she led Ainle down the stairs. At the bottom, the hallway went left and right. The girl turned left and led him to a door with yet another security guard. They were all looking the same -- big, scowling and flat-nosed.

The door opened and a pretty blonde girl in a tight outfit came out followed by a smiling older man. The girls kissed each other on the cheeks before the blonde headed off with her new companion.

Ainle and Amber went into the room, and Ainle saw it was further sub-divided into several smaller rooms. Inside each cubicle was a stereo system, a couple of low chairs and mirrors on three of the walls.

"Money first," the girl said. "It's all about business," she added, smiling an irresistible smile.

Ainle was stressing a little. He was here to find Grace but instead was getting ready for a lap dance.

"Grace is not going to like this," he thought as he reached for his money.

Chapter 28

Grace decided she was not staying, and that was that.

She considered different scenarios. Maybe she could try to trick the guy when he came to the door. If it wasn't the guy from earlier, and it was the three Asian men, she didn't have much hope. But if it was the thin guy arriving alone, she might have a chance with someone who was not expecting anything.

And she didn't have to wait long. The door lock rattled again before opening. There stood the attendant. For some reason he looked bigger than she remembered.

"Hi," she said softly, trying to sound weak and scared. That was the easy part. "When do I get to go home?"

"Come with me," the attendant ordered.

For her plan to work, she needed him in the room. Her heart was pounding not just in her chest, but in her head. Her hands shook. She clamped them on her knees to try and stop the trembling.

"No thank you. I think I'll stay until my husband comes to pick me up."

"No, you come with me." He walked into the room and pointed to the door. "Let's go."

Grace slowly rose from the cot, kept her head down and hunched her shoulders as she crossed her arms over her chest in a posture of submission. She stepped unhurriedly to the doorway and paused. He had led the way the last time, and she expected him to do it again. She waited.

He stepped past her to move into the hallway.

As he walked past, Grace took one step behind to follow, then committed to what might be her one and only chance.

It's now or never.

She came up just behind him and snaked her right arm under his chin. She leapt up, wrapping her legs around his midsection as her left arm shot around the other side of his neck.

He spun wildly in surprise as she grabbed her left bicep with her right hand and sunk the choke deep under his chin, against his throat.

The man slammed back into the opposite wall, jarring her, but it was a fool's move, and she forced the choke deeper.

244

Her leather boots wrapped around his waist and hooked against each other and she held on for dear life as he slammed her against the other wall.

This one made Grace smash the back of her head on the concrete, and her vision starred briefly.

Calen's voice from the dojo echoed in her head.

Come on Grace, squeeze your elbows together.

The attendant reached over his head and grabbed a handful of her hair, pulling hard.

She tucked her head tight into his back and neck, and could smell garlic and stale cigarettes. She could sense his knees weakening, so she squeezed her elbows tighter, her arms aching as he collapsed forward. Together they pounded onto the cement floor.

She knew the choke was as deep as she could get it, but wasn't sure it was enough.

He rolled over, and she held on with her legs crossed and arms sunk as far as they could go.

His body went limp.

She held on, understanding he might be faking, but also afraid to let go. As she strained to hold on, she first smelled urine, then the rancid stench of his bowels letting go as his body released itself into unconsciousness or death. At this point, she had no idea.

She counted to ten, then slowly relaxed her grip, releasing him and then scrambling away, panting and scared.

Her legs wobbled as she leaned against the wall, trying to catch her breath.

"Fuck you," she whispered to the shape on the floor.

Grace got her legs back and headed down the poorly lit hall in the direction she thought she had come the day before. The hallway was empty and closed doors were on either side of her.

She headed down the hall, holding the wall for balance.

What is this place?

*   *   *

"Hey, before you begin, I need a bathroom break."

The dancer looked at Ainle. "Really? Now?"

"Yeah. Too much beer. Which way?"

"Out the way we came in. Tell security, they'll point you in the right direction."

"Thanks. Be right back." He tried to sound cheery, and walked past the security guy. "Bathroom break," he said.

He walked out into the corridor and turned left, then left again. The hallway stretched quite a distance and there were doors on either side. He walked past a few doors and came to an intersection. To the left was a corridor much like the one he was in, and he thought it probably looped back around like a city block.

To the right was a similar corridor, but he thought he could see movement further down in a poorly lighted section barely out of his sight. It looked like a drunk had wandered down from the street. *Probably a lap dance customer coming back for more.*

Ainle stepped back out of the intersection and waited, unsure what to expect.

The person was getting closer and it kind of sounded like he was running his way. The acoustics made it difficult to tell.

Maybe it's security.

Ainle decided the stranger had seen him and was going to send him back, or kick him out of the club.

In for a penny, in for a pound.

He stepped into the corridor to face the threat.

Just as quickly, he realized it wasn't a man -- security or customer. It was a woman, and he recognized the outline.

"Grace! Oh my God."

She rushed to him, panicked. "Ainle, we've got to get out of here."

He saw the wildness in her eyes as she wrapped her arms around him.

"Grace, what's going on? I've been terrified."

Grace, let go of him, grabbed his good hand and frantically pulled. "Come on, let's get out of here."

"Now ain't this tender," a male voice rumbled from somewhere in the hallway shadows.

Without hesitation, Ainle and Grace ran, spinning around and sprinting down the hallway.

                    *   *   *

"It loops around," Mr. Lin said calmly. "They'll end up back where we are. Tim, come with me." He pointed at Rocket. "If you go back that way we'll catch them soon enough," he wheezed and laughed.

                    *   *   *

When they reached the end of the hall it made only a ninety-degree turn to the left. They raced side-by-side down until it ended and turned left again.

"Shit!" Ainle said.

"What?" Grace asked.

"We're going back where we started."

They were trapped. They could hear someone coming from behind them, and someone heading from the front.

As the men appeared in front of them, Grace screamed, "What do you want?"

"You've been sold, you belong to somebody else. You," the Asian man pointed at Ainle, "are stealing from me. She is my property."

"No she's not. Are you insane?" He held his wife's hand. "We are leaving."

"Well, if you can offer a better price than what I paid for her, you can have her. It's just business."

Ainle stood, trying to comprehend what was going on and how to get out of it.

Grace gripped his hand in terror.

"But I gave these guys the money," Ainle said, pointing at the bikers. "That was the deal. I give them the money, and they give me my wife. I held up my end." He tried to sound aggressive and not scared. He wasn't sure how it came out.

"So?" The Asian smirked at him.

"*They* stole from *me*."

"Not my problem."

Ainle was desperate. He had no ideas of what to do. The gravity of the new nightmare was sinking in.

Appearing behind the biker and the Asian man came another. Grace gasped.

Ainle thought she said something like, "But he's dead."

"No?" the smirking Asian man said. "You do not have enough money?" Lin shrugged and looked at the other Asian man. "Take this one and dump his body in the river."

The biker looked at the Asian man. "What the fuck happened to you?"

"She did," the man pointed at Grace.

"Jeez, you shit and pissed your pants?" the biker said.

"Fuck you."

The smirking Asian man lost the smile. "Jack, take him out of here and dump his body in the river, then clean yourself up."

"Yes sir, Mr. Lin."

Jack stepped forward in the low-lit hallway.

Music from the club thumped faintly through the walls as Ainle's thoughts raced. He considered the options.

As the man got close enough, Ainle leapt forward and kneed Jack square in his urine-stained crotch. The impact found its target, and the reaction immediate. The man folded over with a guttural grunt, reaching for his balls, and Ainle set for the next shot at the collapsing man.

But one of the bikers shot in from the side and tackled Ainle before he could reset himself. The two men went down hard with the biker on top and pinning Ainle awkwardly against the floor and wall. The biker got a knee on Ainle's chest as Ainle reached up to grab the man's shirt.

The biker leaned back, out of the reach, and then quickly leaned in and dropped a balled right fist on Ainle's face, sending him into unconsciousness.

*   *   *

Grace reacted without thinking and took a step to defend Ainle, soccer-kicking the biker hard to the ribs.

She stepped back to deliver a second blow when the other biker closed on her from behind, wrapping both his arms around, pinning her hands at her sides. Then he lifted her off her feet, spun around, and slammed her against the opposite wall, pressing her hard against the smooth, cold tiles.

Grace realized her feet were off the ground as the man leaned his full body weight against her. She struggled and kicked and tried to turn, but with no perch for her feet, she only struggled feebly.

"Hmm, you feel good," the man said, leaning his hips into Grace from behind. "This one has a nice hard ass," he said more to Grace than to anyone else.

Grace could see the other biker out of the corner of her eye climbing off the limp body of Ainle.

"Maybe we take turns with you," the man holding her said softly in her ear.

She could feel his breath, smell his beer as one of his hands moved from their bear-hug grip to one hand sliding across her stomach.

"Maybe we even film it and sell it on the net. I bet Mr. Lin has a customer for that."

The Asian man spoke, "Jack, get some help and drag that body down the hall to the harbor entry and dump it. Let us clean this mess up. Tim, that was a very nice punch. You knocked him cold."

The biker let her down, but did not let go, manhandling her towards her holding cell as Jack stood, hunched over, staring at the unconscious Ainle.

As they pushed her back into her room, the biker smacked Grace hard on the ass and said, "I liked that. You and me could have a nice time."

Grace twisted around, furious, intense and filled with hate. It was a combination that took her to the edge of madness, a fury that made her want only one thing -- vengeance.

The biker, maybe seeing the expression on her face and the hate in her eyes, backed out quickly. Her cell door slammed closed, followed by the sound of the lock crunching shut.

Grace pounded the door with her fists and screamed like the insane woman she had become.

*   *   *

Alex and Kat finished their routine on the stage, covered in sweat and breathing hard.

They walked off the stage and men tossed money and comments about how they wanted the girls for a party or a private dance.

Kat was nervous from all the attention and held onto Alex's arm for security.

In the change room, they quickly donned robes, taking seats to cool down and relax.

"Well, that was fun," Alex said as she leaned back and lit a cigarette.

Kat stared into the mirror. "We have four more shows tonight. How do you do it? I don't think I can keep this up." She worried about what would happen if she couldn't do her part.

"Maybe we can find a little pick-me-up. Somebody must have some candy in a place like this."

Kat knew she shouldn't have any, but the craving never went away. She perked up. "Yeah, that would be nice, to keep us going for the next show," she said, deep in rationalization.

Alex sat forward, blowing out a cloud of smoke. "Let me finish this and I'll see what I can find."

"This place might not be so bad after all." Kat sat back and smiled at Alex.

*   *   *

Dragging an unconscious body is a lot harder than it looks, Jack thought. It just flops and hooks onto everything close to it, and seems to fight against you. Even when it's two young men doing the work, it's still not easy.

"Jeez, Jack. Stop a moment, I need a smoke," the other man said in Vietnamese.

Jack stared at his new partner. Even though this kid was a newbie, he was trusted enough to help dump a body in the river. And once this was done, the new guy would be owned by Lin.

Jack was desperate to get rid of the body and get cleaned up, but his fear of Mr. Lin let him know he should dump the body first, then change his clothes. He knew what happened when you let the boss down. This white guy might not be the only one dumped in the river tonight. When the girl escaped from his care, he thought he was a dead man. But now was a chance to redeem his mistake -- in fact he might even get a reward or a bonus of some sort for doing the job for the boss.

"Okay, give me one as well. Then we'll get this done and go check out the girls."

"I recommend you shower first. You stink."

Jack stared at the new guy as he was handed a cigarette. "What's your name?"

"Simon. Why?"

"Because, Simon, make a crack like that again and you'll be swimming with this guy. We clear?"

"Hey chill, have a smoke. I'm clear, my bad," and Simon lit his cigarette before handing the cheap lighter over.

Jack lit the end of his, feeling that the air temperature was cooler here and would become chillier as they moved toward the St. Laurence River. Jack checked his phone, but saw there was no signal down in this area.

In this section of the tunnel complex, the lights were naked fluorescent bulbs, some broken, creating small sections of the tunnel that were in complete blackness. This area was a lot less travelled than others, only used for the rare trips to the river when things needed dumping. They still had quite a ways of tunnel left to reach the harbor access point. The only good thing for Jack and

Simon was that it was a slight downhill slope the rest of the way.

Chapter 29

Grace felt her reason slipping and clear coherent thought difficult to maintain.

She tried breathing to calm herself down, but it didn't work. She tried pacing, but it only got her more worked up.

An image flashed in her mind and it was of her fist smashing into the biker's face, her knee striking the Asian guy in the balls, and that, remarkably, she relaxed a little. When she thought again of kicking one of them, and when she visualized snapping the neck of either of the bikers, she felt her pulse slow. She calmed herself by plotting retribution.

She sat on the cot, hunched over, her hair hanging across her face as she stared at the door, waiting.

Grace hissed at the locked door in a voice that seemed to belong to someone else

"My retribution shall be swift and terrible, this I promise."

*　　*　　*

Kat could hear Alex giggling in the hallway before the door opened, and Alex walked in with a big mischievous smile.

"What did you find?" Kat asked.

Alex reached into her robe and pulled out a small plastic bag containing a nice measure of white powder, holding it up and waving it back and forth.

"Care to sample a little?" Alex asked.

"This is awesome, Alex. Now the party gets started."

*　　*　　*

Ainle slowly began to come to, sensing first the cold floor against the side of his face, and then the smell of shit and cigarette smoke.

Voices spoke in what could have been Cambodian or Vietnamese. He sensed they realized he was coming around.

Ainle was flipped onto his stomach and his arms pulled behind his back. Nylon tie-wraps were zipped tight around his wrists and he was effectively bound and secured.

"Come on," the man named Jack said in English. "We're going for a walk."

One man got on one side, and the other on the opposite, each grabbing an arm and hoisting Ainle to his feet.

The three of them set off down the dark tunnel.

*   *   *

Tim and Rocket sat on the opposite side of Lin's desk and waited as glasses of scotch were poured for each of them.

"Who was that guy?" Lin asked Tim.

"He's from the west, and he stole some money from me."

"Why is he here?" Lin was clearly agitated. He quickly shot back his drink and poured himself another.

"I think he wanted to steal it back again," Rocket said, knocking back his Scotch.

"He came into my business," Lin said. "He came here to steal from my friends and partners?"

Tim finished his drink, reached across the table and grabbed the scotch bottle, inspected the label and poured Rocket and himself another. He wasn't sure Lin was sincere in the "friends and partners" comment, but he would pretend to take it at face value.

"This is fine hooch," Rocket said as he held the glass up to the light.

"Thanks, my other friends from Asia brought this as a gift. It's called *Hanyu* and it is from Japan. Who ever thought the Japanese could make whiskey?"

"Not me," laughed Rocket.

Tim shook his head and smiled because he knew Rocket knew very little about rare scotch. Or any scotch for that matter.

"Listen." Lin leaned forward over his desk. "I have a business opportunity and good men like you could help me, as I could help you. My three friends from Asia are looking for girls and I think I have three girls they will like. The two you brought and the new one in the cell. But now I need three more. Is there any chance of you finding them? There is a lot of money for all of us, and if we leave Mr. Wong out of the deal we don't need to spread ourselves so thin. Interested?"

Lin poured another drink for himself, then poured more for Tim and Rocket.

The boys looked at each other. Tim understood this act of Lin pouring a fresh drink for them was a meaningful gesture.

*   *   *

The two men exchanged words in whatever language they spoke, and Ainle's head throbbed as they continued down the corridor, a hand locked on each of his arms.

Ainle's stomach heaved as he vomited on himself.

The one named Jack, startled, said something that probably translated to *What the fuck?*

In his scrambled thinking, Ainle believed he had a concussion and his body was reacting accordingly. A big part of him didn't care as he was trying to figure out where he was, who was holding him and where they were going.

"Hey," Ainle mumbled through swollen lips. "What's wrong with my arms? My hands are stuck?"

The two men exchanged glances and jabbered something incomprehensible. Then one of them said in English, "Five more minutes and we'll be there, and everything will be alright."

Ainle's head hung forward as he vomited a second time, mostly liquid bile.

"Come on big boy," a man said. "We'll get you some rest in a few minutes. Just keep your feet moving."

*   *   *

Grace heard the door rattle and two new, but older bouncers -- both big, solid men, one with short gray hair and the other bald as a ping pong ball -- brought her a sandwich and water. They set it on the floor.

"Here, have something to eat and drink. Things will work out for you. Eat up! You will need your strength," the gray-haired bouncer said.

Then they backed out of the room and locked the door.

Feeling guilty, as if she were a traitor to herself and Ainle for being so weak, she devoured the sandwich, opened the water bottle . . . and paused.

She held the bottle to the light. Something seemed wrong.

The cap didn't have the usual click when the seal broke on opening.

She examined the bottle, but everything looked fine.

Bringing the bottle to her nose, she sniffed it.

It seemed okay, but then again, what was okay in this upside-down world?

She sniffed a second time, then stuck her tongue out like a kitten and tasted the water.

Was it bitter tasting?

She thought it was . . . or was it her imagination?

She took a small drink.

She tested to see if her tongue felt numb.

Maybe.

Was she feeling woozy? Was her chest tight? Or was it just a panic attack?

Regardless, she didn't want it. She hurled the water across the room, and it splashed on the walls before gurgling much of it onto the floor.

The panic moment eased and she fought to keep her mind focused. The only thing that went through her mind was: *Ainle is dead.*

Then a new thought: *These people are going to rape and kill me.*

The paralyzing, breath-stealing panic consumed her again.

And she stared at the spilled water. She was thirsty and wanted it badly.

*   *   *

The cocaine was clean and strong, and they were excited, hyper and ready to dance.

A dour-faced bouncer came in and asked the girls to follow him.

"Where we going, handsome?" Kat asked.

"Tonight is a special night," he said, still not smiling. "We have some international visitors this week and you have been invited to a private party. There will be plenty of chances to make some bonus cash. So, come with me and you could strike it rich tonight."

Kat eagerly followed the bouncer, forgetting her little bag. Alex picked it up on her way out, shaking her head.

That girl's got some serious learning to do, she thought.

Alex had been around long enough to not let herself get worked up by the life of a dancing girl. She had seen new party girls like Kat before and she didn't like what happened to them. They all thought the world worshipped them and they never realized they were just the disposable toys of rich spoiled brats.

Wealthy kids who cared only for money and for personal gratification only used them and walked away. She had learned years ago that she was just a part of the sick machine. She would have fun and make money with her eyes wide open. And when you thought about it, who really enjoyed their job, anyway? She was just happy to have a job since, after all, it paid the bills.

*   *   *

The scotch flowed and Lin's face had a red glow in the cheeks.

Tim was felt good and leaned back on his chair with his boots on Lin's desk. It wasn't all that comfortable, but he wanted to see what Lin would do.

Rocket swirled the drink in his mouth before he swallowed and thumped the glass on the desk.

"One more, boys?" Rocket asked.

"Gentlemen," Lin asked. "How much do you want for the blonde girl downstairs?"

"I thought you already sold her," Rocket said.

"No, not yet. She is your property. I would not do that to my friends." Lin poured another shot for Rocket. "I have a customer who likes a girl who fights, and he would pay a premium for those qualities. I think she is a good product for a party later."

"Twenty-grand," Tim stated.

"Ten," Lin countered.

"Fifteen," Tim said.

"If you take your feet of my desk, I'll pay you fifteen cash right now."

"A done deal," Tim said as he slid his boots off the desk and sat up.

"Fantastic, fantastic," Lin said adding his wheezing laugh as he reached into his wall safe and handed over three stacks of bills. "Gentlemen," Lin said, smacking his hands together with delight, "there is a party later, and I would love to introduce you to some important people from my old home."

"Only if you get that crazy cough checked out," Rocket said.

And Lin gasped and wheezed one more time.

"Okay, tomorrow, tomorrow, you sound like my wife."

*   *   *

The preparations were almost done. The Hilton Executive suite was decorated and the food and drink were ready. The party was the end point of a week-long negotiation of products for cash, and the three Asian gentlemen had plenty of cash.

Once a year, they were sent to North America to broker a deal for new girls. Money and women were arranged for delivery and money and women were collected. In North America, the Southeast Asian girl is an exotic and sought-after commodity, just like the blue-eyed blonde or the green-eyed red-haired girl from

Europe or North America was a much-wanted desire in Southeast Asia. To the right buyer, the right girl could bring in a large sum of money. Once transported to Southeast Asia, the girl would be rented like a car for ridiculous amounts of cash, and cash only.

Alex and Kat had no idea they only had a day or two in North America. They had already been sold to an overseas buyer. Young, beautiful, sexy drug users were property for a few years, and when they burned out, they were discarded like garbage.

Grace, at 30, was certainly outside of the sixteen to twenty-four-year-old window that most buyers prized, but being an unwilling participant she would bring excellent money for a man with power, control and dominance as his desires. It was a party for those who lived in a world of corruption and vice. It was to be a Hollywood-style party -- not for those who made movies about vice and human depravity, but for those who wrote the book on vice and human depravity.

And this is why the party was set up in one place, but happened in another.

*　　*　　*

Ainle's vision was returning and his balance was starting to stabilize. His head ached, his ribs hurt and he could feel that a few teeth were wobbly in his mouth.

"Hey, where we going?" Ainle asked.

"Swimming," said the man named Jack.

Ainle stiffened his legs, leaned back, and twisted to get away.

The men tightened their grip and lifted Ainle up off the ground to keep him from trying to get away. As the three of them went through pools of light cast from the overhead bulbs, the air temperature was noticeably colder and damper. Ainle thought *I can smell the river.*

Their foot falls echoed as they pushed and pulled Ainle toward the St. Laurence River.

They passed one last opening that offered a passage to the left and right, and Ainle peered into the darkness.

If I can get free, he thought, *I'll go that way.* He saw it as his only opportunity for escape.

The three men came to a sudden stop in front of two large metal doors. Apparently, this marked the end of the tunnel.

Jack smiled in the low light and fished out a set of keys from his soiled trousers, seemingly happy to be at the end of today's journey. He unlocked the oversized bolts, and with a squealing grind, he swung the doors inwards. On the other side was a thick, large gauge screen designed to keep any river debris out of the tunnel access. Twisted bits of dead tree branches and plastic garbage were caught here and there in the grid of the screen. Jack worked the lock on the screen and slid it part-way open, just enough to fit a man. There was a small concrete step, the width of a man's foot, then the black, oily movement of the St. Laurence River as it flowed past.

It was strangely silent.

Ainle tensed and leaned back, sweat instantly forming on his forehead as he stared wide-eyed at the river. The other man peeled a long strip of duct tape and pressed it hard across Ainle's mouth to stifle any attempt to scream.

And scream he did, as well as kicked and flail and twist. His eyes bulged in terror. The bouncers laughed. The man took one arm and Jack the other.

"Have a nice night, your girl is going to join you soon," whispered Jack.

And they pushed him awkwardly, face first into the black waters of the cold, mindless river.

The splash was quick, and in the distance a police siren faded into the night . . . and then silence returned to Ainle.

Chapter 30

The water enveloped Ainle completely. The shock of it all, plus the coldness of the water, paralyzed him. There was the shock of *this is not happening* along with the shock of his impending death, that brought him, temporarily at least, an odd peace, his body alone and lost in this giant river.

I'm going to end up in the Atlantic Ocean.

Dozens of images flashed through his mind in the time it took to go for his body to travel from the tunnel's exit to under the water.

Paralysis -- and its peace -- was soon replaced with panic, and he jerked violently to reach up and swim . . . but is arms were still secured behind his back and he was upside down. The water was remarkably cold, and instantly his clothes were heavy.

He curled into a ball and tried to pull his hands under his feet while still beneath the surface, but they got stuck -- and he panicked and tried to scream.

The duct tape saved him. If it hadn't been plastered over his mouth he would sucked in a couple of lungs full of seaway, and it would all be over.

As it was, his lungs were bursting, needing air, and he was disoriented.

Air, you need air. Exhale and watch the bubbles, chase the bubbles.,"

The voice was from his childhood. That shaggy-haired asshole who had taught him how to swim back in elementary school.

No air, no life, no fight.

He opened his eyes, gave a short burst of air from his nose and felt it travel past his chin and throat. Panic, although it never really went away, was refreshed with the loss of the air, however small. But a sliver of reason whispered: *Panic is going to kill you.*

He curled and tried to let the current roll him. Slowly, he tumbled forward as the river carried him downstream, then he straightened himself and desperately scissor-kicked once, then twice. His head broke the surface and he had just enough time to exhale through his nose before he slipped back under the surface.

He kicked again and got his head clear and took a fast, hard inhale. Snot, water and cold air went in and he went back under and started gagging.

Trying again, he gave several short, quick kicks to keep his head above the surface long enough to get several rapid breaths.

You have air. Slow yourself down, calm down.

This was so easy to think, but as water streamed over his face, he knew he couldn't keep this up for much longer. He would quickly fatigue, sink, and die.

Ainle tried to get his bearings. As the river turned him like a slow top, he looked far across the river to the faint lights of apartments. He looked the other way and saw the bright city lights of old Montreal.

It's like a postcard, he thought as he floated on his back with the languid current. *The city is pretty. But my last vision will not be this.*

He relaxed and let himself sink under the surface, worked his tongue on the tape, wiggled his jaw, and he felt the tape loosen a little. Two more scissor-kicks brought him to the surface, two then three more nose intakes of air, and he let himself dip below the waterline again. Once more he tried working the tape. It loosened further, but didn't release.

Two more kicks.

He tried moving his head to drag the tape against his shoulder, but it didn't work. He took a nose full of water and started gasping and gagging again as water and mucus blocked his nose and throat.

Again, he slipped under.

Two kicks, two kicks, he told himself. Then, sweet cool air got into his lungs.

Cold was overriding everything.

Get out of the fucking water, or you're not going to make it."

The pretty lights disappeared as black-shadowed trees loomed where buildings once were.

Use the current when in a river, don't fight it, the shaggy-haired asshole had called, like it was something only an idiot didn't know. *Accept what God has given you. The current is a gift, just don't go into the middle, boys.*

Ainle flipped onto his back, gasped and breathed through his nose. One shoe came off, and he kicked the other free.

Another breath and he sunk again, two kicks and air, two kicks and air.

It was working, but it was slow going.

Again, two and breath. The shore peeked at him, it was there. Two and breath.

A cold round stone touched a shoeless foot.

Then both feet touched the riverbed.

He pushed off as the current moved him sideways, and his feet caught the muddy, rocky river bed. He managed to stand for a moment, stumbled forward, smashing head-first onto the shore, jarring his neck and jamming his shoulder.

He lay in the shallows, looking up at the stars.

Pain is good. Pain means life.

With arms still behind his back, shirt hanging out, pants barely hanging onto his hips, one sock about to fall off and the other missing, he got to his knees and staggered to the shore before collapsing on the muddy, leafy bank.

It smelled earthy, like home.

A rebirth.

*   *   *

The big neon sign, El Matador, taunted Mike as he looked at it. He shook his head as he looked at Darrel. Both men's faces looked worn and tired in the blue and red glow of the poised neon bull fighter.

"We lost him again," said Mike

"Or this time he's really dead."

"Kinda sad, really. I'm starting to like this guy. Bit of a dummy, but he seems determined."

"Let's go back to the hotel and see what pops up there."

*   *   *

Grace was deep in thought when the lock clicked again and the door slowly opened. Whatever they meant by "party", it was about to begin.

A new guy appeared, not much different from the previous guy, only without the piss-and-shit stained pants.

"Here, wear this," her new jailor said as he tossed a small black dress onto the cot.

"No, you wear it," she said, picking it up and tossing it at him.

He paused at the door, staring at the crumpled-up garment. "I was supposed to take you to your husband," he said. "But I guess not."

Grace was not stupid enough to believe him, but figured there might be the slimmest of chances he was telling the truth. More importantly, though, it would get her out of this stupid room, and maybe give her the opportunity to escape.

"Okay," she said. "Close the door."

He smirked as if she had fallen for his plan, and slid the door closed.

She quickly changed, not liking the dress at all. It was obviously meant to be worn without a bra, which she wasn't going to reward them with, and the hem was high enough to qualify as a mini-skirt. She took the dress off, put her dirty regular clothes back on, and knocked on the door. It was re-opened.

The man gave her the once-over. "You didn't change."

"It didn't fit."

He shrugged, then cocked his head for her to step out into the hallway.

They started down the hallway, and took an alternative hallway. Soon, they turned right, then left through a single steel door and up a set of stairs. She tried to keep the directions straight in case she needed to run back, for whatever reason.

The stairs led them to a thrift shop that sold cheap Asian knick-knacks. The main lights were off and only a couple of security lights provided enough illumination for them to weave through aisles of statuettes of old men fishing and curios featuring waving cats.

Grace reached up and brushed a wind-chime, the sound was soft and delicate.

They exited the store in the rear where a black Lincoln Town Car idled in the alley, the rear passenger door open.

"Come on, dear," the cackling Asian boss said from inside the car. "Everything has been looked after. It has all been a misunderstanding. We are going to meet your husband and you can get back to your little world."

Grace hesitated. She didn't know what to do, was more than a little scared. What she would do for a shower and a drink. Until then, she had no choice but go for a ride.

She slid into the back of the car. A luxury car, except that it smelled of cigarettes.

"You did not put on the dress I picked out for you?" the man said.

"Not my size."

"Really?"

"Too big," she said trying not to sound as scared as she felt.

"Okay. Next time I'll find you something much smaller. Driver, let us get to our meeting."

"Where are we going?" she asked.

"A short drive. Just relax, enjoy."

*   *   *

Grace stared out the passenger window at the quickly changing neighborhoods. She had no idea where they were, but the scene turned from slightly scummy, to the economic opulence of downtown before transitioning into blocks of walk-up brownstone apartments, which in turn were replaced by large homes with even larger yards. Soon, the houses were separated by massive tree-lined multi-story homes.

The car slowed then arced left across the main road and onto a long, gravel driveway. Grace noticed the house was a large country home. The large oak double doors stood at the top of a wide fan-shaped stairway. Large rectangular windows seemed to cover the entire first floor, some of them were open, perhaps to let the evening air flow through the house. Upstairs, similar windows lined the second story and Grace thought the view should be quite nice. The house was situated nicely. Big trees in full autumn bloom on either side helped and no doubt there was a nice big yard around back. A pair of stylish cars were parked out front and several well-dressed men and women were coming and going through the big entryway.

"Is this your home?" Grace asked.

"No, it is not mine. But it is a nice house."

The car rolled to a stop near the front door and the driver got out, walked around the car and opened Grace's door.

What is going on?

She had been told about going to a party, and it was, so far, fitting the bill. Asian men talked and laughed out front. Some stood at the top of the steps, smoked cigarettes, stared at her and smiled. Pretty girls could be seen, dressed in short skirts and tight dresses, showing off their bodies.

The cackling Asian came around the car and put his arm in Grace's, speaking softly.

"You should have put on that dress, it would have made these girls look second class."

"I already have enough enemies. I was told Ainle would be here."

"On his way," he smiled eerily, patting her hand.

Just play along. Figure it out.

She looked around for a place to hide, thinking the trees around the house might be a starting point, but then what?

She just had to get rid of Lin.

Inside, it was definitely a party, far too many people, too many men who eyed her lasciviously, too many young women alternately checking her out and sneering.

Her escort/kidnapper waved to a waiter and spoke in Chinese or something. Grace took in the massive house which was amazing, with enormous chandeliers, and a wide staircase that curved to an upper-level. There were dozens -- if not a hundred -- people chatting and laughing. The waiter approached with a drink tray, and she snagged one, hoping it wasn't poisoned like the water in her cell.

A husky, solidly-built man squeezed by her. His suit jacket opened briefly and she was sure she saw the handle of a pistol in a shoulder holster.

Who are these people?

To add to the surreal scene, she could see a man in a tuxedo playing a grand piano up on the upper level.

To continue the bad Hollywood movie, she recognized the three men from the hotel elevator approaching. They each carried a briefcase and nodded at her kidnapper as they came close. They stopped in front of Grace, looking her up and down, literally from head to toe, and back again.

"This one will do," the tallest of the three suits said.

Grace felt her stomach knot and goose bumps rise on her skin. The man holding her arm felt her tense.

"Have your drink, dear," he whispered.

Grace took a long swallow and finished her glass.

"Can I have another, please," she held out the empty glass. Appearing out of nowhere, a waiter floated in, took the glass and replaced it with a fresh one.

A girl's voice called out -- "Let's get the party started!" -- in a wild squeal from the entrance way. Grace, along with just about everyone else in the room, looked over to see who the attention-grabber was.

The bikers and the two women were standing in the doorway, looking around and smiling. It didn't take long for them to see Grace and her current kidnapper. They nodded, then escorted the girls to the bar.

The man at Grace's side spoke to the three Asian men. "There are your other two, gentlemen."

"Very nice," the tall one said as he watched the girls and licked his thin lips. "Let us go upstairs and inspect the products, sort out the contracts and then we'll get the shipping organized. With this one here," he said, looking at Grace, "this makes ten. Transportation might need a little organizing, but it is a good number. Let us check the quality of the goods, and then we'll be on our way. It is time for us to return to our families."

"Very well, then. I'll arrange an inspection."

Grace felt a chill down her spine like nothing she had ever felt before.

God, Ainle, I wish you were here.

Chapter 31

The "inspection" was arranged in one of the large rooms of the house. The three men from Asia were introduced as talent executives from a new modeling agency and the girls would have an opportunity to get in on the ground floor of this new booming business opportunity.

Grace sat quietly on a rickety fold-up chair, watching the other women, and keeping an eye on the man who stood guard at the door. There was no other way out, best she could tell.

She knew this was all a sham. If the other women didn't look at her with disgust, she might have been able to tell some of them they were in big trouble. They weren't going to be partners in a new, great business. They were the product, to be bought and sold.

Every so often, a man came in and pointed at a couple of the women, and had them follow him out of the room. After a few minutes, they were brought back.

The other girls would ask them what happened, what took place out there. Although it was often difficult for Grace to hear, she understood they were strutted out, photographed -- some with their clothes on, some without -- and brought back. One of the girls was asked to perform "that special talent" and she seemed quite pleased with herself that she took them up on their request. They were then given sealed envelopes with airline tickets and told they'd be taken to the airport shortly.

The man came in, pointed at the girls that had arrived with the bikers, and said "Kat, Alex, your turn." Then he looked around the room until his eyes fell on Grace. "You too."

She reluctantly got up and joined the girls.

Kat and Alex were excited, and when they were brought out, they strutted and danced into the room, flaunting their legs and hips, as well as their sexuality.

Grace, standing off to the side, looked at every window, noticing all the blinds were closed. She saw three comfortable green leather chairs forming a semi-circle around a small table. Pleasant paintings of nature scenes hung on the pomegranate walls. Grace took in the elegant room, and while it was meant to be a warm, welcoming ambiance -- certainly a grand alternative to being locked in a cement cell -- she realized this place was much more dangerous than that underground room.

"Girls, stand over there, to the right," a voice from behind them commanded.

Grace walked where the man pointed, and the other two joined her, one on each side. The one on the left -- she didn't know which was Kat and which was Alex -- turned toward her, smiled and said, "Welcome to the party."

Grace wanted to say *Whatever they say, they're lying.* Instead, she stared straight ahead.

"Okay, ladies. We have a business opportunity for you," a man in the shadows back behind the bar said. A briefcase appeared on the marble top and was opened.

The women turned to see stacks and stacks of money inside. Kat and Alex both gasped and grinned from ear-to-ear. To Grace, it was her selling price.

The man from behind the bar set one of the neat stacks of money on the bar. It was a good manipulation, the perfect stack of money, square edges, straight lines and that nice little band that held all the bills in place. It did its job very well on Kat and Alex.

To Grace, it made her stomach nauseous.

"This could be yours," the man said.

Grace's eyes were disbelieving, the woman on her left looked confused, and the other had her jaw set, lips tight in defiance. She was the first to speak.

"I don't think so."

"Let me explain." The man's voice was calm the way a school teacher would point out an indiscretion to a young naïve student. "You really have very little choice in this opportunity. The money is real, it is everywhere, but you need to know how to find it." He paused dramatically. "I know where to find it."

Grace looked to the woman on her right -- Alex? -- and shook her head.

"We have a modeling contract for each of you," the man added. "And this is what you can make when you join our modeling agency."

"Shit, sign me up," Kat said. "Where we going?" She walked over to the money. "Somebody give me a pen."

Alex followed her, putting her hand on Kat's shoulder, Grace walked over, partially out of curiosity, but also to not stand there by herself. A contract had been placed on the bar beside the money. The man handed Kat a Monte Blanc pen. She grabbed it, smiling as she signed.

"What's your name?" Alex asked the man behind the bar.

"Zichou," he said.

Grace stood where she was and didn't move.

A tall, slim man stepped forward, from out of the shadows. "We fly out tonight. We need you in jeans and regular shirts. Time to change and then we'll start traveling the world. This is a six-month contract and we'll have you back in the spring. Then, if all goes well, we'll talk contract renewal. Welcome to the team. You may call me Mr. Quach."

Grace went cold, wrapping her arms across her chest for warmth. Quach's eyes were spooky, unblinking. How did these

282

girls not see it? Were they that desperate? Greedy? Were they really that stupid? She had seen foolish students in her classroom, but she always believed they would find the good path. Maybe she was wrong. Is this what happens when they refuse to learn? Is this who they become -- so cold men could prey on them?

Even though Grace did not sign the contract, the three of them were escorted out and taken down a short hallway, walking into a room where a pair of suitcases were waiting for them. The room was painted a dull orange hue. It had a small bar to one side and Grace noticed the expensive looking scotch bottles. Strangely, she felt like taking one. She had never stolen anything in her life, but now she was thinking about slipping one off the counter -- even though she had nowhere to put it.

Things have really changed.

Grace scanned the room. Like the other room in the back, the door was the only way in and out. Certainly, there was someone on the other side, guarding it.

"No bags, honey?" Alex asked Grace, snapping her out of her trance.

"I'm not going anywhere," Grace said. "You're idiots to think that any of that money is for you, or that anything they said was true."

"No, we signed contracts," Kat said.

"Don't be so stupid," Grace snapped back. "Did you read it? You just gave up your bodies -- your lives -- for what?"

283

"That's real money, they really are modeling agents," Kat replied.

"Where is the money? Did they give it to you? No, because it's not real. They're not real."

Kat's mouth opened, then closed. She looked more confused than ever.

Grace kept at her.

"You will never return to Canada. You're going to die a drug addicted hooker in some brothel in Thailand or Vietnam."

Grace glanced at Alex,

"Come on, you must know what's going on. They're going to make you pay for your plane ticket, for your food, for everything. They will promise you money, but at the end of it all, you will owe them. Where the hell are you going to stay? When do you get paid? How are you going to get around? By limo?"

Alex looked at Grace while she slipped one long leg, then the other, into her jeans and pulled them on. "How do you know this?" Alex asked.

"They held me in a fucking cell, just two hours ago. They beat up my husband and for all I know, he might even be dead."

"Well, that's you," Kat said, sneering. "Not us, we're the talent. Welcome to the team, that's what they said. They mean it, I can tell."

Grace shook her head. "You're going to find out too soon that I'm right, and then it will be too late.

"How do you think you're not going?" Alex asked. "What are you going to do?"

"Jeez, not you," Kat said. But she was looking uneasy. "I have to leave, I shot that guy back home. I can't go back, this is my chance to change things."

Fury rose up in Grace like she had never felt before.

"That was my husband, you bitch!" Grace raced across the room, shot her left arm straight out and clamped her hand around Kats throat.

Kat gagged and stumbled backwards, thumping hard into a dull orange wall as Grace pulled her right arm back to deliver a solid punch.

The door swung open. "Hey enough!" yelled the man.

Grace slowly let go of Kat's throat and backed away.

Kat slid down the wall and crumpled to the floor, holding her throat.

"You're a freak," Kat said from the plush carpeted floor. "I'm going."

Grace walked away and slumped down onto a gaudy pink armchair, her heart was pounding, her breathing chugging in and out of her.

Alex looked at Grace. "You better not try that on me, I'll slit your throat."

Grace looked over to Alex from her chair. She pushed her hair out of her eyes with the back of her left hand. It felt oily and needed washing. "You have a knife?"

Ainle was lying in river mud and on cold stones. He curled his knees in to his chest and tried to roll up and stand. His first exhausted step sent him stumbling in the darkness and he went down hard on his left shoulder. A large stone jammed into his ribs and drove the air from his lungs.

He lay for a minute sucking in the cold air, aching, getting stiff, with a chill setting into his body. He felt like a pathetic loser. But he couldn't give up.

Once his breath was back, he rolled again, got his knees under him and stood upright, standing wobbly for a moment. Carefully, he placed one socked foot ahead of the other. The mud was slick and cold. He stumbled again and fell forward, bracing for a hard impact, but ended up in mud and tree roots.

I'm out, he thought. But as he lay there, drained, wet, and cold, he thought of Grace.

He curled again and crawled, inching himself through mud and leaves until he felt a patch of grass. He tried to get his hands under his feet again, but he just didn't have the flexibility. After almost getting his hands permanently stuck under his feet, he resigned himself to getting back to the hotel looking like an escaped prisoner of war.

*   *   *

"Listen," Alex said, folding up the knife and sticking it in her back pocket, "if you don't want to go, fine. But don't fuck it up for us."

Grace decided to take another tact.

"Look," she said. "You're beautiful women. Gorgeous. You probably always wanted to be a fashion model. Who wouldn't? I know, once upon a time, I did. And while Asia is not Paris or Milan, it is a great opportunity to get away from what you've been doing. Now there's me telling you everything you want is a lie. It doesn't make sense. But deep down you know that what I've said rings true. After all, these people seem like agents for a fashion place, in this big house that looks the part. It's all a nice façade. If this were real, they would have brought you to a Manhattan skyscraper, not some fancy private home in Montreal." She paused. "None of this is real."

Something she said seemed to click with Alex. Kat just looked confused.

Grace felt a chill, slumped in her chair and stuffed her hands in her pockets. She felt the small piece of soap and remembered it was her symbol of rebellion.

"I'll not stop you from going. I can't stop you. But, there is no way you will get that knife on an airplane. Everything will get screwed. Why don't you let me have the knife and you might be able to help me."

Alex laughed, "Yeah, right."

"No, I'm serious. Everybody gets searched on those flights. When was the last time you were on a plane? When was the last time you were on a plane, Kat?"

"Just the flight here."

"Well, that's a domestic flight, it's not the same as going from one continent to another. Think of all the terrorist types. They search every bag. They'll find that knife." Grace looked at Kat. "You're not getting out of the country, or even the fucking airport. Not with that knife. It's that simple. I know you're not stupid. I'm sorry for some of the stuff I said, I was just angry. I'm pissed at all this shit. I was kidnapped, held against my will, my husband probably murdered. You do your own thing, I don't care what the fuck you do."

"You're one crazy bitch," Alex said, smiled and moved to finish with her suitcase.

The door opened and the cackling, wheezing Asian was followed by Mr. Quach, announcing, "Okay ladies, it's time to start your new lives."

Alex walked slowly over to Grace, held her hand out and helped Grace climb up out of the plush pink chair. "I think I understand you," Alex said.

"Thanks," was all Grace could manage, but she stood up.

Alex opened her arms to give Grace a hug. As they embraced, Grace felt a hand slip into the waistband of her jeans.

Alex pulled away and looked fiercely into Grace's eyes. "I'll miss you crazy lady." Then she leaned in and whispered, "If we get out of here, we'll need that money."

"Enough of the love, ladies. We have a journey ahead of us. You can do more hugging when we reach our destination." The man gave his wheezing laugh.

The girls stood awkwardly as the men stared at them.

Grace put her mouth close to Alex's ear and whispered, "Look at how they watch us. I'll kill the big fucker first."

Chapter 32

Ainle staggered across the cold wet grass towards the lights of the city. Stopping to catch his breath, he sniffed at the air, catching the scent of burning wood. It felt good. The cold had him shivering uncontrollably and the thought of a fire was strong enough to pull him forward.

He paused in the wooded darkness. Socks hanging off his feet, shirt muddy, untucked and plastered to his shivering body. All he wanted to do was curl up somewhere warm and sleep. If he turned his head, he thought he could hear voices. Ainle pushed himself forward.

As he came over the rise, the light of the flames flickered in the darkness and the small group sitting around the fire fell silent as he stumbled toward them. He collapsed between a grizzled old man and a frightened teenager.

"Help me," Ainle growled to the old man.

A woman's heavily accented French voice said from across the fire, "Do what he says, help him before the fire burns him."

The young guy and the old man looked at Ainle. The teenager got off his wood stump and guided Ainle onto it.

"He's cold."

"Martin, give him your coat," the woman commanded.

The young man took off his heavy coat and draped it over Ainle's shoulders.

"Daniella, his hands are tied."

"Well, untie them."

"I can't. They are plastic. They need to be cut."

"Hunter," the woman said, "please cut the plastic with your knife."

A blade came slowly from under the old man's heavy coat, and easily sliced the plastic tie-wraps.

Ainle groaned a thank you and held his swollen hands towards the heat.

"Thank you, Hunter," Daniella said kindly.

The old man nodded and put the knife back in its hiding spot. The three people watched Ainle.

"Martin," Daniella said. "Continue reading the scriptures while our new friend warms himself."

Martin began reading in a stumbling, awkward voice that was still looking for itself. *"You shall lay your hand on the head of the burnt offering and it shall be acceptable in your behalf as atonement for you.* Leviticus."

Martin's voice droned on about atonement and punishment as Ainle dried by the campfire. It might have gone on for an hour. He thought about how bizarre this all was. The punishment of sinners, how appropriate was that. Was he a sinner? Of course he was. He had stolen drug money, lied, used violence, made choices that caused his wife to be stolen from him and imprisoned. His arrogance had been a major driving force. He needed to reverse his path, he needed his old life back.

He didn't realize he had been mumbling out loud and the river people had been listening to him.

"You can never go back and we all know that," Daniella said. "We can only get salvation by being accountable for our wrongs."

"Who are you people?"

"We are just travelers who are trying to find our own salvation for we are sinners and this is how we pay. We are shunned from society and we have a chosen to help where we can, who we can. Tonight God has sent you to us. We give you fire and help you on your path, and this helps us on our path."

"What is my path?"

"Only you know that."

"How do I know? Everything I've done lately have been pretty screwed up so far."

"Right your wrongs, seek balance. Return the stolen, ask for forgiveness, free the imprisoned. Remember, my God is both vengeful and kind. This is balance. You come from the water, we give you fire. Balance. Your coldness becomes warmth. Balance. Seek balance and atonement will find you. Now, if you are warm, you must go and find what you are looking for."

Ainle stood, handed back the coat, looked to Daniella, and said, "Balance."

She smiled, nodded and said, "Go."

"Thank you," he replied as he turned and walked away from the fire on stiff legs.

He followed a rough path away from the river toward an empty park and parking area. The night had turned the parks from busy hub of family activity into a barren unfriendly space.

"Balance," he muttered to himself as he hobbled on.

He traversed the parking lot and crossed a road and began to weave his way up through the streets, only barely aware of his appearance and constant mumbling. If anyone were to see him they would they think he was a mentally ill homeless man.

"Next stop, the hotel. I've got to find Grace and make things right. Got to make things right. Got to find balance."

* * *

Kat stared at Alex and Grace. "What's with you two?" she said. "Are you sisters now?"

"Maybe," Grace said.

"Well, I'm getting on that plane and I'm making it big, so fuck you and your husband."

The big Asian turned to the wheezer and smiled. "I'd pay extra to watch that," he said.

"Sorry Quach, he's dead. I had him thrown in the river."

"Well, those two make a cute couple," Quach said, nodding his head towards Alex and Grace.

Grace felt at a profound sadness that her fear had been confirmed. Ainle was dead. She had never felt so far from home and alone as this moment. Images of Ainle's beating and being dragged away plagued he. And now, combined with the thoughts of him being dumped into the river, sent her into a deep sense of loss. She felt defeated and empty. What was next? She knew what was next. She was witness to many serious crimes and something from an ancient part of her brain knew she was not getting out of this place alive.

Grace turned to Alex and spoke softly, "They lied to me. They told me I was coming here to see my husband. But he was already dead." Tears welled up in her eyes. She had to look away.

"Come on, show us some of that fun you girls like to have when there's no men around." Quach set down his briefcase, opened it and peeled out two hundred dollar bills, slapping them down on the low table.

"We don't have time for this," Wheezy said.

"Hey!" Quach yelled. "You two, dance together and this money is yours." Quach stood with his hands on his hips.

Grace didn't want to dance, wasn't going to, but thought the more she complied, the more the men would relax, and she might see a way out. She tentatively put her hands on Alex's hips and stepped awkwardly to one side then the other.

"We're in big trouble."

Alex placed her arms on Grace's shoulders and continued the fake dance. "Where's the other briefcase?" she asked. "I'm sure there were two of them."

"Must be in that other room."

Kat sprung up from her chair and pointed at the two hundred dollars. "Hey, where's my money? I'll dance."

Wheezy spun with lightning speed and smacked Kat across the jaw with an open palm. Kat yelped like a puppy and tumbled to the floor. She curled her legs into her chest and held her hand to her face and began to sob.

Alex and Grace watched, but kept moving.

"You owe me money," the man yelled at her. "When you pay back my plane ticket, then you get paid."

Quach laughed. "Nice one, Mr. Lin. Now you two -- that's not dancing, move those bodies. Let's see some hips, nice and slow."

"Well, sister," Alex said in a soft voice. "If we're getting out of here, you better make your move soon, 'cause I know where this is going."

"Yeah, I thought you might."

"I've been in this kind of spot before. He'll offer more money and demand we get naked and put on a show. So, unless you're into having a little intimate performance with me, we better think of something."

Grace's mind was racing while she did a slow grind. She felt humiliated, angry, violated and violent.

Alex pushed Grace back to arm's length and moved her hips towards Grace's and slowly pressed herself against Grace.

Grace barely noticed as she looked past Alex at Mr. Lin licking his lips and it reminded her of a prehistoric lizard, cold and hungry.

She looked over at Quach. He was big, his face flushed over his expensive gray suit -- and she clearly saw him as the sex slave trader he was. Alex spun Grace around and she saw Kat weeping like a broken child and her anger boiled within her. Grace gave him her best attempt at a sexy/pouty face, and it must have worked as Quach beamed.

Kat was shaking in sobs, a hurt little girl and it was easy to see anger boiling within her.

Grace turned to face Alex and pulled her close and placed her mouth to her ear. "Lead us to the big guy, the one called Quach."

Alex leaned back and looked at Grace. "Your eyes are on fire, I see hate in there."

"Yes ladies, that's more like it." Quach cheered them on and loosened his tie. "Lose some of those clothes, ladies."

Alex and Grace slunk closer to Quach, and Alex turned her back, pressing herself into Grace, then arching her back. With the practiced hand, she pulled her white shirt up and over her head. Grace reached into her waistband with one hand and pulled the knife out.

Alex turned to Grace and wrapped the shirt around Grace's neck.

Grace reached up and placed her hands on Alex's.

Grace used the shirt to hide the knife.

Alex turned again towards Quach and his eyes were fixed on their body movements.

Grace unfolded the knife under the white shirt and stayed behind Alex's undulating smooth back.

She slid and reached her empty hand around Alex's stomach like a caress and placed her mouth at the back of her neck, whispering, "Closer."

Alex put her arms up and onto Quach's shoulders.

"I'll fuck you both," he said with a low grunt.

Grace felt the power rise up in her, and, in a flash, her anger became madness and rage.

The knife shot up from behind Alex and Grace thrust it into Quach's throat.

Surprise, then shock made him freeze momentarily, and in that instant she dragged the blade across and through his jugular vein. She clamped her free hand into his hair and hot blood sprayed across Alex's face and chest.

Quach gurgled through his open throat as his knees gave away. His eyes bulged out as he reached up to the gaping wound in a futile effort to close it up.

Blood poured out of him. His mouth moved the way a fish would move its mouth when out of water.

Mr. Lin stared at the collapsing Quach.

He blinked madly. Blood was everywhere.

He reached into his jacket.

In what seemed like one fluid movement, Kat leapt off the floor, grabbed a bottle from the bar and swung with both hands at the back of Lin's head. There was a sickening smack, and Lin fell face-first into the growing pool of Quach's blood.

"Son of a bitch!" Kat yelled out at the two bodies on the floor. "Now this is a party! Drink up girls, we're in the shit now."

Alex retreated to the pink chair, shaking and covered in blood.

Grace was leaning over Quach, horrified at what she had done, even if there had been no other choice.

Kat, out of fear or relief began to ramble. "There's no going back now. Looks like my modeling career is over before it started -- story of my fucking life." She popped the lid off the bottle in her hand and took a swig. "Here girls, take a drink.

Looks like you need it. Alex, time to clean you up and stop that shaking -- you're freaking me out."

*   *   *

"Now that's some good looking money," Tim said as he set his beer glass on to the table.

Tim and Rocket were relaxing with Khoi, one of the Asian traffickers, in what could be referred to as an old-school man cave. A giant eighty-inch TV on a wall played porn. Big, comfortable leather chairs in the middle of the room hosted the three men around a solid low wood table with a large stack of cash in the middle. In the back corner, a small oak bar and a large pool table with blue felt sat empty and waiting. The men were smoking cigars that were expensive and delicious.

"So, let's get this straight. Two to four times a year, we bring girls out here and you'll pay this much cash?" Rocket asked.

"Exactly," Khoi said as he sucked on his cigar. Khoi might have been the youngest of the three, but had the hardened face of a much older man. "Thailand has all kinds of business. Quach is downstairs with your girls getting them ready. Lin from El Matador has access to a market that demands girls from North America. I also have a cousin that visits Poland, Bosnia and Serbia, but the girls there are cheap and dirty and have been through the rape gangs, so they are not the best quality. North America has grade 'A' meat. We pay premium prices, you make

299

premium money and so do I. So does Quach and Zichou. My children go to expensive American schools all because of this new market and money. We look after each other."

"How do you do it?" Rocket asked. "I mean, it must be complicated."

"We own airport security, customs agents, police, even Interpol agents. All you have to do is bring your girls to Lin and you walk out with a large stack of good money, clean money, every time. So, let us raise a drink to our new venture, a new partnership."

The four men raised their glasses and drank deep. Success makes men thirsty.

Chapter 33

Grace vomited.

"Oh my God, I can't believe this. What have I done?" She heaved again, but only a little yellow bile came out, falling into the giant blood pool.

Grace felt she was on the edge of hysteria and panic, Alex was in shock, and Kat had gone crazy.

"Okay," Kat said as she pulled the gun from out of Lin's shoulder holster. "The gun is mine." She looked over the weapon, turning it in her hands like a handyman inspecting a new tool. "This is just like the one I shot that fucker Grundy with."

Grace looked at Kat, who took another drink from the bottle.

Alex was still shaking, but not as bad.

Grace handed the crumpled shirt to Alex. "Here, put this back on."

"I'm going to get the other case of money," Kat stated, and with the gun in hand, she marched to the door.

"Wait," Grace said. "Help me with Alex. She needs to be cleaned up and I do too."

Kat put her hands on her hips, the handgun appearing huge in her small hands. "Okay mom, whatever," and she walked out of the room.

Grace got a damp cloth from the bar and started to wipe Alex's face and shoulders. The blood smeared more than anything, but she got a good amount of it off her face. With the blood gone and makeup washed off Grace saw how innocent Alex was at that moment. Her blue eyes were dull, drained. A single tear slowly rolled down her cheek.

Grace leaned in and placed a light kiss on Alex's forehead the way a mother would on a small child.

"Hey, it's okay now," Grace said as she helped Alex put on her shirt.

The gunfire was muffled, at first, but Grace recognized it well enough, and the crack of the next shots snapped Alex out of her state of shock. The two women looked at each other. They each seemed to know what the other was thinking, and they headed for the suitcases. Time to get changed.

Alex grabbed a dark blue sweatshirt that said *Montreal* on the front and gave it to Grace. Then she took out a gray hoodie for herself with the word *Canadiens*.

"We look like tourists," Alex said.

"Good," Grace replied.

"Is Kat dead?" Alex asked.

"No, she's indestructible."

Kat pushed the door open and stood in the doorway holding the gun in one hand and a black shoulder bag in the other. "Got it girls," her smile beamed.

"Kat, what did you do?" Alex asked.

"Look," she said, pointing at the bag with her gun. "Money, money, money, money, money, money! Let's go to Florida and party."

Grace was at the small sink at the back of the bar washing her hands and knife, and she thought of that play from Shakespeare where the wife couldn't get the blood off her hands. Things had spiraled out of control in a matter of seconds and she felt her reason slipping.

Get it together.

She splashed water on her face, took a deep breath and turned around. Kat was standing there, gun in hand, a briefcase of cash on the table and a carry bag on her shoulder.

Grace saw an innocent child that had no idea of the seriousness of the situation.

Alex sat in the chair, staring straight ahead. She looked like she understood the danger they were all in.

"Alex, you okay?" Grace asked as she folded the knife and placed it into her pocket.

"No, I'm not okay," Alex said. "Well, we have to get out of this house."

"Hell yeah," Kat picked up the bottle and took a swig.

"Okay, dump out the clothes from Alex's bag and put the money in there. It'll be easier to carry in one bag."

"What are you going to do?" Kat was offended at being told what to do.

"I'm going to try and figure a way out of here."

Grace fished the neatly folded little piece of paper out of her pocket. She had seen a phone behind the bar and she went to it hoping the thing actually worked. She dialed the number and waited.

As it rang, she wondered why she hadn't called the police. It would make more sense, she thought, to call the police. She had that funny feeling, that intuitive vibe that said she didn't know who to trust. She could always call the police later.

"Hello."

Abdullah's voice had that calm tone that seemed to come from another lifetime.

"It's Grace. I need help."

"Grace, my goodness. Are you all right? Where are you?"

"I'm okay. Well, I'm alive anyway. I'm in Montreal at a house where they sell people."

Grace explained as much as she could to get Abdullah up to pace.

"My dear, remember, do not count your husband out. Speaking from experience, hope is a very important quality. Sometimes it is all we have."

"Thank you, Abdullah. I will be in your debt."

"No, do not think like that, but first we must get you and your friends out of that house."

"Okay."

"If you cannot shoot anybody else it will be better for you."

"Okay."

"You say it is a big house. There must be a back door, walk out the back and take a car and go to the harbor."

"The harbor?"

"Yes, the people you are with are very bad people -- but you know that. What you don't know is they have long arms, so do not trust the police."

"Oh, God."

"I am a religious man, Grace. But God is not with anyone now. God is only watching, not helping. Bad things have happened and God wants us to solve them ourselves."

"Yes."

"Can you remember this? If not, write it down, but don't lose it."

"Okay, I need a pen." Grace looked to Alex and Kat.

Kat was dumping the money into Alex's carry bag.

"Here's a notebook with the money," Kat said, leafing through the pages. "It's all in Chinese or something."

"Is there a pen or pencil?"

"Yep."

"Thank you, Kat," Grace said, taking it from her.

"You're welcome," Kat said, smiling.

"Alright, I have a pen."

"Grace, did I hear you say there is a notebook with the money?"

"Yes"

"Keep that, you never know."

"Okay."

"Get to the harbor and find entrance four. Look for the freight ship Abulkader. Bashir, you remember him? He is in Montreal and is at the ship. Get on board and there will be room for you. The ship leaves before morning, so you must hurry."

"Where is it going?"

"Europe, France. Do not worry, once you are on board the ship you will be safe."

"I am in your debt."

"Perhaps, but do not worry now. Call your family from the ship, but not until then. I will call your hotel and leave a message for your husband to tell him where to meet you. Let us hope he receives the message before you set sail."

"Thank you."

"Do not thank me until you are safe. Now, leave that house, be careful and may God be with you. Now go." And the phone went silent.

"Okay girls, we have a plan." She purposely sounded more confident than she felt, knowing that everything Abdullah had told her was easier said than done. Go out the back. Without being seen? Take a car. How? Go to the harbor. She didn't even know where they were, and if she did, she still wouldn't know how to get to the harbor.

"What is it Grace?" Alex asked, timidly.

Grace gave them a quick overview. "But we've got to leave now."

"What, are you kidding?" Kat said.

"Let's just get out of here," Alex said from the chair. "We can't sit here."

"Florida, baby," Kat said. "We need to really party."

"Kat, you don't have a fucking passport. You can't go to fucking Florida."

"Then I can't go to fucking France either."

"They won't check until we get there," Grace said. "It's a boat, not an airplane." She felt like she was dealing with a fifth grader.

She looked at the two men on the floor.

"We need to find car keys and take a car. I'll check this one," she said, pointing at Quach. "Kat, you check that guy," she said, nodding to Lin.

Grace knelt and fished around in the dead man's pockets, not sure what kind of scuzzy things she might find. But the only thing in there was a set of keys. Almost simultaneously, Kat came up with a set as well.

"Alright," Grace said. "Let's find a back door and see if we can get ourselves a car."

Kat took one more drink from the bottle and poured the rest of the whiskey out on Lin's unconscious body.

Lin moved slightly, groaning as the liquid roused him.

Grace lifted the bag with all the cash. It was much heavier than she had imagined.

Kat stuffed the hand gun into the waist band of her jeans, just like the gangsters on TV and went out of the room first, turning right towards what seemed like the back of the house. Alex followed, with Grace bringing up the rear.

Music was thumping somewhere upstairs, and she could hear men laughing from a room somewhere.

*   *   *

"What's the holdup with Lin and the girls?" Tim asked after the laughter died down.

Rocket was sipping his beer and staring at the money.

They were sitting with their new friend, an older Asian gentleman who had been introduced as Raymond. Despite his small size and slight build, he was clearly older than the others,

308

and the man in charge of the events of the party. His neatly trimmed gray hair and perfect fitting light gray Hugo Boss suit jacket and black tie gave the appearance of a man much younger than his sixty-six years, most of which were spent in some form of criminal adventure.

"Lien," Raymond ordered, pointing at another Asian across the room. "Go see what's taking Lin and Quach so long."

Lien set his drink down and resented being ordered in front of these North American thugs . "Okay," he said as he stood up and pulled his jacket over his turtle neck shirt. He stopped in front of a mirror and straightened his new jacket, it was something that he was quite proud of. They had all shopped in Montreal when they had arrived and the girl who had helped them in the Hugo Boss store had been so excited at the chance to sell top line clothes and to collect an excellent commission. And when they paid her in cash the poor girl had almost wet herself. Lien laughed to himself as he stood and regarded his reflection. He liked what he saw, the dark purple turtleneck shirt under the light blue almost gray herringbone sports jacket fit perfect. That girl really knew her stuff.

*   *   *

Lien opened the door and walked through the house to get Quach, Lin and the girls. He liked the music that was playing -- techno-pop from Korea. Two pretty girls giggled as he passed, and he smiled at them. Young Asian men nodded to him. They were the young guns with their fast cars and even faster women that were eager to move up through the organization. They were him a few years ago.

A handsome man with a tray of drinks paused and Lien took one of the scotch glasses. Business was good. He always surprised himself when he thought about his role in the organization. Taking girls to another country should have bothered him, but it didn't. He loved it. He loved the deception, the travel, and most of all, the money. After all, he was just a provider of goods. He was no different than the person who provided the alcohol for the party.

At the top of the stairs, one of the security crew stood watch and nodded as he walked past and descended to the basement. Quach was probably sampling the product. It was Quach's weakness, but he thought *We all have a weakness, I certainly have mine.* He smiled to himself knowing the gambling tables of Macau would be waiting for him when he got home.

The music from upstairs became a repetitive low, dull thud. Lien knocked on the door where Zichou was organizing the finances and travel plans. Raymond was the brains. Quach the controller, Zichou the organizer and Lien . . . he was the sergeant. He held it all together and kept things moving, just like any sergeant in any military. He got things back on track, got things done.

Lien knocked again on the door, a little surprised there was no answer.

He walked on down the hall to where the girls were getting prepped. He knocked on that door.

No answer.

He knocked again, harder.

Still nothing.

Lien tried the door handle and found it was locked.

He stood for a second. Even if Quach was playing with the girls, he wouldn't lock the door. He never did before.

Something was wrong.

Lien's brow furrowed. Something was definitely not right.

He stepped back from the door, raised his right leg, and delivered a front-kick, hitting the door just beside the door handle.

The door shuddered briefly, but didn't open.

He repeated the strike, releasing a deep yell as the door jamb splintered. The door swung open.

Lien stood in the frame and instantly took in the monstrous scene.

Quach was face down in a giant pool of blood.

Lin was also face down nearby but was alive, able to lift his head.

Lin stared at Lien with uncomprehending eyes, puked and then flopped back down.

The girls were gone.

Chapter 34

This place is huge.

Grace led the group of three as they seaarched for a back door. Kat found a room that was nearly all glass. Grace decided it was their way outside. The three girls stepped into the room and stopped, looking for an exit among the exotic plants and the floor-to-ceiling windows.

"Wow," Kat said as she looked around the room, "I've never seen anything like this."

"It's a sunroom. Rich people have tea and read the paper. There," Grace pointed to a small round table with two chairs, "This would be a nice place to relax after a day of work or have a coffee on a Saturday morning. It's not fair," she said.

"What's not fair?" Alex asked.

"This whole thing. We work hard, and they lie, cheat and steal to get this." She paused, deciding she needed to get back to the task at hand. "I think we need to get outside and get away from here."

"No problem," said Kat as she picked up one of the small tea chairs and hoisted it over her head. With all her might, she swung the chair at the nearest window.

The glass seemed to pop and the entire pane showered shards out into the black back yard.

The three women stepped out of the sunroom and into the cold evening air.

*　　*　　*

At the sound of the smashing glass, Lien looked up from Quach's body. He had to see what that was. He started walking towards the sound, taking out his phone and dialing Raymond.

When Raymond answered, Lien said in Mandarin, "We have a problem. Quach is dead, and I don't see the money. I don't know where the girls are."

"Okay, I'm on my way."

*　　*　　*

Raymond looked at the bikers and thought about telling them the situation then chose against it. If the police were going to be involved, which looked like a possibility, he would dump the blame on the bikers. The less they knew the better.

"Gentlemen, I have to sort out a transportation issue, please excuse me. Enjoy the cigars -- they are from Cuba."

Raymond rose from the table, checked his pockets, felt his gun under his arm and disappeared into the hall closing the door behind him.

*   *   *

Tim and Rocket drew from the cigars and looked at each other.

"What do you think, brother?" Rocket asked between puffs on the cigar.

Tim stubbed out his half-smoked stogie and looked at Rocket. "Too good to be true, too good to be true."

"Yeah, something is screwed up here. These guys are a dirty bunch."

"Let's slip out of here and get back to our bikes. I need a ride."

"Cheers to that mate. This fancy hooch is nice though."

"True enough, let's finish these and make out farewells."

*   *   *

The tree-lined back yard in the moonless night was almost pitch black.

"Which way?" Alex asked softly.

"This way," Grace guessed, holding Alex's arm.

The three of them walked quickly to their left and followed the wall of the big house, hoping to make their way to the front where the parked cars were. Soft yellow lights glowed from long back windows, providing a path to the corner of the house. They paused and looked down into the dark pathway that led to the front.

Slowly, they crept past a large air conditioning unit, then garbage bins that were neatly lined up, then small cypress trees, and finally they reached the front corner of the building.

Grace set down the carry bag and peered around the corner, seeing the cars parked in the huge yard. She pressed a button on the key fob, and from the line of cars, a horn started blaring and lights flashing.

"Shit," Grace whispered as she fumbled with the fob to stop the horn and pulsing lights. "Alright girls, lets go."

*   *   *

Lien was standing at the broken window of the sunroom when he heard the car horn go off. He dialed his phone.

"Yes," Raymond answered.

315

"I hear a car horn. Check the front, I'll circle around from the back."

"Okay."

Lien stepped out onto the broken glass and paused for a moment, looking into the dark yard.

Did they go to the woods or to the cars?

If it were him, he would have gone to the darkness, but he had to think like a woman. He decided these girls were not equipped wilderness survival, even though the woods were more like a park. That, and the car horn, was clue enough for him.

He ran down the back of the house, moving towards the cars. At the corner, beside the cypress tree, Lien could see the girls heading to the line of cars.

They were close to getting away with the money.

"Hey, wait!" he shouted as he launched out from shadows.

*   *   *

"Quick, get in," Grace said, panicky as the man at the side of the house started running their way. Also, from the corner of her eye, she could sense another older man running out of the front door. She wouldn't be surprised if both had hand guns drawn. She would have to expect that.

Kat opened the back door and Grace heaved the heavy bag onto the back seat.

The running men covered the distance quickly. "That's not your car," one of the men shouted, raising his gun.

The other man raced up. "You belong to us -- you do not leave unless we release you."

Grace was at the driver's door, frozen. Alex held onto Grace's left arm as Kat stood defiantly to Alex's left, her hands around her back.

"Come on girls, back to the house," the first man ordered.

"No," Grace said.

The second man put his gun up to Alex's head. "Come with us now."

"Fuck you!" Kat yelled. "You don't have the balls. You won't do nothing."

Alex's head exploded, with brain and skull spraying over Grace and onto the side of the car.

Grace screamed as Alex's lifeless body crumpled against the car on its way down to the pavement, coming to rest like a discarded doll.

In an instant, Kat pulled the handgun from the back of her waistband and shot the nearest man square in the chest. He staggered back one step before his legs folded, dying before he hit the ground.

The other man spun away, going down to the ground as Kat tracked him and fired, missing. She fired again, but the gun only clicked. Kat hurled the empty pistol at the man, missing him too.

Grace was standing in shock from with blood spray, skull fragments and brain tissue on her face and shoulders.

The man on the ground fired another shot, apparently missing everything.

Kat pushed Grace hard into the car yelling, "Fucking drive!"

Grace snapped out of it, scrambled into the vehicle, fumbled with the keys, then found the ignition as Kat lurched into the back seat. The engine came to life, and Grace stomped on the accelerator.

The rear wheels spun wildly, the car fishtailed and gravel and dirt sprayed as the silver Mercedes raced out of the driveway and into the night.

*   *   *

From the upstairs window, two men watched the events unfold.

"I think it's time to go home, brother," Tim said.

"Yep."

"Let's hope these fools don't connect us to that mayhem."

"They might try."

"Rocket, you got keys?"

"Nope. Don't need them. That older looking SUV on the left over there should be easy enough to boost. Won't be my first stolen car."

Tim was feeling a little shocked at what transpired -- and it was more than the loss of the money.

"He should never have done that to Alex. She was a good kid."

"Well, Kat gave him a good one. Got to respect that."

"Yeah, she's definitely got some spunk in her."

"You know, those Asians are going to hunt them down."

"Well, if she ever gets back to Vancouver, she is definitely forgiven."

"She's one of us now," Rocket said as he turned from the window.

"You remember your first killing?"

"I remember them all."

"Me too. Those are lessons you never forget."

"We should go."

"Yeah, time to get home."

*   *   *

Jacques LaForge had been enjoying his night at the party. He had sampled a little cocaine and was eyeing the girls. There was some serious money being tossed around and enough had been sent his way to keep the local police cruisers out of the neighborhood for the night. But now, shootings and killings meant he needed to disappear or the party was over for good.

He watched the panic unfold all around him while he slowly went out the front door. All he had to do was get in his car and drive back home. Jacques pressed his key remote and climbed into his car, started it and drove slowly out the main gate. If he took his time he'd be in the city in thirty minutes. He looked in the mirror and saw cars race his way, then past him. "You are a lucky one," he said to the mirror. "Chanceur."

As the cars raced past he knew he had to see where they were going. "Maybe I'll just tag along to see what happens next."

*   *   *

"Can you believe this?" Darrel said in disbelief shaking Mike awake.

From their place in the van they watched Ainle limp up the street, socks half off, clothes still wet."

"What the hell is this?" Mike was just as amazed as Darrel. "Is this for real?"

"Guess he's not dead."

*   *   *

After an hour of walking through the quiet streets, Ainle made it back to the hotel. His feet hurt, he was shaking with cold, and was in a foul mood. It helped him focus on Grace.

"Mr. Larcon," the bellman said from behind his desk. "What happened?"

"I fell in the damn river and I lost my key," he lied, feeling the warmth of the lobby soak in. "Can you help me get in my room? I need a bath."

"Of course, I'll get you squared away."

Ainle was sure the bellman had seen many things in his time at the hotel, but really? Falling into the seaway had to be a new one.

At least Edwin -- that was what his nametag said -- was discreet enough not to ask more questions. He just talked about the change in the weather while they went up to the room.

Once let into his room, he asked Edwin to wait a moment, and he fetched a five, passing the tip before saying, "Merçi," then closing and locking the door. He finally felt warm for the first time in hours and safe.

Ainle saw the light flashing on the hotel phone. His heart leapt. It had to be Grace. He took a moment to tear off his soggy, ruined clothes before pressing the message button.

But the voice that came through the speaker wasn't from Grace. It was a man.

It took him several seconds to realize who was speaking.

Abdullah calmly told Ainle what was going on: that Grace and the two girls, who they ran into at the mussel bar were heading for the harbor to board a cargo ship.

It all seemed unreal.

Ainle sat naked on the end of the bed and put his hands on his head. *"Grace is alive, but I have lost her. It is my fault. I have made all the wrong choices that have messed up our nice normal lives. How wonderful it would be to have normal back. Actually, just to have Grace back."*

He stood up and looked at himself in the mirror. He was a mess. His ribs were bruised and his thighs had purple welts on them. His lips were swollen and cut. He tried to look himself in the eye, but could only handle it for a second before looking away in shame.

He took a deep breath and gasped as a shooting pain in his ribs raced up his left side. At least he could feel pain. He could have died, Grace could have died, and it would be all on him. That would be real pain.

He wanted a shower, but knew there was no time. He washed up the best he could in the bathroom sink, then put on a pair of tan khaki pants, a white t-shirt and a green crew-neck sweater. He grabbed his cross-trainer joggers, their passports from the wall safe, money and credit cards, and stuffed them into his pockets.

Ainle stood for a second and looked about the room, thinking. He picked up the hotel phone and dialed Abdullah's number, but only got voice mail. He waited, then after the beep said, "I owe you, thank you," and hung up the phone.

He took one last look around the room, and one last look in the mirror. This time he was able to hold his own gaze.

"From this point on, if anyone hurts my family, I will destroy everyone and everything."

He knew his path had only one direction. Balance had to be restored. It was what he had heard from the river people. But how exactly?

He would figure that out as he went forward. He had to.

Chapter 35

The house in the country had become a scene of chaos. People in the neighborhood were aware there had been some major problems and were choosing to get clear of the place rather than stick around. There had been gunfire, after all. Who knew where the bullets would go if they started up again.

Lien was getting up from the parking lot with the handgun in his right hand. He looked at it, wondering why it had jammed.

One of the young guns from the party -- Lien couldn't remember his name -- had apparently seen the entire shootout unfold and figured this was his opportunity as he came running up all excited. He was young and crazy enough to run full speed into a shoot-out.

"I have a car," the young gun offered.

"Good, let us get those females. Rewards are always waiting for those who seize opportunity."

Lien looked at the young gun and saw the irony of life. He used to be the young gun and now, at 30, he was the old guy.

Raymond was dead and the details of the customs agents, the Interpol flunkies and anybody else they owned was in that carry-bag. It had been stupid to bring it, but it was the magic key to their fortune. A plan that had backfired. If that bag ended up in the wrong hands, business was over and they could all be dead.

On the other hand, it boiled down to simple business. It was his chance to move up.

"This is my car," the young gun said, pointing to a Mercedes 350 SEL.

"I'll drive," Lien said, snatching the keys out of the young gun's hands.

*   *   *

Tim and Rocket blended in with the madness and slipped out the front door, heading for the SUV they had seen from the upstairs window. Using a brick from the flower garden, Rocket smashed in the passenger window. Pulling out some wires, he connected the right ones, and the dashboard lights came on and the engine fired up.

"What about the steering lock?" Tim asked.

"Watch this -- your daddy taught me this one," Rocket grabbed the steering wheel and with arms that were extremely comfortable pulling wrenches, torqued left, then right, then left again, cracking, then breaking the steering lock. "Old school strong-arm steering," Rocket said with a childish grin.

"Slow and steady, brother. Let's just sneak back like regular folks," Tim suggested.

"You got it, Martha," Rocket chided.

Rocket drove smooth and steady down the driveway. As they approached the large swing-gate, a car raced up behind them, its headlights bright in the rearview mirror.

Tim glanced out the side window to see Lien clutching the steering wheel and fly past them, out into the street, red taillights doing their best to disappear into the night.

*   *   *

Trees blurred by in the shadowy darkness as Grace hung on to the steering wheel. Alex's blood and brain tissue were still plastered to the side of her face and hair. She began to shake uncontrollably and the car began to weave as she sawed the wheel back-and-forth, fighting to keep control.

"Jeez, keep it together. You're going to kill us," Kat said from the back seat. She reached up and put her hands on Grace's shoulders, squeezing gently.

Grace eased off the accelerator just a little and got some control back.

Kat took the opportunity to clamor between the two front seats and slide into the passenger seat next to Grace.

Grace began to sob and moan as she thought about what just happened. She rubbed her arm across her nose and brushed something away from the area between her nose and lip. She stared in disbelief trying to comprehend what she was looking at. The realization that it was a jagged portion of Alex's skull freaked her out. She thought, "Alex lay in a crumpled heap, but part of her is with us in the car, splashed on our skin and hair, and chunks of her are falling off my face." This caused her to shake. The trees on one side of the road seemed to come closer, and a moment later, closer still.

In effort to get back on the road properly, she over-corrected, and branches rasped the side of the car as gravel rumbled up into the undercarriage.

Panicking, she slammed on the brakes, bringing the Mercedes skidding to a stop sideways in the middle of the road.

All became quiet, except Grace's heart, the sound of which seemed to be thundering in her head.

"Well, that was fun," Kat said. "You okay?"

"Uh . . . Yeah, I think so. Sorry."

"You may want to get this pointed in the right direction."

"Yeah, I will. Just need to catch my breath."

"No, I mean you should do it now."

Grace looked at Kat, confused, then saw the young woman was looking past her, down the road from which they just came. She turned to look.

Car lights appeared in the far distance and were closing in quickly.

"We should go, Grace."

Grace looked back at Kat, not comprehending. The girl's face was strangely lit in the cabin of the car.

"Pick it up, they're chasing us," Kat yelled.

"What?" Grace said.

Kat leaned over and looked at Grace for a moment before raising her hand and smacking Grace as hard as she could across the face.

"*Aahhhh!*" Grace shrieked.

"Get a fucking move on, you stupid bitch!" Kat screamed back.

Grace became aware of the more intense light coming across Kat's face, and saw how serious she was. When she looked out the side window, she saw the bright lights of a car on her left slowing as it crept up to them.

"Come on, baby," Kat coaxed.

"Okay, okay, got to drive," Grace said. She stepped on the gas gently at first just to get moving, but when the car behind tapped the rear bumper, and the wheel shuddered in her hands, she stomped the accelerator to the floor. They were instantly pressed back into the leather seats, and the lights behind became less intense.

"Yeah, now you got it," Kat said, excited.

"Okay," Grace said as they now raced towards the city. "We need to get to the harbor. Can you find it?"

"How? I mean, no."

"Here, use this map thing," Grace pointed to the navigation system on the dashboard. "It's got to be a touch screen or something like that. Just push things and see what happens." *That car is still back there,* she wanted to add, but didn't. Instead she just said, "Please hurry."

Kat started to play with the navigation system. Grace was starting to feel a little calmer, the car's speed and stability gave her a sense of confidence, but the other car was still back there and she had no idea how to give it the slip.

They were now coming into the outskirts of the city, and the road became a little busier with late night traffic.

"Where do we go, Kat?"

Apparently, Kat was not having any success with the navigation system.

"Push the button that has the microphone or speaker thing," Grace said, glancing at the console.

"Destination please," a British-accented female voice asked.

Grace spoke up, "The Montreal harbor, please."

"The Port of Montreal?"

"Yes, the Port of Montreal."

In a few seconds, a map in full color appeared on the screen, the route highlighted in green.

"Okay Grace. Get ready. We need to make a left turn at the next light."

"But it's red."

"Afraid of a ticket?" Kat leaned forward, looking left and right, checking for traffic. "It's clear, hit it."

Grace floored the accelerator and the car shot through the intersection, veering left, the traction and stability control system this time kept them from spinning out.

"A couple more blocks and we'll need to turn."

The traffic was getting heavier as this part of the city changed from low warehouses in a business district into the taller buildings of a commerce district.

"Right at the next light," Kat directed.

Grace took the corner quickly, but cleanly.

"Alright, we're getting closer, baby," Kat said as she glanced between the map and the street.

Grace could feel her pulse in her temples, her face felt tight where Alex's blood had dried, and she flexed her hands, trying to relax. She glanced at the rearview mirror, saw lights, but wasn't sure. "Is that car still behind us?"

Kat pivoted around in her seat and craned her neck. "Yep, he's still there. What's the plan?"

"Plan? I don't know."

"Okay, you need to lose him."

"Yeah, I know that. How?"

"I don't know. But he's going to kill us. Try looping this thing around the block or shooting down one of those back alleys. Something like on TV."

They arrived at the harbor with the car still behind them. The entrance had a tall fence and several gates -- some for transport trucks, others for harbor employees, another for visitors and tourists.

"We want number four. Is he still following us?"

"Yes he is. Don't forget, this ain't your car so, if we have to, fucking bag it. You need to take a left at the end of this Papineau street and then we'll end up on Notre Dame, and entrance number four should be on our right."

* * *

What the hell?

Lien had been hanging back for a little while now and was pretty sure they knew he was following them. It didn't matter to him if they knew. He wanted his bag of money back, but he especially needed the notebook.

"Where are you going now, ladies?"

He backed off a little more to give the impression that he had given up, hoping the girls would make a mistake and get themselves in a dead-end. This part of the city was old and the streets were dark. Lien knew this would be a nice place for the girls to die.

*　　*　　*

"Okay, turn left at Pie Street," Kat said, sounding a little too excited.

"Calm down Katherine, calm down," Grace said before she cranked a quick left turn.

As the car lurched, Kat looked over at Grace and smiled. "I haven't been called that since I was little."

"What next?"

"Right, then another right."

"Hang on," Grace said, following directions and ending up on Viau Street. It was quiet, just a few small cars parked against the low curb. She found a parking space big enough to fit the Mercedes, slowed and pulled in, shutting off the lights and the engine.

"Now what?" Kat asked.

"We wait a bit, see if that car is following. Then we have to get ourselves into the harbor. There's a big ship called the Abdulkader -- or something like that -- and it's going to France."

"Wow, first China, now France. I feel like a world traveler."

They sat in silence for a few minutes, the only sound the ticking of the engine as it cooled. The minutes dragged and seemed longer than they really were.

"When does the ship leave?"

"In about an hour. If the harbor isn't that big, we should find it fairly quickly. I hope."

"That bag is pretty heavy. It might take longer than we hope."

"Yeah, I was thinking that too." Grace looked in the rearview mirror as she tried to wipe the dried blood from her face.

"Look," Kat said.

A dark sedan drove slowly from right to left on Notre Dame. Grace saw there were two men in the car. It went out of view.

"Come on," Grace said. "Grab your stuff, let's go."

*   *   *

"I need a taxi, please," Ainle said to the bellman.

The cab pulled up quickly -- surprising since it was after 3:30 in the morning. Ainle slipped the bellman five dollars as he climbed in.

Ainle leaned forward and said to the driver, "Port of Montreal, terminal four, please."

*   *   *

"Away we go. Follow that cab," Darrel said.

"Ain't this a wild one." Mike put the little van in gear and pulled out behind the cab. He hung back about thirty meters and settled into a leisurely ride.

*   *   *

The girls walked in the shadows of the tall old building to the street corner. Just across the road and a little to their right, a big blue sign with a white number four lit the terminal entrance. A small booth was next to the entryway, and it looked like someone was inside, reading a newspaper.

"So, we just walk over and into the entrance and down to the boat?" Kat asked.

"Sounds like a good plan to me," Grace said with a fake smile.

"Maybe we'll need to bribe the gate guy. Just in case."

"Sure, why not. Just in case." Grace dug her hand into the carry bag and took out a neatly stacked brick of money. "Here, only if we need to. People kill for less."

"Okay, thanks mom," Kat said, rolling her eyes.

"Sorry, I'm scared."

They walked out of the shadows, crossed Rue Notre Dame and went directly to the Terminal Four entrance.

*   *   *

Jacques watched the girls from his car. He was curious about the heavy bag they carried. He knew it had to be important. But, where could they be going? He started to open his car door when he spotted the two young gangsters from the party.

"Merd," he said. "Now what?"

*   *   *

Lien and his passenger watched the girls walk across the street from a block away. They were walking quickly, but he could tell the weight of the bag was a bit of a problem for them.

"Let's get them," the young gun said.

"Okay, but let them get into the harbor first. It's too open here. We must be careful. Hunting men is not the same as hunting women. That skinny one is crazy and the blonde is cunning."

Chapter 36

"Bonjour," Grace said as politely as possible.

"Bonsoir," the old gentleman in the security booth replied. *"Qu' est-ce que vous faites ici Mesdemoiselles?* What are you doing here, ladies?"

"We are meeting my husband and we are taking a cruise to France."

The old gentleman looked suspiciously at the two girls. "Pardon?"

"My husband set up an adventure holiday for the three of us. We are going for two weeks on a cargo ship. It's the new way to travel. We have our passports," Grace lied. "Do you need to see them?"

"*Non, non.* You will need them on the ship. Me, I would take a plane and be there in eight hours, not ten days. Let me guess. This is your husband's idea." His blue eyes sparkled, offsetting his tobacco-stained teeth. "You must love him very much."

Grace nodded, "Yes, yes I do."

He smiled warmly and returned the nod. "Follow the road all the way across the train tracks. Then, there will be large containers for cargo, and then the harbor, and then your ship. I believe it leaves within the hour. So, do not leave the road -- it is dangerous here. We have trucks and trains, but no aeroplanes." Again, the warm tobacco smile.

"Did my husband arrive, already?" Grace asked.

"No, you are the only adventurers tonight. *Bon voyage, mes belles.*"

"*Merçi,*" Grace said, looking at his nametag. "*Merçi Bernard.*"

The girls walked up the road, the weight of the bag causing Grace to lean to one side. The smell of diesel fuel filled the air and the loud clangs of metal-on-metal rang down from the rail tracks off to their right. Rail car wheels squealed as a massive, slow moving train approached from the left pulling big grey boxcars and long black oil tankers.

Grace felt the need to look back the way they had come. Part of her was hoping to see if Ainle was coming . . . and there they were. Two men, dark outlines silhouetted by the streetlights.

337

Were they the ones from the party?

It was hard to tell, but they were walking with determination towards the security booth. One pointed at the security booth as the other stood with his hands on his hips looking towards the train.

Then she saw a muzzle flash.

She was pretty sure it was a muzzle flash. She couldn't think of what else it might be.

The train's horn blared loud as the cars slowly rumbled through the crossing, blocking the girls' path over the tracks.

Grace spun back towards the train as the two men started their way.

The train's horn blared again and both girls looked up at a smiling mustached man who was waving at the pretty girls from the cab of the engine.

Kat smiled and waved back.

"Come," Grace yelled over the noise of the rolling train. It seemed to be picking up speed.

Grace grabbed Kat's arm, and they ran down the tracks to try and get in front of the train, but once they left the paved road, the surface turned to gravel and stones.

Running became stumbling, and it wasn't long before Grace sprawled onto her hands and knees, the bag of money tumbling ahead of her.

There was no way they were getting in front of the train.

"Do we go under?" Kat yelled over the squealing railcar wheels.

"I don't think we can make it."

"What about the little ladders on the ends of the cars? They aren't going that fast."

Grace paused and looked back down to the road, seeing that the two men were now at the crossing.

"Okay, get up there, I'll give you the bag."

The rail cars continued to rattle and the metal wheels screeched against the rails.

Kat grabbed hold of the railing at the end of one of the boxcars. She skipped once and pulled herself up onto the ladder, and then onto the narrow platform that framed the end.

Grace hoisted up the carry bag and Kat grabbed it with one hand while the other held onto a big, round crank wheel. Grace grabbed the rail, but it was tricky because the railcar seemed to roll left and right as it moved down the tracks, and the gravel was loose, like walking in sand.

Grace did a small skip just like Kat did, but lost her footing and slipped. Her hand clamped tight and held on as she was dragged alongside the train. She saw the rust-colored wheels rolling on the rails, staring for a second, almost going under the wheel.

She tried to scramble up, bouncing her knees off gravel until both feet found ground. She ran one step, then two and jumped, getting one foot onto the bottom rung of the ladder. She pulled herself up onto the narrow platform.

"Shit Gracie, almost lost you there," Kat said smiling.

"Fuck, that hurt," Grace said, wondering if she was bleeding somewhere.

From the confined space between the two rail cars, she could tell the train was starting to pick up its pace.

"Now we jump, Grace."

"Jump?"

"Yeah -- jump, tuck and roll. Easy." And Kat leapt off the side of the rail car, still holding the carry bag. She landed in the gravel and tumbled to a stop coming to a rest sitting upright and clutching the bag.

Grace followed. The impact wasn't as bad as she expected, but the tuck and roll became more of a flat thud and a grind to a stop, belly-down.

Winded, she got up and limped over to Kat, who was dusting herself off.

"Come on, Kat. Let's get to those big metal boxes. We'll hide in there and then find that ship."

They scrambled across another set of tracks, took a quick look back, didn't see anyone following, and made for the rows of stacked sea containers.

* * *

Watching the murder of the security guard was enough for Jacques. The choice was either get involved or leave. He weighed

340

his options and knew he should stay, but there would be too many questions. As he put the car in gear a taxi pulled up and he watched the husband get out and move into the harbor area.

And to make things worse the mini-van with the cowboys was stopping back from the cab. He couldn't believe the husband did not see it. Now he knew he had no more options. It had to stop here. He got out of his car and felt for his personal handgun from under the driver seat.

*   *   *

"Mike, that's the Dodge of one of those Frenchies."

"Here he comes. Watch his fucking hands, man."

Darrel got out the passenger door and called to Jacques to stop. A trains horn blared as Jacques fired two rounds through the windshield killing Mike instantly. He then spun left and fired two more rounds into Darrel, both bullets smacking into his chest. Quickly he scanned for the brass casings and found all four. He scooped them up as the taxi disappeared into the darkness. He saw Ainle approach the security booth, *How could he not see what had happened?*

It was a blessing. "Fuck it," he said and walked over to the Charger and stuffed the gun back under the seat. Slowly he put the car in gear and drove up a side street. He needed to find a bridge and toss his gun. Things were getting crazy, it was time for a holiday.

*   *   *

Ainle's taxi pulled up just short of the Terminal Four entrance. He paid the driver and walked to the security booth. The blood splatter was clear before he got close.

He peered carefully into the booth and turned away quickly from the sight of the old man. Half of his head was broken away where his right eye should have been. The body lay folded awkwardly in a large pool of blood that appeared black and grotesque in the late night.

A train was just leaving the crossing up ahead, and he turned from the scene of death and began running down to the rail crossing.

At the crossing, he stopped and looked to the left, seeing only rails, darkness and railcars sitting motionless. To the right, he could see two men getting up from the gravel along the side of the tracks as a train rolled away to some unknown destination.

Ainle watched, not understanding what was going on as the two men started to run towards a stack of sea containers. They slowed at the edge of the tall metal boxes and then crept cautiously as if looking for something. Or someone.

He stood there wondering what was going on. After the day and night he and Grace had gone through, it had to all be connected. If this is where Grace was going, then whatever these men were up to, it couldn't be good. They probably killed the booth attendant, and were now looking for someone else.

According to Abdullah's message, the ship was supposed to be on the other side of the containers. *"Across the tracks and past the rows of containers. The ship has been loaded with cargo, and it's ready to sail."*

Fuck them," he thought as he began to jog down the road to the far edge of the stacked containers. The first one was a light blue color. They all had tough corrugated metal sides that were cold to the touch and stacked three containers high. He looked up briefly and guessed the stack must be thirty feet high casting long shadows and adding to the darkness.

Ainle peered around the first corner and caught a glimpse of what he thought was Grace and another woman dart behind the next row of containers. He was just about to call out when the two men from the gravel at the tracks followed the women. Both had pistols.

Ainle saw the two men go in different directions. It looked like the taller, thinner of the two went the same way as the two women. The other went farther down, away from where he was standing.

All he wanted was to see Grace. He had to get to her. He had to save her.

Ainle went to the next row of stacks and stopped as he heard footsteps pounding his way.

He waited, in a shadow, listening, unsure what to do. *Where were they coming from? Where should he to go?*

He decided immediately that he could stand in fear, or confront it head-on.

He stepped around the corner and -- like the week before -- Kat plowed hard into Ainle, and they both went tumbling down. Grace then tripped over both of them, sprawling onto her already bruised hands and knees.

Grace thought this was it, they were caught and dead.

Kat sat up, looking wide-eyed at Ainle and said, "Deja-fucking-vu." She scrambled to her feet and darted around the container and into the darkness.

Grace stared in disbelief. "Abdullah said you'd make it, but I thought you were dead."

"Not dead yet, baby. Come on, let's get over into the shadow." He got up and led them where Kat stood. "Who is following you? What's going on?"

The three of them stood and listened to the sounds of the harbor as the girls caught their breaths.

"Those two want that bag," Grace said, pointing to what Kat was sitting on. Kat looked up and winked. "They will kill us all to get it, it's that simple. We need to get on that ship and we don't have much time. It's leaving with or without us."

"I have our passports," Ainle said, knowing he sounded lame.

"Thanks, honey," Grace smiled at him.

"What's the plan?" Kat whispered from her seat on the carry bag.

"I'll hide," Ainle said.

"Nice plan," Kat interupted.

"No, they don't know I'm here. They come for you and I'll surprise that guy, take him out. We out number them three to two, then we'll out number them three to one. Then we go to the boat."

Kat looked to Grace.

Grace looked back to Kat and said, "Okay. Let's do this."

Ainle slipped around the corner of the container and crouched in the darkness and waited. Grace and Kat stepped out into the space between the containers and stood just at the edge, also waiting.

It didn't take long for one of the men to see them and start into a sprint.

Grace held onto the carry bag in one hand and held Kat's hand with the other.

Grace watched the dark figure close the gap. Adrenaline was racing. Grace whispered, "Ready?"

"Ready."

"Here we go."

Grace pulled Kat with her and they ran past Ainle towards the next row of containers in an effort to work closer to the ship.

Ainle watched them labor across the open space to the next set of containers knowing he had to restore balance to reach some form of atonement for the mess he had created.

The young man turned the corner, not expecting Ainle's right fist. The man's front teeth were knocked down his throat as his knees folded and he fell into unconsciousness.

*　　*　　*

It took the girls longer than expected to get to the last row of containers. The weight of the bag made them stop once or twice to shift the load and then to start off again.

They got to the last row of stacks and worked their way through the gaps to the harbor side of the containers. The ship was not far. Yellow lights lit the ship's hull. The lower part of the vessel was red and sat low in the water. The main superstructure was white and rust streaks had left long trails down from doors and portholes.

There was movement around the ship, men starting to leave the deck while ropes and cables were being reeled and secured. Railings were being checked as sailors did the last preparations for the long ocean voyage. The only way onto the ship was the aft stairways that led crew and passengers up to the main deck and superstructure.

Kat stood behind Grace. "Where's your guy?" she asked, softly.

Grace ignored this for now, looking over the ship and seeing Bashir at the top of the stairway. He was tall slim and dressed in an open collar white shirt His olive skin was sleek with sweat and he looked concerned. It looked as though he was waiting for them.

"Let's wait a little, then we'll make our move."

The walk over to the ship was going to mean leaving the shadows and running out into the open of the well-lit dock. Then, there was the slow climb up the stairway and onto the ship.

"Alright, Kat, let's move a little closer."

Grace pulled Kat slowly down the side of the containers to the edge of the last one. Then they stopped.

Something was wrong.

Kat was breathing in her ear squeezing her shoulders. Grace's heart pounded in her chest. She breathed in long and deep through her nose to try and calm herself. That's when she noticed it. The distinct aroma of cigar. The last place she smelled that was from the house in Montreal.

He was near.

Her heart raced faster and pounded harder as she fought back panic. She felt the urge to just run, but they had guns.

She felt for the folding knife that Alex, poor Alex, had given her.

Slowly she took the knife out of her pocket.

Kat started backing away.

Grace quietly opened the knife and held it in her right hand, down at her side. She put the carry bag down and took two delicate steps away from the corner of the container. Her heart raced and blood rang in her ears, sweat broke out on her forehead. She felt light-headed and thought she might faint like in some stupid old movie.

*   *   *

He heard them coming and waited. They had split up to circle around. He had guessed they were trying to get to a ship, probably the nearest one. It looked like it was preparing to sail soon, maybe within the next hour.

He waited for them to come to him. They had to cross open ground and that's where he planned to take them down, snatch the bag of money and get the hell out of this forsaken place.

But the woman had stopped.

He took out his gun, he didn't need to check to know it was fully loaded -- he could tell just by the weight.

Gun in hand, he stepped around the corner, saw the two women backing away, raised the gun and moved forward.

*   *   *

Suddenly, the man was there, gun up and menacing. He stumbled like he was trying to tackle her, but the bag of cash had gotten in his way.

Wildly Grace lifted her right knee in an effort to avoid being tackled. The knee caught him square under the chin as he

348

looked up at her. His balance abandoned him and he stumbled forward, trying to grab her.

She swung her right arm in a wild arc at his back and she felt the knife penetrate somewhere between his ribs.

It made her feel nauseous, her hand clamped around the handle. She yanked it out as he collapsed to the cement dock.

Grace stared, frozen for a moment.

Kat grabbed her arm and pulled her around the writhing, moaning body. Kat picked up the bag, half-dragging it as they bolted across the open dock to the ship.

In seconds, they arrived at the foot of the ship's long, steep stairway.

Bashir tall and strong with determined eyes called down to them, "Ladies, hurry, we leave in minutes."

"Where's Ainle?" Grace yelled.

"I do not know. But I do know the captain received word there is trouble here, and he will leave without you."

Grace looked back from where they came and saw something spooky -- or rather, didn't see something that spooked her: The man she stabbed wasn't where they left him. She thought at first that it was the shadows playing tricks with her eyes. But he was gone.

"Grace, where is that guy? Where the hell did he go?"

"I don't know, we just need Ainle."

Grace looked up the stairway and saw Bashir checking his watch.

*   *   *

Ainle's hand ached. He was sure he had broken something with that punch.

He could see the girls at the foot of the ship's stairway. Other than his hand, he felt good -- they might just make it after all.

From out of the darkness, a fist caught him, glancing off his jaw.

Ainle's vision flashed white as a foot came out of nowhere and caught him straight in the groin. It felt like his balls had been stuffed up into his throat. He dropped to his knees.

"My name is Lien. Where's my money and note pad?" the man said as he kicked Ainle in the side.

Ainle covered his head and rolled over into a fetal position. He was kicked again and again in the ribs as he tried to get to his feet.

He was mostly up when a punch to the face sent him reeling back. If the storage container had not been there, he knew he would have gone down . . . and probably for good.

Ainle looked up at the wild-eyed man, and something told him the man seemed labored or in pain as he appeared he could only attack him from one side. Maybe he was just toying with him.

*   *   *

Grace dropped the bag and ran towards the fight. A woman insane. She hadn't come this far to lose the one and only thing that mattered.

Lien heard her coming knew everything was going his way.

He waited, baiting her. As Grace closed the final distance, he spun and drew his handgun from his shoulder holster and pulled the trigger, shooting point blank.

What he didn't expect was the crazy girl directly behind her who leapt over the one he just shot, sinking her thumbs into his throat.

The woman screamed as she bit into his face ripping a chunk of cheek off, then spitting it back at him. He screamed in pain before she sunk her teeth into his nose and crunched cartilage. Her thumbs dug deeper into his windpipe. As he turned his head, she bit into his ear and ripped half of it off. He spun around trying to get free, but her legs had wrapped around him and clamped down hard.

Ainle pushed himself off the container as his vision cleared enough to see Kat biting and clawing the man's face.

Grace was lying on the dock, not moving.

A coldness took him to a hell he didn't know existed.

Lien shook and twisted and screamed, trying to dislodge Kat as they staggered towards him.

Ainle paused, then side-kicked at the knee that was supporting Lien and Kat. The leg buckled, and Lien went down, Kat still clamped onto him.

Lien used an arm to try and push off the ground and Ainle targeted the back of the elbow. He again side-kicked and destroyed the elbow joint as Kat was inserting a thumb into one of Lien's eyes.

Lien's squeal of terror was high pitched, and it snapped Kat and Ainle out of their insanity.

Ainle grabbed Kat by the collar of her jacket and dragged her off the shaking form of the tortured man.

"Let him live," Ainle said. "He's a broken dog, and we've crippled him. Better for that one to live than to be given the peace of death."

Grace writhed on the pavement and they both turned to her.

"Gracie, Gracie, please don't die," Kat said, suddenly crying.

The round had hit Grace high on the right shoulder, and blood was blooming like a mad flower on her shirt.

Ainle lifted Grace off the ground, cradling her. Then he got her over his shoulder and hurried to the ship's ladder, with Kat taking the bag.

"Grace just don't die," Kat pleaded.

Grace rolled her head to one side. "Thanks Kat. You're my sister now."

Ainle continued to hurry as best he could with his wife slung over his shoulder.

"Ainle," Grace said from behind him. "You saved me, just like in the story books."

"Hey, Kat saved us both."

*   *   *

The next morning, Grace awoke to a slow, thudding rumble and steady gentle movement. It was the soothing motion of a fully loaded freighter in calm water.

Ainle had his back to her, looking out the porthole, drinking coffee. Kat was sitting at the side of the bed pretending to read an old paperback.

"Hey you guys," Grace said, sitting up. "Where are we?"

"We're just sailing past Quebec city. It's really nice. The ship's doc fixed you up. You're like me -- the bullet missed all the important parts. You're going to hurt for a few weeks, but it's clean."

Grace felt the dull pain in her shoulder, but it wasn't nearly as bad as she would have imagined.

"So, here we are on a ship," Ainle said. "There is nobody to report the shooting, and I think the doc has fixed more than one bullet wound in his time."

"I'll have to thank him," Grace said.

"There's plenty of time for that. Kat and I counted the money last night. It's just over two million, cash. Maybe not enough to retire on, but we can relax and get some sun."

Kat reached her hand to Grace's. "Can I get you something?"

"Water or tea would be nice. Thank you."

Kat smiled and left.

"Listen," Ainle said when Kat left the room. "That black note book, I think it's in Mandarin or Cantonese. And there are all sorts of numbers."

Grace frowned. "I know. Abdullah told me to hang onto it. He said it might be important."

"I'm sure it is filled with all kinds of secrets."

Kat returned with two mugs of hot tea.

"Here you go. Careful it's hot."

"Thanks. So where are we going?"

"France," Kat said. "We're going to France! I'm so excited. Will you teach me some French so I can sound cosmopolitan?"

"I sure will, Katherine. *Bien sûr.*"

Made in the USA
San Bernardino, CA
01 April 2016